TO LOST NATO'WA!

"Now, men, ye have the proofs ye asked for. I leave it up to you. Ye've hunted whales with me on both sides of the earth. But this will be no whale hunt. It's lives we hope to save—the lives of men and one white woman, who dared to follow her man into the North. 'Twill be a voyage more full of peril than any cruise ye ever took before.

"I'll not belittle the danger. First off we seek a land that we know nothing of except by hearsay. The ice lies thick betwixt us an' this Nato'wa. What may befall us when and if we find it, no man knows. 'Tis certain sure we'll meet with savage men—benighted devils who love the sight of white men's blood.

"And for reward . . . the old Grim Reaper will be waitin'. Of us now gathered here, 'tis certain sure some won't return . . .

"Yet on the other side of the accounts is this: if 'tis God's will that we return with tidings of the lost and proof for other men that there is land beyond them barriers of ice, the world will carve our humble names in bronze. And men of future times will link them names with Peary, Stefansson and Roald Amundsen—Lord rest him in his unmarked grave!"

KIOGA OF THE UNKNOWN LAND

by

William L. Chester

Introduction by

Thomas D. Clareson

DAW BOOKS, INC.
DONALD A. WOLLHEIM, PUBLISHER

1301 Avenue of the Americas
New York, N. Y. 10019

Cover art by Richard Hescox.

FIRST PRINTING, MAY 1978

1 2 3 4 5 6 7 8 9

DAW BOOKS

PRINTED IN U.S.A.

Introduction

by *Thomas D. Clareson*

Blend together a hundred dreams which have haunted man's imagination and given shape to his popular literature: one result is William L. Chester's *Kioga of the Unknown Land,* the fourth and last of the epic adventures of Kioga, the Snow Hawk, in the wilderness of the unknown Arctic continent of Nato'wa, homeland of the American Indian. During its original publication as a serial in *The Blue Book Magazine* in 1938, the blurb to its fifth installment placed it in "the great tradition of Verne and Haggard." It is a classic example of the so-called "lost race, lost land" novel which developed as a response to widespread pubic interest in archaeology, geology, anthropology, and the last wave of exploration during the late years of the nineteenth century and the beginning of the twentieth. Of more importance, Chester gave those adventures of Kioga a distinctly American flavor separating them from Haggard and even Edgar Rice Burroughs.

Nor should the reference to Verne go unnoticed, for the entire action of the series is set in motion by the spirit of scientific inquiry. In the "Prologue" to the first novel, *Hawk of the Wilderness* (1935, 1936), James Munro, a "famed anthropologist and Amerindian enthusiast," journeys northward to verify personally evidence he has obtained. He hopes to settle "that most enigmatic and much-argued of puzzles—the origin and pre-Columbian history of those true Americans, the Indians." (One must not forget the heat of that argument. At one time they were identified as the Lost Tribes of Israel; at another, after the discovery of the extensiveness of Mayan and Incan ruins, as colonists from Atlantis.) Chester also responded to the deep-seated interest in polar exploration and the Northwest Passage by locating Nato'wa far within the Arctic circle in strangely warmed waters beyond the ice barrier.

Significantly, these choices do not seem to result from the casual decision of a commercial writer. Apparently they rise from a deep concern on Chester's part. In the 1930's during a period when in fiction, as a film, the only good Indian was a dead Indian—as the villain of *Hawk of the Wilderness* says explicitly—Chester stands unique among popular writers because his narrator laments that the Indian cultures were "swept away life chaff before the invasion of the Europeans. . . ." Nor is this a chance remark. Once in America the Snow Hawk's first request is to visit a reservation; there he sees "the remnants of a red-skinned race living with all the wild, contented liberty of animals caged." At the opening of the second novel, *Kioga of the Wilderness* (1936), angered by "the tragedy of a great race in slow decay," he leads a group of Indians through Canada toward Nato'wa.

These matters provide essential background for the central image of the four narratives. As is well known, even after the American continent had been spanned, the frontier kept its hold on the American imagination. Increasingly in popular fiction since World War Two the yearning for that new land has taken the form of exploring either the far reaches of the galaxy or the depths of the "inner space" of the human psyche. Chester gives local habitation and a name to the older dream, for Nato'wa remains a "virgin forest-land unknown to civilized man." It is the Edenic continent that was America in the eyes of so many early colonists and European travellers. It is the America extolled particularly by the early explorers and mountain men. One reader may see the frontier and Nato'wa in terms of fantasies of escape from the restrictions imposed upon the individual by society. Another may see them in terms of a rejection of the modern urban-industrial civilization which had already taken its fundamental shape a generation before Chester wrote. For Kioga, who had freely roamed the northern wilderness, "was not all of civilization a prison?"

Whatever else, Nato'wa serves as an epic stage for the deeds of the Snow Hawk. Chester has molded him from the stuff of heroes. He is actually Lincoln Rand, only son of American medical missionaries whose small ship had been driven by storms against the reefs of Nato'wa at the turn of the century. Orphaned when his parents were killed by a war-party in a raid on the Shoni village where they had been accepted, he is raised by his father's close friend, the Amer-indian Mokuyi, whose own infant son had died in that same raid. His physical prowess arouses the jealousy of his youthful companions who injure him so that for a time he limps. But through the love of Aki, the bear cub, he escapes into the forest where the she-bear Yanu adopts him. He tells James Munro of his youthful wanderings with the bear people in such tales as "Unharmed, He Dwelt Among the Forest People," included in *One Against the Wilderness* (1937). Not only is he physically restored, but he gains a cunning and a kinship with nature surpassing that even of the Shoni themselves. Thus, although he has been an out-sider throughout his youth, the tribal elders recognize his abilities and offer him a place on the tribal council. He unites the seven Kindred Shoni Tribes against their enemies and becomes their war-chief. He is a figure out of myth. Just as he calls up innumerable legendary warrior heroes, so, too, he may resemble superficially such modern figures as Mowgli and Tarzan, but because of the care with which Chester has drawn upon the American background, Kioga is his own man.

Kioga of the Unknown Land (1938) brings the saga of the Snow Hawk to its climax. It resolves the love story of Kioga and Beth LaSalle—which has linked the plots of the novels together. The incursion of the crew of the *Pirate* allows Chester a last denunciation of the predatory nature of "a wild mob" of supposedly civilized men as they seek gold. But the central action of the novel grows out of a puzzle, another scientific mystery. Once again James Mun-ro has found evidence of an unknown race, "the People of the Tusk . . . A mighty culture, oldest on the earth." (Be-cause they have blue eyes, he links them to the Mandans.) One can miss the importance of what Chester does. So well has he established the "reality" of Nato'wa that within one "lost land" he ventures to create another—beyond the cloud-capped Tamasili, "the Mountains-that-have-no-tops." His audacity succeeds.

No summary can capture the vivid detail of the action, nor should it try before the reader has joined Kioga, the boy Tokala, James Munro, and the narrator as they pene-trate the "Vacant Lodges"—caves in the mountains—find their way through the subterranean tombs of the kings of the People of the Tusk, and emerge into the land of M'Anda. Individual scenes and characters remain in the mind's eye: the tunnel which the People of the Tusk have excavated for generations in an attempt to follow their legendary kings into the outer world; the haughty and beautiful Loalli, Princess of Ayal. But it is Kioga the Snow Hawk who holds center stage in "the City of the Kings," for only his wit and courage and strength can prevent rebellion, can save himself and rescue his friends.

In publishing *Kioga of the Unknown Land,* DAW Books has rescued from the obscurity of the pulp magazines of the 1930's one of the most imaginative and memorable American lost race novels.

The College of Wooster
Wooster, Ohio

CHAPTER 1

"Stanley Kirk, so far as we're concerned, your life's not worth a nickel if you make the trip you're talking of. Try Lloyds. They'll insure anything. But it'll cost you doggone high, my lad."

So spoke my friend and old insurance counselor, whose name I won't divulge for simple reasons. We sat at after-dinner coffee in the Promenade Café. Spray from the fountain beside Prometheus whisked cool upon us now and then. Spiring toward the evening sky, there rose the giant of the famous New York rendezvous which bears the name of Rockefeller Center. Out on Fifth Avenue gay throngs strolled up and down, or lingered above and around us, looking down upon the diners with the tireless curiosity of sight-seers.

My friend took no notice of this. "You are asking us to underwrite a venture outside the field of insurable risks."

"Well, let it go, then," I said, with a trace of unwarranted resentment. "Your darned insurance companies have no imaginations anyhow."

"Be realistic," was the answer. "We don't deal in the imaginary. We deal in risks that show some likelihood of going right—not a voyage to an unknown land that is bound to end in disaster. We've carried you at reasonable rates while you were prowling in India and half the other countries on the globe. But those places are known, at least. This land you rant about—Nato'wa—it may exist, for all we know. But deliberately to take a ship into the ice packs in the Arctic is suicide—and suicides are not insurable."

"Insurable or not," I answered, "Munro's lost up there somewhere, and I propose to find him. Hang the risks."

"Munro was an explorer and a scientist," my friend reminded me unnecessarily. "He'd know how to take care of himself. You ought to realize that. As manager of his museum you've known him long enough."

We finished our coffee in silence, and parted with a perfunctory handshaking. He took a path paved with insurance figures and walled with interest tables, the path of safe-and-saneness. My course began by leading up old Fifth Avenue and ended in tremendous adventure in a strange new land. My friend, I later learned, died victim of a motor accident; while I, brushed by death a hundred times, lived on to record these extraordinary events.

Make no mistake: I'm not its hero. I only tell a strange tale, much of which I saw, part of which I was. More often still I recount facts as they were later told to me, and frequently infer details which never have been told. When the story is finished, and a long-blank spot is filled in on the map, the newfound land of Nato'wa, discovered early in this century and known to white men less than a decade, will be a synonym for adventure on a last frontier.

The name of Lincoln Rand, a physician by strange fate turned discoverer, will rank with those of other greats whom death deprived of the high honors, due to great achievements. For Rand it was who cleared an old riddle from the slate of science by proving Nato'wa to be the cradle of the red-skinned race called Indians.

Rand's diary first told of the timbered mountainous wilderness, of its fierce wild beasts and savage men; and of its climate, tempered by warm currents; and of his little son, called by the Indians Kioga the Snow Hawk, born to rove a wild hawk of the wilderness, indeed, an outcast with only shaggy forest denizens for company, until qualified by his fighting sinews to become the greatest warrior in all the Shoni tribes.

Added to Rand's accounts will be the journal of James Munro, explorer-archaeologist, who journeyed to Nato'wa on his own account to verify the natural wonders of which Rand's writings told. Far more than a dry array of scientific facts, this journal is a document whose pages overflow with strange adventure. It tells of Beth La Salle, the young American girl who dared to seek and be reunited with Kioga whom she loved; of Dan, her younger brother who sailed upon the *Narwhal* too, and of all the others of a fearless company.

Boldly they set forth, attained their goal, set up their fortress in the wilderness and met Kioga once again, only at the last to see the *Narwhal,* seized by a discontented few among the crew, putting out to sea.

Marooned, their fate might well have come to be another mystery of the North, but for the lucky chance which brought the *Narwhal* back into the ken of civilized men. The faithless crew aboard had long been dead when we found them on that frozen funeral ship. But before the *Narwhal* caught fire, burned and sank, James Munro's journal was recovered along with other papers, and with it undeveloped photographic films, exposed in far Nato'wa. And into my hands these records properly came, to become a part of the famous collection of New World historical objects housed in the Munro Museum in New York City, of which I exercise control in Munro's absence.

Until the night two years ago when I was swept into the rushing events of great adventure, I had not lost a single item of Munro's collection—of which perhaps most priceless were a map and chart found on the *Narwhal.*

No ordinary map and chart were those two precious papers. The one pertained to new land in the Arctic called Nato'wa; the other to the ice-girt reefs and stormy seas which held the outer world at bay from that dark land until the present century. Upon that map and chart, survivals of Munro's ship *Narwhal,* were pinned my hopes of succoring my famous friend.

Another ship, the whaler *Bearcat,* and her skipper Captain Scott, were at my service—of that Scott's telegram had just informed me.

Days of feverish preparation were past; little remained but to close the museum, set the burglar alarms for which the building is intricately wired, and gather up the map and chart by which our expedition would be guided. These were in a vault, below street level, where I now went.

Entering the vault room by the great oak door, I paused instinctively, conscious of something untoward. The vault yawned open, just as I had left it, but suddenly the answer came: Through the vault room, usually dry and stuffy, there blew a breeze, cool and fresh with the tang of rainy damp. This draft came steadily from a place behind the open vault door. Swinging the door through a quarter-circle disclosed a little heap of broken masonry before a hole leading outward from the building—the unused inlet of a coal chute to the bins which the vault had long ago displaced. The bars across the cemented opening had been sawn through with a hacksaw, attested by metallic granules lying near; and on the floor a drying footprint still was partially visible.

Someone besides myself was in the museum! That much I realized; even as I snatched out the revolver which I always carried when alone in the museum, from behind me came a sound and then a heavy blow, glancing from my head to shoulder. I went down, stunned an instant, recovering sufficiently to see vaguely a form flit past, a cylinder of paper in one hand, not easily identified.

My own voice sounded, strained, unnatural:

"Stand where you are! Don't move!"

And then I fired, one quick blind shot.

I heard a muffled yell. Something flashed before my eyes and hit the wall behind me with a thud. Then came the slamming of the oaken door, the sound of running footsteps on the stairs that led above. I followed, still in half a daze, yet cautiously. Wind blew through the upper hall. The outer door hung open, and a curtain of rain fell just beyond. I burst upon the rain-wet street, with its shadow-rows of anemic city trees.

From other avenues came the roar of elevated trains, the bray of auto horns out in a great city, as the after-theater crowds turned homeward. To give blind chase to the marauder of the evening would be useless. Returning to the museum, I saw traces of blood and found the vault in confusion.

A sum of cash and gold and silver ornaments were left behind. The marauder had been no common thief of works of art or historic value. But that on which I counted most was gone—the map of Nato'wa's eastern forestland, and with it the chart of perilous reef-filled waters on its coast.

Who the marauder could be remained a mystery, never solved by police, hospitals or neighborhood doctors, whom I notified at once that a wounded man was wanted in connection with this burglary of the Munro Museum.

But of the midnight visitor, this much was certain: He was small of stature and slim, else he could not have wormed his way into the museum via the coal chute. He was resourceful, cool and cunning, as proved by his quick escape and self-effacement. He was not one to halt at violence—as witness the blow on my head and a thin, keen knife stuck in the jamb where I had stood. His wound was in the left hand. A dark print on the wall proved that. . . . Little did I dream under what circumstances I should encounter this unknown marauder again!

To lose the only extant map and chart of our new land was a dire blow, the first of many still to come against the rescue expedition. The question now resolved itself to this: Deprived of map and chart by which to sail and take his bearings, would Captain Scott stand by his original agreement to sail the *Bearcat* into the unknown?

To settle that, I set out for the Pacific coast at once.

CHAPTER 2

" 'Tis unfortunate, aye, now it is, that the scalawag got the map and chart." The words were Captain Scott's, uttered in the cabin of the whaler *Bearcat,* straining her hawsers at a pier in Seattle seaport. They came from lean-grizzled jaws, brick-red from many years at sea in chase of Moby Dick.

Scott was little changed since our last meeting. A little frostier on the leonine head, a little more lined about the lips, but shoulders just as straight, the eyes as keenly bright and blue, the grip of hands, weathered red, just as unstinting in cordiality. Hard-bitten was Captain Scott, hard-bitten too the words with which he followed that remark to me:

"But map or no map, lad, we'll seek your unknown land. For if there's land up in the polar quadrants, as ye claim, the *Bearcat* is the ship to find it. And scrape my hull, I do believe in this Nato'wa place ye speak about! What's more, to set your mind at rest, my ship is at your service, and I am too. As for the crew—" Scott paused to suck reflectively at his grimy white clay pipe.

As he paused, the third man in the cabin leaned across the table. Some forty-seven years of age, he was the opposite of Scott in every outward way. His hands were white, well-cared for. His skin was pale, his face new-shaven, his clothing of the latest style and cut. The corporate boards on which he sat as a director were many. In John Ford La Salle we both beheld a man of means and culture and refinement —but something more as well, which made us kin: a well-conditioned body, open, clear-eyed glance, and an inner consciousness of courage and great resourcefulness. To him life had been prodigally kind, until the blow which fate had struck against him through his children, both of whom had been lost with James Munro. His voice, accustomed to command, now spoke in very different tones:

"This risk you've volunteered to take, Captain," he said to Scott, "is more than I dared to expect. If you find Beth and Dan for me, you'll never need to put to sea again."

"Belike ye speak of cash rewards," returned Scott, eying La Salle quizzically.

"If money will repay you, all I've got is yours," the other answered fervently.

"'Tis clear ye do not understand my nature, sir," Scott told him bluntly. "With all the gold of Croesus in my hold, I would not quit the sea. I'll take my pay in satisfaction at seeing ye reunited with your kin. Reward—ah, bah! 'Tis not much longer I have got to sail these earthly seas. For fifty years I've chased the whale. Now comes a chance at sixty-two to write my name in hist'ry. Stow all that talk of payment, sir. But if, God willin', we reach this unknown land, mayhap they'll put my name upon the map and call a bay or river after me."

La Salle spoke gruffly, as men oft do when deeply moved: "I'll shake your hand on that." And in the quiet of the *Bearcat's* cabin, they gripped and wrung, a bargain made whose outcome none of us could have imagined.

"But what about a crew?" La Salle asked anxiously.

"We'll put our cards right on the table," Scott said. "And let each man decide it for himself." He turned to me. "Ye'll have the movin' pictures, I suppose? Good. Set up your contraption. That piece of sail will do for screen. I'll call my men."

The crew were soon assembled and introduced to us; we shook hands all around. They were a quiet lot, not given much to talk, but with the sea's roll in their gait, horn on every palm.

"Be seated, men," said Scott. "Ye've not forgot the *Narwhal* with her dead men's crew which we found some months ago off Alaska. Ye've also heard a lot of Nato'wa, a new land in the Arctic. That ship took Dr. James Munro to that new land. And with him went Miss Beth La Salle, and Dan her brother. Not one of them returned. Marooned, they are in need of help, somewhere up in the north. I'm goin', with the *Bearcat*, on a search for them. But since 'twill be a risky business, ye've each and every man a right to know the facts before ye sign up for the voyage. Kirk, here, will tell ye anything ye want to know." Scott nodded, and I took the floor, and looked from man to man.

Finally one Tim Sullivan spoke up: "I do not fear so much the danger," he said, "or I would not love this trade of whalin'. I've been around the world, I have, from the Amazon to Zanzibar. But never have I heard of this Nato'wa, until here lately. Beggin' your pardon, but how d'you know it's not a wild-goose chase you're goin' on?"

"You've said it, Tim," another said. The remaining men nodded silently. "What's to prove this land is not a dream?"

Force of habit sent the question to Scott, who had his answer ready, gesturing toward me. "Kirk, now, will show the pictures made from films found on the death-ship *Narwhal.*"

Directing their attention to the sail-cloth screen, I dimmed the lights, pressed a switch which set the small projector humming. The screen came alive, with clear and perfect moving pictures.

We saw a schooner, now moving through a sea of ice, now wrapped in spinning mist, while jagged reefs passed by on either side. Next came a scene which showed the vessel almost wrecked, at anchor in a landlocked harbor. Each scene bore a caption assigned when all the films had been assembled. Shots of a volcano, and steaming springs were titled: *"Heat from inner earth makes Nato'wa's climate temperate."*

Another caption: *"Birds and animals of Nato'wa."* We saw a long-haired tiger prowl through a jungle of evergreen scrub, weighted down with snow. Came next a rare scene—a puma striking down an elk doe.

You could have heard a pin fall in that cabin as the picture changed to an eagle striking down a great white swan amid a burst of silvery feathers; a moose splashing up a river bank; a bear climbing in a treetop.

Then followed river scenes, showing canoes loaded with dusky paddlers, their backs gleaming as they labored. The caption here read: *"Wild forest tribesmen of Nato'wa cousins of the American Indian."*

Then came a sudden blank. One film had reached its end. I turned the cabin light on, by its light to insert a second film. The faces of those men had changed, and bore expressions of absorbed interest, wonder—and lingering doubt. But to a man, their imaginations had been set afire.

The film was quickly changed, the room all dark again.

And now the ropes and rigging of a ship appeared in the near foreground upon the screen. Beyond its rail a seacoast was passing by. Ashore a band of men stood near a cannon, which belched a ring of heavy smoke. So startling was the realism of being on that ship and being fired on, that some of the men who watched the scene dodged instinctively. The picture-ship was shaken, and the image blurred. A direct hit had been registered by the distant gun.

Ashore a handsome young white woman, garbed in buckskin, moved into focus, to stand beside a man of striking proportions. Thus, on a bit of celluloid, preserved for us of the outer world, was a perfect group picture. I threw its enlarged "still" upon the screen, pointing out four fingers: "This is Beth La Salle, and this is Dan."

"My son and daughter," came the elder La Salle's voice in explanation.

"Third from the right is James Munro, the scientist, whom you all knew."

"Aye! Aye—it's him!" muttered Sullivan excitedly.

"And this," I continued, indicating the most imposing of the group, "is Lincoln Rand, known among those tribesmen as Kioga, the Snow Hawk."

Rand's was a figure to command interest, envy and admiration: straight, tall, formed like a living bronze. His splendid torso was naked to the waist; in one hand was a hunting bow, and at his back a quiver full of arrows. Here was the ideal form of the hunter-warrior, combined with the features and expression of a well-browned civilized white man.

"That is the key man in our search," I emphasized. "Wherever Kioga is we'll find the others, modern pioneers on a new frontier, in danger of their lives and needing help."

Thus in vivid pictures were the *Bearcat's* crew acquainted with those we sought, and leaving the final "still" upon the screen I gave way to Captain Scott, who uttered then the longest speech we ever heard him make.

"Now, men, ye have the proofs ye asked for. I leave it up to you. Ye've hunted whales with me on both sides of the earth. But this will be no whalehunt, mind ye. It's lives we hope to save—the lives of men and one white woman, who dared to follow her man into the North. 'Twill be a voyage more full of peril than any cruise ye ever took before.

"I'll not belittle the danger. First off we seek a land that we know nothing of except by these pictures and hearsay. The ice lies thick twixt us and this Nato'wa. What may befall us when and if we find it, no man knows. 'Tis certain sure we'll meet with savage men—benighted devils who love the sight of white men's blood.

"And for reward—wait, wait! I have not done. To compensate ye for the toil, the old Grim Reaper will be waitin'. Of us now gathered here, 'tis certain sure some won't return. I may be one. Let that sink in."

There was a silence, unbroken save by the breathing of men within the *Bearcat's* cabin. Scott continued:

"But look ye, men! I would not press a mother's son to go with me against his will. Yet on the other side of the accounts is this: If 'tis God's will that we return with tidings of the lost and proof for other men that there is land beyond them barriers of ice, the world will carve our humble names in bronze. And men of futur' times will link them names with Peary, Stefansson and Roald Amundsen—Lord rest him in his unmarked grave!" Scott paused again to light his cold pipe and sucked noisily, the only sound now heard, except the hoot of a passing tramp, outbound on some more prosaic cruise into the Pacific.

La Salle sat drawn and pale, waiting on the verdict of these men. Scott's crew sat round the great hewn table, slow of thought and slower still of speech, impassive and expressionless. But every word had sunk in and to them the grizzled old whaling skipper added, on a harsh note ill-masking a deep emotion: "Now lads, this ship is mine. I own her keel to truck, and I've committed her from peak to sternpost. But who so of us does not wish to go along, let him speak straightly now.

" 'Tis only fair to say that if ye do refuse, locatin' a new crew will force the voyage over for another year. The best of men are not found in an hour or a day."

Having delivered himself of that, Scott stood up. "Now men, go out and talk it over with yourselves. Muster on the foredeck in an hour. Them as would rather not sign up, our ways part at this dock, and God bless every man, no matter what he does!"

The men filed out with little speech, for whaling men are seldom long on words. An hour passed. I made some notes. Scott filled the cabin with strong smoke and never spoke in all that time. La Salle paced nervously, suspense almost too much to bear, for one more year might mean the difference of life and death to those he loved, lost somewhere beyond the shoulder of the earth.

Punctually on the striking of the bells, we three went forward, where the men had gathered.

Two of us held our breath. Scott spoke succinctly to each man in turn.

"Now, Sullivan?"

"Sure, sir, an' did ye think I'd ever quit the *Bearcat?*"

Scott swallowed hard. "Pete Silver, engineer?"

"Them engynes would not turn for no one else, sir."

"Tom Codd, what do you say?"

"Who'd feed those bloomin' lubbers if I did not go?"

"Sven Svenson, I'll hear from you."

"Huh! Ay go, by yumpin' yiminy, fur the hell of it!"

"Macgregor, you speak up, man!"

" 'Tis vurra cerrtain ye'll ha' need o' Scottish blood—savin' coal or cash or lives, Macgregors shine."

Scott's voice shook slightly as he spoke the name of Otto Stumpf.

The stoutish German wiped his shining brow.

"*Ja,* sure I shtay. You hadt to ask old Otto?"

Scott stood up stiffly, his blue eyes very bright, and one more name to call. "Washington Madison Grant, what say you, lad?"

A negro youth stood proudly up to his full height of five feet two, black as the ace of spades, his frizzled pate agleam like ebony.

"A cullud man stood nex' to Peary at de Pole, suh," he said, with swelling breast. "Ah aims to repasent mah race in dis a'venture—ya-as, *suh!*"

A moment Scott swept them with his bright blue gaze, then turned to John La Salle triumphantly, and full of pride. "Of their free will—not one held back. I could have told ye."

Then John La Salle did that which made them all his friend. From one to another he went, and shook the hand of each in turn, without a word. And not one looked him in the eyes, for everyone could see that they were misted dim.

Scott's voice was heard. "All right, then, lads. . . . The tide is high. We're sheathed with double steel up in the bow, for buckin' ice. Stand by your posts! We sail within the hour."

Aboard the *Bearcat* the undercurrent of excitement was running high. The ship herself was of that spirit, tugging with impatience at her moorings. The men sent up a cheer, dispersing then each to his place of duty on the ship.

From up in the bow La Salle and I saw Scott mount the bridge and heard his voice call the command.

"All right. Cast off!"

Cast off! What pregnancy of things to come was in those simple words! Cast off—from land, from friends, from civilization itself, to voyage forth upon a quest upon which men may never go again, to succor life and find a new land on this earth. Risk all, share all, whether the reward was gold and glory and far-broadcast achievement—or sudden, unrecorded death.

Now with a great splash her lines came in. The capstan pawls rang merrily in the rings. The whistle roared; the screw began to beat. Another shout rose, echoing here and there about the ship. The *Bearcat* had begun the noblest of her many sailings, a joust with sea and Arctic ice. A few souls on the shore beheld and heard. But none of them, in that hour long past, were gifted with a knowledge of her mission.

Farewell to Puget Sound—farewell America! The great Pacific swelled beneath our keel. Now Ketchikan, the Gulf of Alaska, Akutan Pass, the Isles of Shumagin, Indian Point in far Siberia—all fell behind. South Head, the black rock of East Cape and North Head too—one by one the far outposts of men dropped astern. Through stormy Bearing Sea the *Bearcat* plowed, passing between the Straits into the Arctic Sea, beyond the Diomedes great and small.

All went well aboard the whaler, proceeding at reduced speed when heavy fog enveloped her.

CHAPTER 3

"Schooner ahoy! Board on the starboard quarter!"

The cry keened down from the crow's nest, and Scott looked back toward the horizon, now all but cleared of fog, to scan the indicated vessel closely. "A trader, headin' for the Siberian country to dicker with the Deermen and the Chukchees," was his first opinion.

Whereas the *Bearcat* already stemmed the floes, which crowded her on every side, the schooner, by a lucky choice of water lanes, gained on us steadily. Several hours found her abeam, some miles distant; but to our signals she made no answer. Scott scowled at that, for by the courtesy of the sea, we were entitled to her recognition and reply, if nothing more. But presently conditions in the ice checked both ships; and once again a light haze drifted between us.

Eager to try my skill at maneuvering on the ice, I asked Scott's sanction for a visit to the stranger, which he at first refused on grounds of danger. But as the fields continually grew more solid, he finally gave way, on my suggestion that the other might be in some kind of distress—a curious soft spot in this hard-bitten man who more than once had saved life on the seas.

"Go, then, if ye're set on it. Tom Codd will go along. Do as he says—he knows the way of ice and how to get about on it. But do not let 'em see ye, on the stranger. I mistrust that ship. Honest men would be more friendly in the North. Go warily."

So, while the *Bearcat* stood a little off the ice to drop a boat, we armed ourselves, then oared across the patch of open water, made fast our craft beside the ice-field, and took to the ice. Across its tumbled jagged waste we trudged, Scott's warning in our minds; and as we slowly neared the other ship, I left Tom Codd behind, armed with his rifle. Under cover of a crag which hid us from the ship and most of her from us, I then went on alone to find the stranger anchored just beyond it.

From my point of vantage up atop that mass of ice, I peered almost straight down upon her passengers and crew. A more villainous-looking lot had never walked. One little group stood watching a wrist-turning match between two sweating contestants, jeering or cheering the changing fortunes of the contest. Amidships several gamblers sat round about a cask, playing cards upon its end, and pausing now and then to fill tin mugs at its spigot. Some bore pistols; others wore knives at belts. All save one or two were dour, cold-faced, unshaven men, typical of North Country riffraff.

Voices rose in drunken argument, ending in savage curses and the smack of fists on flesh. Somewhere a woman laughed shrilly and soon appeared, a fading blonde; with her were two others not more attractive, familiars of that roistering gang.

The captain of this unprepossessing lot was gazing forward toward the gang whence came the sounds of shouting, laughter, the squeal of a cheap fiddle and raucous chords of an off-key accordion, sounds oddly out of place in this vast sea of wind-carved, wave-driven ice, emphasizing the littleness of man and all his acts.

Now a tall and burly man stood shakily upon a cask to drink a toast. At its shouted conclusion: "To the land of gold and Injins! May we find the first and exterminate the second!" a laugh rose, subsiding as he continued: "To the land where they ain't no police or Mounties to interfere with honest men—may all its redskin squaws be beauties!"

Some one cheered lustily, but a rumble of congesting ice drowned out the others.

Then suddenly my eye was caught by one at whom I could not help but start, with an odd feeling as of recognition. Yet not exactly that, for to my knowledge never had I set eyes upon this individual before. Scanning him closely, I cudgeled memory for the clue to his identity, which remained elusive, until his left hand, bandaged heavily and carried in a sling, came suddenly into view.

That set the wheel of identification turning. Slim and snakelike in every movement, the man was little heavier than a boy, but keen and shifting eyes in a swart, flat Asiatic face, marked him for what he was—a deadly little *fer-de-lance* if looks meant anything at all. Here, I felt sure, stood my marauder of the museum, thief of the map and chart by which this vessel sailed.

The thoughts I had begun to entertain were now confirmed: the goal of this wild mob was identical with our own! With this assorted gang of men the first wave of empire had begun. Nato'wa, a new frontier and the last of earth's pure wilderness, was fated to be the brawling-ground of this tough hybrid pack. Wanted men, seal-poachers, desperadoes, dregs of the Alaskan and Canadian wilds, with their slattern women—here they were, a shipload of the wastrels who seek escape and profit on every new frontier, and come to reap where other men have sown. And in sheer force those aboard the ship outnumbered the *Bearcat's* crew almost five to one, every man armed.

Some joked and laughed. But the word most often heard was *gold*. It was this yellow lure which enticed them from the comforts of more temperate climes into the deadly rigors of the North. Reluctantly would the scientific world accept the facts of a new land as genuine. How swiftly had these gold-seekers snapped up the merest rumor!

Save for the rowdy horde on deck, the schooner appeared to be ship-shape. Shifting to where I could command a better view of her forward decks, a gun could be discerned, covered by lashed canvas—relic, no doubt, of rum-running or smuggling days in other seas near other coasts. What arms she had below, and her resource in ammunition, could only be conjectured—presumably enough to make her formidable even to the larger *Bearcat* if it came to fighting.

My thoughts turned to the stolen map and chart, lacking which the *Bearcat* was already handicapped. Somewhere upon this ship were those useful papers. With knowledge of their hiding place, it had been well worth the greatest risk to attempt regaining them. But to pass unseen among that crew of ruffians on deck was now impossible, and rumblings of the ice close by forbade my lingering much longer.

My gaze returned to the little Asiatic; and suddenly, across the space, his eyes met mine. At once he yelled out shrilly, snatched up a rifle and fired point-blank.

Half-blinded by a burst of ice kicked up by his shot, I turned and ran, glad of my strength and great activity. And though there was no pursuit. Codd and I scrambled at top speed across that chaos of shifting ice—now surging heavily under heel, and cracking with the sound of bursting bombs. Long fissures fingered among the floes, and plates and slabs of ice up-ended in the path, agleam like shining armor. Staggering across that uncertain footing, we slowly neared the looming *Bearcat,* its ports aglow like oranges, a welcome, solid-looking stronghold, where eager hands made haste to help us to the decks.

Captain Scott heard my report, and nodded grimly, muttering: "I told ye she was up to nothing good. Ye acted wisely in comin' back without riskin' your hide against the odds aboard of her. They have the map and chart, which I would give my ears to have. But they'd not part with them without a fight. And fightin' might be costly—more so to us, who are outnumbered and outgunned. Ye have Munro's description of the reefs and landmarks, in his diary. 'Twill have to serve."

Another fog soon fell. Terrific rumbling in the ice began. When the air had cleared again, the schooner's masts had vanished. By now accustomed to her presence, the crew were startled. Scott explained her disappearance with a grim simplicity. "Change of wind and ice-pressure are quick finishers. I've seen the like before. The ice will crack a ship open like a walnut. Or maybe she caught a wind we did not feel and a lane we did not see, and slipped away."

It was not a pleasant thought to realize that while we lay in comparative safety, almost within view another ship with human souls aboard might have gone to the bottom. Scott would have put a rescue crew upon the ice, but now the floes were in upheaval once again. And from this day onward we were too much occupied with labors of our own to give much thought to others. . . .

Favored by wind and weather, we had thus far come well on our voyage. With similar luck another week would have seen the *Bearcat* in that unknown temperate sea which surrounds Nato'wa. But the tremendous hostility of the Arctic now became apparent. The elements showed their teeth. The ice closed in, dashing our hopes of a quick passage.

Day after foggy day the stout ship rammed against the floes, quivering in every rivet with the endless impacts. Crash after crash shook her stem to stern, while sometimes we made but a few miles a day, or again logged a fair northing when open leads were found. Ramming, backing, ramming anew, forcing her prow high up on the floes and by sheer weight of hull crashing the ice beneath her—it was *Bearcat* against Arctic, and the stout old ship seemed to shudder with awareness of it.

The outcome was a gamble, an agony of uncertainty, ever under it the fear that we might be beset, locked in the ice, unable to reach Nato'wa before another year or two had passed—if ever. The precedent for such a fate was ample.

Nor dared we slacken our efforts; for in the Arctic, of all places, ships must hasten or be doomed. Behind, evidence of the whaler's struggle, a lane of brash extended back into the fog—small ice broken up by the ship as she bulled her forward way in a weary, endless monotony of struggle amid a vastness of space, shut in and isolated by fog and ice, motes in a blind universe.

But not an idle hour, even at such times as we were becalmed or ice-girt. There was the language of the Nato'-wan tribes to be learned from Munro's self-made dictionary. There was his diary to be studied, that we might work out some substitute for the stolen map and chart, by which to find our way or arrival in the new land.

The ice began to triumph. The *Bearcat* made no headway. Heavy fogs froze on her, overlaying spars and decks with transparent cloth-of-silver—a beautiful dress which must be chopped and hewn away lest she grow heavy above and liable to capsizing. Two shining hummocks raised their peaks towering off her port bow. She listed some degrees, first one way, then another, as the ice-pressure shifted.

A frigid, stabbing wind blew moaning in from the southwest. This wind it was which had piled up the ice now threatening the ship, which had already yielded forward below the forecastle, admitting much water.

Weary and discouraged, we had but an hour of sleep that night. The *Bearcat* groaned in all her joints, and trembled as the ice made good its throat-hold on her stem. La Salle walked the cabin floor silently, his face a study in despair. He would be brooding on the nearness of the end, with Beth and Dan still unaccounted for, unaided.

Scott and his men were all alert, ready to abandon at a moment's notice. Already a store or provisions had been swung overside to be lowered at a signal.

Close to disaster though we were, I somehow dropped to sleep—and awoke on hands and knees against the wall, a crashing, roaring sound in my ear. The ship pitched sickeningly and rolled with awful heaviness. She must be going down!

La Salle and I rushed up on deck into the light of early dawn, ready for the worst. Instead—

Instead we saw the ship transformed. The ice was melting from her. The crew were cheering lustily—strange conduct from men aboard a foundering ship, until one saw the cause. The floes had broken up; their roar and thundering was what we took to be the *Bearcat* being crushed. And our *Bearcat* was a prisoner no more. Her roll had come from sudden release of icy grip upon her hull.

North and west stretched out the open sea, clear save for a few growler bergs on one of which a fur-seal swayed sinuously. Gone was the frigid southeast wind that snatched breath from the throat and pierced as with a blade of ice. From north and west there blew a steady breeze, still cold, yet cold without conviction, like the first breath of spring in milder climes.

Who could forget the glad music of water trickling from where ice had been, the crash of bits of ice to deck, and the promise of that welcome wind so wonderfully tonic, moderating by the hour, magically opening the way to the tired ship! And on its breath was the faintest trace of what we sought, a hint of growing things, of green-clad spaces on mountain heights—of *land!*

Born of contact between warm air and colder waters, great billowy banks of mist surrounded us. The breeze dispelled them, leaving only wisps above the sea. The northern sun rose very slowly upward, ember-red, coloring the mists with its own warmth. The growler on which the seal still perched apparently took fire. The seal, as if in fear, dived off, a purple arrow plunging into a sea of golden melting incandescence.

All on board gazed at the sun, rising like a beacon of hope after our long despair. But of a sudden one of the men glanced toward the southeast, exclaiming in astonishment: "The schooner!"

Emerging from the ice some miles behind, evidently under auxiliary power, was the ship we had sighted in the pack.

Scott scratched his grizzled jaw and eyed her, puzzled.

"Now will somebody tell me—how the devil did we miss seeing her? And how did she come all this way from land ag'in' such wind and ice? She's sure had better luck with the winds and the water lanes than we. Mostly, though, I calculate she's done it by following in our wake under power, taking advantage of the lane we've broken. She's up to no good, either."

"Good or no good," I said, "we can't prevent her. The seas are free. And don't forget—"

"She carries a gun forward, aye!" the Captain interrupted darkly. "For what, if not for trouble? Certain, not for shootin' seals!"

"If it comes to a fight, sor," offered Tom Codd eagerly, "we'll give it to 'em, that we will. We've got the whalin' gun, don't forget, sor, an' bomb-lances aplenty. What's good for whales'll do for them."

"It isn't fight they want," Scott barked irascibly, "not for leastways. There may be further ice, for all they know. And while we're here to break a way for them, they would be fools to fight. Unless I miss my guess, we'll not see hide nor hair of 'em—not for a while at least."

His words proved true. Long before coming up with us, the stranger wore away; nor did she change position that day, so far as we were concerned. Next morning found her nearer, and sundown under the horizon out of view.

But she had a useful chart. We must reckon, from Munro's meager diary notes. Nato'wa's probable location and the only channel into land. We would meet with her again.

No land had been raised as yet, but the ice-belt was now behind, the outermost ring of Nato'wa's defenses stormed and carried. We were within those temperate seas which washed the coast of our goal, whose waters were so full of life the eye could scarce record it all.

Fur-seals and sea-lions swam past in countless herds. Wherever there was ice, walrus squatted amid their harems. Scott's eyes bulged at sight of schools of blue whale broaching fifty yards abeam. Had we been hunting oil, we might have killed a hundred.

The spars and masts were filled with black-backed and ivory gulls. Solemn puffins, with gaudy red and yellow beaks and feet, veered in flight or dived for fish. Clouds of murres flew past uttering the odd murmuring cries so like their name. And over all, fierce preyers hovered—sea-hawks and robber-ospreys, killing right above our decks.

The sun wheeled under on a glasslike sea. The *Bearcat* steamed full speed ahead. All hands breathed easier with the ice astern. The tension of dread had lifted. Forward, the bow-watch raised his voice in song.

Dawn revealed a derelict on the starboard beam, haven for a cloud of sea birds. Hulks multiplied as we neared Nato'wa's reefs. The sea was fairly sown with them. Many rode high up, remarkably preserved. A huge white owl perched on the topmost point of the foremast—fierce harbinger of the land we long had sought. The morrow found us steaming near the outer reefs, taking soundings constantly.

Then suddenly the loud cry, *"Land! Land ho!"* came floating from the masthead. All hands rushed to the forward rail, and peered into the north. A momentary lifting of the fog gave us our first glimpse of a towering headland.

Who says that inanimate nature may not speak in a voice which man can understand—he has never stood as we did, silent, each man wrapped in his thoughts, while Nato'wa, the unknown, mysteriously strange and unaccountable, sent forth her silent threat.

Over all that distance the fascination of it reached out, gripping every man. It was as if some strange deep gift of prescience had been vouchsafed to all of us; for all who stood upon this solid iron deck had sensed that many would leave their bones forever upon that farthest, loneliest land in all the world.

Lacking our chart, on which we earlier had placed such dependence, we had to use Munro's slim written description of the entrance to the channel in the reefs. Cross-bearings on two rocky spires convinced us we had found the place of entry. At less than two knots headway, the iron prow of the old whaler nosed between the outer rocks, groping forward into the labyrinth.

A fog blew off the land, obscuring all that lay ahead. Words scarce convey the perils to be run by any ship which seeks to brave the reefs, fogs, storms and tides which guard Nato'wa from approach by men of the outside world. Our passage through the polar ice-pack had been child's play, compared with threading these dread obstacles.

The fog grew heavier, and ropy twists of murky vapor serpentined about our decks, which soon were drenched with it. Sounds and men's voices were amplified peculiarly. Beyond the rails the sea was hardly visible, except in glimpses when the floating mists would part.

Now and again the cry, "Rocks dead ahead!" would sound, then Scott's voice shouting down the speaking-tube—bells were too slow in this emergency. It was a feat to navigate this iron ship through waters which had been dangerous to ships but half her size. Her weight, an asset in the ice-pack, was a drawback here, increasing as it did her draft.

There was no sleeping now. Scott kept his post, listening for the leadsman's calls. The screw beat slowly—*thrum-thrum-thrum* and once it rang upon the rocks, a deadly sound. The rudder creaked on its post; the endless workings of chains within decks were audible.

Then came the storm. Out of this northern cradle of evil weather, it rushed forth with a screaming wail, to strike almost unheralded—a fierce and freakish storm of wind and hail which careened the *Bearcat* with its first breath as if she were a little fishing smack.

Tall seas rose towering blackly up, and charged against the rocks like snorting bulls. Harsh gray waves bared foaming fangs and snarled along the rails. Their crests of churning foam snatched off by wind, stung our cheeks like scatter-shot. Both starboard boats were torn astern in half a minute.

Straws driven through solid planks—men speak of that when tornadoes strike. This night we saw much worse. Small granite chips imbedded themselves in the hardwood of the *Bearcat's* mast—that near was she to shore. Poor old Tim Sullivan, forward in the line of duty, was cut down, mutilated as by machine-gun fire, by these hurtling shards, dead and riddled in a hundred places by that shrapnel-blast of jagged little stones.

Two anchors out, a hawser by some miracle of seamanship got across a wedge of rock—but still the *Bearcat* dragged. Wind and tide and growing darkness, all combined to drive her on the razor fangs of rocks that waited, bared, to tear her bowels out. A loud report like cannon fire was the hawser parting, snaking back in murderous recoil like some gigantic anaconda. Pete Silver, making fast an after hatch, was caught in its hempen toils and snapped a hundred feet into the churning sea.

Then the bow port anchor chain let go, striking fat red sparks in angry showers from the windlass gypsyhead. One hook still held, but not for long. A sudden twisting lurch dragged out ring-bolt and deck-beam bodily. No time to slip the cable, let alone make fast a finding buoy. The anchor was already gone, and with it twenty feet of decking, with salt sea rushing through the gap.

Then with a crushing jar the *Bearcat* piled up on a reef. Her hour was near—no man but knew that. Scott hurled an order back. A single word was heard—"*Whaleboat!*"—and in a moment out it swung above the roaring sea.

There was one tense moment when it seemed that this boat, like the rest, must go to pieces on the *Bearcat's* hogging side. Then came a momentary lull; and we piled in, Scott last of all.

Snatched by a huge wave, the whaleboat fled the ship's side and hurtled shoreward, grounding in twenty minutes on a rocky beach, between two great rolling combers.

Pell mell we all sprang out and grasped the gunwales with intent to draw her up on shore. But the second roller caught her, twisted—and stove her into matchwood on a rocky ledge.

Captain Scott gazed back upon the quaking corpse of his beloved *Bearcat*. She hung between two rugged spurs of rock, each one of which had bitten into her. Immense seas slammed heavily against her. Inch by inch and foot by foot the stout old ship gave way, her plates bending under weight of water and her own great tonnage. Each breaking wave struck with the sound of hollow drums. Then with a crash, down came her iron-fitted foremast, striking fire from a donkey engine as it fell.

And after that, as if her pride were broken, the *Bearcat* resisted little more.

"She's goin'!" cried Scott in a husky, choking voice. The ship hung trembling. A cumulative sea was roaring in, its force redoubled by the compression of two rocky walls. We heard it strike, an anvil-blow amplified a million times, a crash as of a thunderbolt. Then almost with a mortal sound there came the scream and screech of tearing steel—and the *Bearcat* was gone, her shroud the mists, her sepulcher the roaring reefs.

Upon the wash of that great destroying sea there was a spar, a length of mast; and when its undertow had sucked away; a life-ring with the name *Bearcat* on it floated out among the ridges, testimony one day, perhaps, to an outside world, that the *Bearcat* had met her end.

From somewhere near, beyond the towering cliffs behind, there came a muffled hollow roar. As one the little party turned to face the formidable challenge of Nato'wa. Deep anxiety clutched the boldest hearts among us. Nor could even experience on another planet have prepared us for the stupendous novelty of the events to come.

Somewhere near here, within the next few years, the Russians on the *Krassin* would prove to the world existence of warm currents in the Arctic. The *Sadko,* too, seeking land not seen since 1810, would radio of milder currents and signs of land unsighted hitherto. Russia, too, would break a northern passage for her fleet to win ready access to the East, across the shoulders of the earth. How long before men of the Soviet would come upon Nato'wa, as had we?

As if the *Bearcat's* loss were not enough, now, bitterest draft of all, we saw that hated schooner coming through the reefs, and lying to behind a rock near by.

"She made it, sure enough," said Scott heavily. "Satan himself must have manned her wheel."

Storm-marked, and with canvas in hanging shards, she otherwise was sound and whole. Where the greater *Bearcat* had gone down, this lesser ship of wood, by virtue of her shallower draft, had weathered through.

Feverish activity marked the dropping of her anchors. Two boats were quickly lowered. Into them men sprang to the point of overloading, burning to be ashore, apparently and searching for the yellow lure that brought them here. But tragedy raised its head that early. One of the men, slipping on the ladder, lost footing and fell into the sea beside the ship. A swirl of water, a mottled shape rolling belly up, a long-drawn screaming cry choked off with dreadful suddenness; then the unlucky man was jerked under—by a shark? Less hastily thereafter, the disembarking continued.

"What is that name?" asked Scott, squinting at the ship's sharp prow.

"Pirate," I answered.

"Pirate, hey? A fitting name, with them cutthroats aboard! But let's be movin'. We are not fit for fight like this."

Shouldering our salvaged few belongings, we turned along the cliffs, seeking to keep out of sight of those upon the *Pirate.* Until we had achieved perhaps a hundred feet of altitude along the slanting cliff ledge, in this we were successful, then suddenly a chip of stone flew from a ledge above our heads, and there came a sharp report from down below.

Several times again they had our range. Otto Stumpf, red-faced and sweating with the steepness of the climb, gasped and clutched his arm. The shirt stained red with blood. A jeering cry rang out from down aboard the *Pirate.* First blood was shed, and more would follow.

Scott shook his hairy fist. A bullet whistled past his head.

He joined the others in a more prudent course, crouching low and hastening along to where a broadening of the ledge enabled us to hug the wall beyond their rifle range. . . .

Scaling the lofty coastal cliffs at last, we had our first glimpse of the forested interior—a wilderness without parallel on this present-day earth. Far to the north it stretched, a bold terrain, sloping down a mile or two from where we stood, then rising up in hills beyond, and finally, in mighty sweep, soaring swiftly toward a range of mountains in the distance. And everywhere the earth was clothed in splendid forest.

Somewhere, miles back in the interior, there flowed a river known as the Hiwasi, which took its rise in that distant range, flowed seaward, then after a mighty bend flowed parallel to the coast from east to west, and reached the sea far to the south of our landing-place. By striking due north, we should attain its banks.

The heavy thickets raised almost impassable barriers to our movements, and so we sought dry steam beds leading downward from our rocky eminence, following along such pebbly courses until at last they led to flowing water, little higher than sea level and flowing slowly toward the south.

What stream this was we did not know; but on its bank we made a camp—a raised stout barricade of fallen logs and pointed branches as a protection against the forest brutes whose footprints lined the mud and sandy margins.

Alternate sentries guarded the slumbers of the others all through that first night in Nato'wa, but naught occurred to give alarm. By firelight, with our one ax and patient labor, we fashioned a raft of logs, already fallen, lashed these together with stout vines and then cut pushing-poles wherewith to urge the clumsy craft along its way.

A great canoe had been far preferable, entailing but a fraction of the labor in propulsion, but time was of the essence, and anxiety to reach the River Hiwasi uppermost in mind. A good sound tree of proper size and shape was not easily found. Nor had we means whereby to gouge it out, excepting fire, which in our state of mind was much too slow. And so we made poor shift with the materials we had.

Our plan was now to push against the current of this lesser river in a north and easterly direction, hoping that its upper reaches paralleled the main stream of the Hiwasi, on opposite sides of the same divide or watershed. Hours of laborious upstream poling on the succeeding day brought us into broken water, not navigable farther.

From what I recalled of records lost, we here must cross the backbone of a minor mountain range, somewhere beyond which flowed the Hiwasi and the Acopi, its tributary. Armed with man's first weapon, a simple new-cut club, I climbed the nearest ridge, and from its eminence beheld the silver shimmer of a river far below. Nightfall found us at its bank. Scott suggested:

"Dig in right here. Set lines for fish. Make our headquarters fit to live in and worth defendin'. Then seek the trail of Munro and his people. But one step at a time."

It was good counsel, swiftly acted on. Of broken rock, laid solidly, and roofed above with thin poles interwoven with foliage, a rude blockhouse rose slowly, commanding views upstream and down.

Necessity mothered strange invention. On lines made of odd bits of string and unraveled clothing, Scott and his men set out the few fishhooks one of the men produced from a pocket case. Insects formed a bait which good-sized fish took eagerly. The wilderness, thus far was kind to our cause.

On the bank La Salle and I, with fire, ax and patient labor, fashioned a dug-out canoe, wherein to seek the secrets of the lower river.

"He goes swiftest who travels alone," Scott quoted, to agree with me. "Let Kirk attempt to find the trail, or clues to it, while we are workin' here, and so no time is lost. Moreover from studyin' the di'ry, he knows more of this land than any other, and so has better chance to find that fort, where likely they returned."

To this the rest agreed; and on the third day I set forth alone down river, convinced by many signs, that this was truly the Hiwasi, somewhere below the Shoni village of Hopeka and the forest fort in which our friends had stood a seige.

Here was on every side, a most impressive forest. Great buttressed trees walled in the river, crowding to the very edge. Ofttimes, where creeks debouched into the main stream, they were thickly screened with giant roots, forming gloomy tunnels, leading back one knew not whither. The river had carved the rocks and banks into a thousand kinds of caverns and lurking places.

In midstream, islands large and small, all forested, cut off full view ahead. In many places a dense growth, rivaling the mangrove of other climes, clutched earth and rock in its grip, binding all together against the times of flood.

In density almost tropical; in all other ways a northern forest like the Siskiyou a hundred times perfected—such was this wilderness of Nato'wa. Throughout the forests there were well-trod trails, but not the kind that human animals tread—if they would live. In Nato'wa, men follow the river routes, and thus I had my first glimpse of Fort Teskatuna, to call it by its Indian name.

Situated high up on a wooded river island, its northward wall alone was visible from below. Spanning the river from the cliffs opposite the island, an immense forest tree bridged the gorge. Where this had fallen, the wall had crumbled. Immense and rope-like vines had now begun the work of binding up the wound. Birds nested in the toppled giant's branches, which still sprouted green in places where the life-stream from the roots had not been broken. From embrasures in the north wall, black-mouthed cannon still protruded.

Concealing my canoe upon the island shore, I began the steep ascent through undergrowth and trees toward the hilltop island stronghold. Near and far, harsh-cawing ravens rustled through the branches in their heavy flight. At last the frowning south wall was in view. And as I stood beholding it, the gloom about me seemed to deepen. The trees nearby assumed strange goblin shapes. At a light touch upon my shoulder I started, then relaxed. It was a twig, which fell to ground.

Skirting the base of the wall, gaze roving its lofty height for means of ingress, I came finally to its battered double gate, locked from within, defying every effort at entry here. Around the corner of the south wall, surmounted by its tower, a steep trail beside the west wall was the only path by which an enemy might hope to storm.

Up this path I clambered, clutching protruding roots and stumps, to surmount the west wall and look upon a raised work, strongly built to defend this vulnerable point. Then I scaled the bastion with some difficulty, and dragged myself atop of it, commanding then my first view of the fort's interior.

Directly below was a rock basin containing a water supply. This trough stood at one end of an interior quadrangle, lined on three sides by a series of connecting rooms, built of heavy timbers and equipped with loopholes staring at the inner court. The thick roof of these rooms formed a broad platform directly behind the wall proper, which was pierced by embrasures for strange crude cannon. At every cannon stood a heap of iron balls. Watch-towers, at southwest and northeast corners, eyed the outer approaches narrowly through rifle-slits. Little more was visible due to the gloom elsewhere in the shadowy interior.

Utter silence met the ear, the silence of a dungeon or a tomb. But suddenly the skin about my ears and scalp was tightening, a tingle quivering down my spine. One reacts thus, sometimes, without knowing why, prodded by something beyond himself, some ancient instinct whose operation helped his line survive down to himself, its end. No question—this was a warning. And as I stood waiting for I knew not what, a shrill and piercing shriek rang echoing within the walls, weird and blood-curdling—a human voice or a frightful mockery thereof.

I took a further step, searching the shadows for sight of him who had awakened the silences. Seeing no one, hearing no further sound, I took yet one more forward step. Once more that shrieking voice rang wildly out.

"Stand back!" this time it cried, in a tone so full of warning that inadvertently I obeyed.

"Who's there?" I asked of the unseen, with simulated boldness. The answer was a curious muttering and cackling, as of laughter. The sound this time came from within the court; and cautiously climbing down to the platform, thence by a rough log stair into the darker quadrangle, "Who are you?" I repeated.

The answer was another burst of muttering from the nearest doorway, followed by *"Stand back!"*

Scarce knowing what to make of such a greeting, I sought to humor the speaker. "Look here I won't harm you. Who's there?" And suddenly switching on my light, I played its beam about inside the nearest room.

A grisly scene met the eye within. Human bones lay all about the floor. My heart froze in me.

A single pistol hung upon the wall, near it a powder horn and bags of ball and patches. Here was a weapon, like the cannon, fashioned within these very walls by ingenious men, to whom no obstacle had been insurmountable.

Taking down the arm I poured powder in the muzzle, pushed down a leather patch, dropped in a bullet, atop of this pressing another plug. Priming the pan and drawing back the hammer with its sharpened flint, I turned toward the door of the adjoining room, feeling much more secure thus armed. On opening this, a second door beyond slammed loudly. The unknown must have gone before, since he was not here, in what appeared to be the powder-room.

Passing into the third room, I heard a rustle as of garments, but this time no door closed. Advancing to its far door, I covered the loophole with my cap, so that whoever was beyond might not observe me seeking further arms. But in this—a workshop, apparently—not another gun did I see.

Turning back to the door, I laid hand upon its bar, and seeking to draw it open, stood back dumbstruck. The door was fastened by a heavy draw-bolt—bolted on *my own side!* Whoever had gone before me had either gone through solid four-inch planks of oak, or by way of the loophole in the door, through which I could hardly thrust my arm!

As if beholding my state of astonishment, from beyond came a burst of laughter. Someone seemed doubled up in paroxysms. Words followed, as incongruous as those which went before.

"Gold, by gum!" was what it sounded like to me, and then a child's voice calling, *"Here, Nugget! Here, Nugget!"* followed by a shrill whistle, as of someone calling to a dog.

But now such things made sense. Flashpan, eccentric miner, once the *Narwhal's* cook, and Tokala, the little Indian lad from America, were the sole occupants of the fort; for their voices had just spoken. But why the barred door and their reluctance to show themselves?

Drawing back the bolt, I flashed my light into a kind of living chamber. The room was empty.

Determined to end the farce, I passed successively through two other rooms, both unoccupied. In the third I heard again that rustle as of garments and drew back startled. A number of wide-winged bats rushed out into the court. The rustle seemed explained. But bewildered by the total absence of those whose voices I had heard, I made one last attempt to fathom the mystery.

"Flashpan," I cried out urgently, "if that is you, come out! Tell me what happened to the others."

A child's voice this time spoke from outside. If I was not mistaken, once again it said: *"Here, Nugget!"*

This was instantly followed by a guttural voice muttering a

few rapid words which I could not at once distinguish, so low were they. Perhaps imagination suggested it, but in a flash it seemed to me the words were these, in native Shoni: *"Kill him! Kill him!"*

Prepared for anything, I cut my light and pointed the pistol through the door I was then opening and peered beyond. As quickly I slammed it shut, for finally I had seen something move. I threw the bolt and looked through the loophole, grateful for these ponderous walls.

A great tiger was entering the fort by way of the huge tree-bridge. Looking not to right nor left, the heavy animal prowled out of my view along the platform. Soundless on his cushion pads he passed above my head; yet the stout timbers trembled as he went. Just next the door of the adjoining room a stair led to the quadrangle. Down this creaking path the tiger came in one great step.

The others, whoever they were, might not have seen the beast approach. I raised a shout. "Tiger! Watch out!"

At sound of my voice, the great male checked. Neck fringe ruffed out, black lips retracted, the four great canines drawn apart, thus with a husky snarl grating from the glistening throat he stood a moment, taken aback by my strange light.

The pupils of his eyes contracted visibly in the light. I saw and recognized a man-killer. The fangs, though long, were worn, the cutting teeth quite black with age. And yet the huge brute was in full strength, and fat with good living—on human flesh? And I, lacking that rough-hewn barrier between us, had been his latest prey.

As if in answer to the shouted warning, there came once again that crazy repetitious yell: *"Stand back!"*

Ignoring this voice, the fierce beast thrust his muzzle against the loophole. His reek encompassed me; his fetid breath blew hot into my face. Then from his cavern of a chest he hurled a roar that struck me not like sound-laden breath, but more like something palpable, flinging me bodily back flat against the inner wall.

Fear? Yes, I knew fear, and shame is absent when I tell of it. I am no coward. Yet I stood twitching, utterly paralyzed by that thundering voice. Not only I—the very walls and ground shook too, objects rattled on the walls, bits of masonry dropped from the ceiling.

Hitherto I had known only the more silent tigers of the Far East, who challenge but infrequently. Tonight I heard the tiger of Nato'wa giving voice, forcing his awful tones from belly-deeps to jaws—not once or twice, half-heartedly, but time and time again for full five minutes, as even lions do not do, meeting echo with answer until the fort quaked to the thunder of it.

Shaken and quivering, at each successive roar I felt my flesh turn cold, despite the mighty barrier between that brute and me. Then I saw one great paw intruded. The hooked claws fastened on the loophole's edge, scoring the hardwood like chisels in wax. Shaking the structure with mighty efforts, the great cat desisted, to pad back and forth.

Watching its orange and black side-stripes pass, I thought at last of my pistol, and leveling it when the muscled shoulder came in view, fired. I heard the spark of flint, the *puff* of priming powder and a result like the burst of a roman candle—but no report. The bullet had somewhere rolled out of the barrel and I had put aside my bag of bullets. The gun was useless to me.

For the moment the tiger was gone. But ten seconds later he clawed at the very door by which I had reentered. The killer must have retraced my own prowlings, beginning at the open door of the arms room. Baffled by the heavy bar, again it returned to the quadrangle, snarled through the port, crouched to lap water at the trough, and returned, roaring anew.

What had become of the others in the fort, whom I had heard but not once seen? Had the tiger come upon them?

And now I understood, with vast relief, the implications of those human bones scattered in the arms room. My friends had not, after all, broken taboo. Instead, the fort was the den of this man-eater. Hither he brought his victims, to be devoured at leisure; and when he went out stalking others, the ravens cleaned the bones.

But what of the voices? All that night I sat hungry in the dark, chilled to the bone, with the man-eater roaring before my door, and only my thoughts for company. And troubled thoughts, not knowing who occupied the fort with me, nor why its previous occupants had forsaken it, nor whither they had gone.

When the beast at last departed, I slept. But toward morning the mysterious voice spoke up again: *"Stand back! Stand back!"*

Looking from the loophole, I turned away, revolted. The

tiger's prey lay there—or what was left of her: a Shoni woman.

Fearful of meeting the beast in the quadrangle, I passed through the several rooms, securing the doors as I went, and going warily. The beast was gone. I was free to seek a further clue to our missing friends.

In the quadrangle was a line of mounds, near the north wall. Memorials roughly burned into the logs told a story:

Ianko, Son of Tessaco,
Died in Action,
July 17.

Meliko, Mother of Sekowa,
Killed, by Stray Bullet,
July 23.

Other mounds showed the clawmarks of wolverines, baffled in their ghoulish digging by solid slabs of stone laid atop each body. There was evidence of the fort's long seige—broken arrows sticking from the walls, with here and there a bullet embedded, or flattened and lying on the ground.

What tragedy had befallen Munro and the rest? Capture by Indians? Death in the forest, such as I had only just evaded the previous night? Climbing to the platform, I sought some answer to the riddle there.

In the towers were no clues. Quartering the platform, I found nothing new. Pausing beside a cannon, I cudgeled my brain for a sane answer to the mystery of the speaking voices, when suddenly, almost at my elbow, there rang forth the first voice I had heard, repeating the identical cry.

Then from the cannon's mouth, as if in sudden fear, a raven darted, with a rustle as of garments, to flap heavily in air, alighting atop the wall nearby. It regarded me boldly with the shrewd gaze of its cunning kind, its bright yellow eye glistening like a jewel. Its large beak open; simultaneously I heard Flashpan's voice, muttering miser-like:

"Gold, gold, gold—"

Staring at the raven, I had to force myself to accept the demonstrated fact. Then memory served me, and I knew the truth. It was this mimic-bird's voice which had spoken. The voice of a natural wild mocker, however indistinct, parroting the cries and simple phrases it had often heard repeated, had baffled my wits until this moment.

If I recalled aright what I had read in Numro's diary, this bird was one of Flashpan's several pets, and should answer to the name Bonanza. I tried it, and the bird answered with a cackle, and a child's voice calling and whistling as to a dog.

Once more calling the creature by name, I extended an arm. Without hesitation it jumped to my wrist. One mystery was solved. Another only deepened. What might this dark bird yet tell if only it could speak intelligently?

"Speak, Bonanza, speak," I urged cajolingly, stroking its glossy back, and using a phrase it must have heard before.

"Spik, Bonanza!" mimicked the pet, then fell silent. I waited, hoping. The raven screeched, and scratched its head and preened.

Then, *"Hide it in the breech!"* the raven murmured indistinctly. Gibberish, I thought in near despair, then suddenly stood inspired as the raven jumped from my arm to its cannon, entering as it had appeared, *in the breech*. That woke me up, gave me the needed clue.

Luring the raven forth anew, I perched him on the wall and explored the cannon's mouth. With regret I removed a rough nest of sticks, reaching in the full length of my arm and finding—nothing. But on directing my flashlight within, I saw what made my heart leap—some kind of skin-wrapped package, bound with leather thongs.

Notching a ramrod found close by, I hooked it in the thong, and drew forth that bundle. Carefully replacing the nest, I bore the package to the arms room. Then throwing out the grisly human relics which cluttered this place, I unbound the package and turned the light upon the contents.

Here were maps, sketches of wild beasts, some nuggets of pure gold and various odds and ends—ornaments and other things, valuable no doubt. And then—a note, upon a page torn from a little copy-book. My search approached its end: the writing was in the round hand of Dr. James Munro. It read:

> *At last! Today the Indians brought another tusk, carved like the one long lost. Translation of the markings on its full length of nine feet, speak of a strange and mighty race of men, who call themselves the People of the Tusk, and dwell somewhere in Nato'wa, no one knows where. Perhaps soon we shall—*

That far I read, when suddenly my light died out, the batteries gone dead. The short Arctic day was near its close. Half-darkness invaded the room, although the quadrangle outside was light enough.

I paused, about to light, if I could what seemed to be a home-made oil lamp that hung upon a wooden peg. Some inner warning bade me turn. I froze almost to stone at what I saw.

The door had just swung in, responding to a heavy outer pressure. Beyond, a feline giant, the hair singed from a black-and-orange-striped shoulder, was dropping on all fours into a crouch, with indrawn breath and open-hanging jaws. The curved incisors gleamed like dark-stained ivory. Largest of the tiger-kind found anywhere on earth, met within its own environment by one unarmed and taken by surprise, and having not a twentieth of its jungle strength—what chance had one mere man against this stalking creature of the night?

Now crouching low and watching me with eyes like burning greenish moons, it placed one broad, round paw within the room, and from the bottom of its mighty chest unloosed a roar that jarred paralysis into my limbs anew.

A moment more and I had been poor carrion, like that other mutilated thing which I had seen. But as the striped tail jerked up in prelude to the killing spring, there came to ear a sharp loud *crack!* much like the explosion of a pistol. The brute turned fiercely round, snapped at the air, colliding with the doorpost as it spun, and half withdrew hindforemost to the quadrangle.

A yell escaped me then, of fear and wonder mingled. For almost on the lashing tail a human form dropped from the upper platform—a figure unmistakable for any other.

Fine, clean-cut features on a dark and shapely head, a pair of green-blue eyes with fiery intrepid gaze, a torso bronzed as any Indian's. Wide-shouldered, lean of waist, long-limbed—with coil-like muscles indicating almost boundless strength and bottomless endurance. I knew him at a glance, the man we sought—Kioga, the great Snow Hawk, thick spear in one hand, coiled whip in the other.

The snarling cat had not come fully forth, when with a move too quick for eye to follow, the long spear, hurled with mighty force, drove through its body near the shoulders, point emerging red upon the other side.

Transfixed upon the shaft, the tiger reared, blood frothing from its nostrils. Before it rose erect, with a lightning spring its human foe clung closely locked upon its neck and shoulders, beyond the easy reach of clawing paws.

End over end the lean brute threshed in paroxysms, its flat hips thumping on the hard-packed earth—and still the man-form clung, linking it round with legs of steel.

My blood ran wildly at the sight of two fierce animals locked in struggle for the mastery, in such a scene as had not been witnessed since man first strode upon this ancient earth. Surely no other human being had ventured near that pain-crazed brute, a dozen times the more dangerous for the spear it carried.

Despite those cable thews, how long could human flesh and bone avail against that jungle juggernaut?

Now both upon the ground lay tangled. The great fanged jaws gaped wide, the pulsing human throat almost within their compass.

Belatedly I sought to aid the man who dared to stake his life that I might live; and rushing forth, struck at the savage head with clubbed gun—and missed the mark. Ere I could strike again the tiger's eyes went blank, the long form stretched out limp. . . . That well-shod spear had done its work.

But at its side, half under it, Kioga lay as silent as the lifeless tiger.

I took one great paw in my grip and sought to drag the carcass from Kioga. With all my strength I could not move that heavy body. The man lay still. Dead? What had death and that fine form in common? It could not be—and it was not.

Kioga stirred. Light came to his eyes. They saw me standing there. He spoke.

"Who are you?"

"Stanley Kirk," I told him, bending over. "A friend of James Munro. Are you badly hurt?"

He smiled, displaying white and even teeth, by way of answer writhing from below the heavy brute, and saying with a little laugh: "He was too old to do much harm."

Bending at its side, he withdrew his spear, set it aside, and laying hold upon the beast's hind-legs, half lifted it and dragged it quickly within the arms room, its former den.

I had not even budged it with my utmost strength! Kioga shifted it as easily as the brute itself had dragged its human prey into the fort the night before. Blood welled from claw-wounds in his shoulder; but ignoring this, he turned to me.

"How came you here?"

He listened to a brief account of the *Bearcat's* coming—but to my eager query as to Dan and Beth he made no answer.

"Your people, are they armed?" he demanded.

"Our weapons all sank with the *Bearcat,"* I admitted.

"That must be remedied. The Shoni tribes are at each other's throats. The fort was stripped of almost everything, as you can see. We cannot remain. The Shoni warriors were on your trail, and can't be far away. Follow me, and later we can talk."

He turned, picked up his lash and bow, strode out into the quadrangle, and led the way along the upper platform to the north wall and the tree-bridge joining the island to the shore. From here the reasons for the fort's abandonment were visible—two wide and V-shaped cracks, already overlapping, which might at any moment expand and slip half of the structure into the river eddies in the chasm.

When we were halfway across the rough-barked, toppled giant, the Hiwasi swirling far below, two graceful long canoes appeared in view, cruising obliquely up across the currents. Another also could be seen, bearing in tow the clumsy dugout I had hidden.

Lean-bodied muscular savages of copper hue propelled them with long paddles toward a sandbar just below the bridge. . . . My first view of Nato'wa's native people, whose ferocious caliber so soon would show.

From the fort behind came a shrill, almost inhuman yell. Three feathered heads appeared above its wall and saw us almost out of reach and swiftly making good our escape.

Faintly came the twang of bows, more loud the shrill of arrows whistling past our ears. I felt a sudden stabbing impact in one thigh; and glancing down, beheld a shaft of wood protruding from the muscles, its flintpoint red with blood. Already, at this early stage, Nato'wa thus first marked me with a lifelong scar as of her own.

Glancing back, the Snow Hawk saw me slip, with one leg crumpling. He checked, returning instantly. Before I could protest or urge him to go on alone, he picked me up, as lightly as a child is carried, and passed beyond the bridge into the forest.

He went perhaps a hundred yards along the route of average men, the thicket-tangled lower forest. Then bidding me hold fast, he climbed among the ledges of a cliff and mounted rapidly where a chamois might have found foothold with difficulty. The first low branches of the forest trees here almost brushed the rock, and into them Kioga sprang, without visible preparation.

Now all was changed. The solid earth was well below, a bending, ever-shifting hand- and foothold beneath; yet never for an instant did he pause, nor seem to hesitate when choice of routes lay open. Up, through the forest, midway, above the higher terrace, then into the very topmost canopy he went, bearing me as if I were no extra weight. Then, the trail broken for all pursuit, he transferred back among the rocky ledges once again. Not even he could climb into the sky.

A forest stretched before us toward a misted valley. In the crowns of several trees hawks had their nests; far in the blue great condors circled slowly. This was Kioga's favorite solitary realm, up where only hawks and eagles dwelt.

Depositing me upon a shelf, my back against the cliff, Kioga examined carefully that arrow sticking through my thigh. With hands that were sinewy but wonderfully gentle, he cut the shaft with his knife and drew the two ends out. Gashing an outreaching limb from a certain tree nearby he waited for the sap to exude, then thickly smeared the wound with that.

Scant thought and no attention for the cruel gouges on his own brown shoulder, but first thoughts for the hurts of another—that was Kioga as I knew him then and ever afterward, through the cruelest buffetings of strange fate that were to come.

"Now we can talk," he said at last. "Tell me about your ship and how you came here."

"Gladly," I responded. "But first, what of Munro and the La Salles?"

"Beth and Munro are safe with some of my Indians. But Dan—Dan is missing. He is impetuous and sometimes rash; we were in need of meat, and he went out armed only with a rifle, to fetch some in. When I left, he had been gone too long to suit any of us. I came back for some weapons left behind, thinking to meet him on the way. We quit the fort when its spring dried up and the foundations began to crumble. In search of Dan, I saw the Shoni warriors pursuing someone more cautiously than usual. I came before them to your canoe, and trailed you—and found you at the fort."

CHAPTER 4

"I killed last night at dusk," Kioga told me. "There should be plenty left. Wait here until I return."

Thirty feet—perhaps much more—below, a branch thrust out. Stonelike, Kioga dropped down through the intervening space, broke his fall by seizing its springy end, and forcing it to a lower branch, let go. The limb sprang back. The man was gone, as soundless as an owl that drifted past on velvet wings.

And on that lofty perch I lay, a man of civilization, wondering at the fortunes of the recent past, grateful to my very depths for the sweet boon of life, so near extinction a few short hours ago.

An hour passed. Wind in the pungent evergreens; notes of wild birds fluting clearly through the branches; the bugle calls of elk far on some distant ridge; an eagle soaring by, a fawn in its talons, bleating—these were the sounds; with now and then from far below this waving green, as from the ocean's depths, a heavy sinister note, a tiger challenging.

A shadow fell across the ledge. Turning with a start, I saw the Snow Hawk standing there.

"This much was left," he grinned, "because it smelled of the smoke from the fire I cooked it with."

He flung a leg of roasted venison on a flat of rock, and cut thick helpings from it, placing these on slabs of birch-bark taken from a bundle, made of new raw deerskin, the hair inside. From this also he took wild sour plums, sweet acorns, pungent cress, still wet with water from the brook it grew in. None knew better how to live in the forest. Never did a meal go down more easily.

And when the wilderness repast was done, we knew one another better; and the Snow Hawk looked forward to a meeting with Scott, La Salle, and my party at the block-house. That planned, we slept, and on the morrow started out, Kioga bearing me earthward as easily as some creature to the branches born.

Striving then to walk, a single step convinced me of its inadvisability. Kioga, glimpsing these poor efforts, called an instant halt, amid a thicket of forest close beside the river.

"There is a better way, in which you'll not need your legs," he said. "The Shoni shall donate a good canoe. They do not know it, but they shall."

Another hour passed while he was gone. When he returned, it was by water, in a long canoe, a dugout larger than my own. I climbed aboard with difficulty, took up a paddle and bent to labor with the Snow Hawk, our course upriver.

"Rocks right ahead," I warned Kioga, who smiled, I knew not why. But following his gaze, I saw two long and narrow wolfish muzzles appearing in the undergrowth nearby.

Wolves they were, but fiercer, more ravenous than any known to hunters of my other world. With long stiletto fangs gleaming white, they slowly emerged with back-laid ears—tall as Irish deerhounds, yet true wolves in all but their exceptional size. Lean, gaunt, wicked-eyed, they moved as one toward the rocks in the river, as if to cross by leaping from one to another.

Then suddenly the rocks rose in amazing bounds, revealed as a herd of river-bison, until now unaware of stalking peril in the thickets. With awkward haste they fled, bounding all about us and dashing water into our craft. But already the killers had seized and hamstrung a fat young cow.

A hundred times since then I have seen the wolves of Nato'wa kill. But each time is like the first. One does not harden to such stark ferocious cruelty.

Now the wonder was begun. That which earlier was unseen thrust itself upon the eye. Here what had seemed a bayou darkened by driftwood was in fact black with thousands of wild geese. Elsewhere along the river banks animals rose up to give us way, or calmly watched our passage. At every turn we glimpsed a moose or two, and caribou in bands lingered on the sandbars. The veldt of Africa, the grim Dekkan of India, hold no such plenitude of birds and beasts as may be seen each day in dark Nato'wa, most populous of wildernesses.

Pausing at a point some way northward, Kioga glanced quickly up and down the river, then raised a net of leafy vines and drew the craft beneath its screen. A cave mouth gaped darkly just behind, into which the canoe moved, obedient to Kioga's pressure of the blade.

There came a rasping sound, the smell of smoke, a spot of red glowing in the darkness, then suddenly a spurt of flame, and in one hand Kioga held a light, the product of his friction bow.

The cave was deep, with several chambers. The Snow Hawk disappeared, returning with a great armload of weapons. Some were rifles, rough but cunningly put together and fitted with flintlocks and firing-pans. Others still were pistol-length, and all were of a shape and size recalling weapons surviving from the War of Independence.

Returning from another trip, Kioga deposited leather bags of shot and horns of black gunpowder. "We stripped the fort of everything," he said. "Flashpan carved the stocks and bored the barrels. Munro made the powder of raw materials from the forest deposits from mineral springs."

I chose a pistol and a rifle for myself, slung horn of powder round my neck, and fastened bullet-pouch at belt. The remaining weapons filled the craft between us. On top of them Kioga tossed two heavy leather bags. Thus laden, we set off again.

When the rough angles of the blockhouse appeared, a hail told us that we were viewed. The place gave forth its occupants, among them John La Salle and Captain Scott. Their glances were riveted upon Kioga, with curiosity, admiration and wonder intermingling.

Acknowledgments followed introductions. The quiet Snow Hawk made a good impression. La Salle stood forth to grip Kioga's hand and to ask:

"My daughter, Beth—and Dan?"

"She is safe and well," Kioga answered. "Dan has not returned from a hunting trip, but—he should be able to take care of himself."

La Salle went pale at that news, then pulled himself together. "Thank God, Beth is safe!" he managed fervently. "When shall we see her?"

"As soon as I can tell her you are here."

His fears allayed, La Salle now eyed the splendid form before him. Of all that stood there, perhaps only Kioga and myself knew what was in his mind. Kioga bore his scrutiny and appraisal with a level gaze that did not waver. Then once again La Salle put forth his hand. The gesture marked his acceptance of the other, both as a man, and as the man his daughter loved.

Kioga then distributed the arms from the canoe among Scott's men—one rifle, shot and powder to a man, and from the leather bags brought buckskin shirts and caps of fur, and smoke-tanned moccasins to replace the tattered relics of our seamen's clothing. When the change was made, a band of men stood there who henceforth were to be frontiersmen of Nato'wa, modern only in their memories of civilization, for all apparel and equipment seemed of some bygone day.

The Snow Hawk left not long thereafter, and all that night I heard La Salle moving restlessly about the blockhouse. In the morning his voice called the glad news: "Turn out! They're coming!"

His words were hardly necessary. Each man was on his feet, and looking through the morning mists at an argosy both strange and picturesque, approaching.

It came in close formation, a swift and compact unit, prepared at once for war or peace, four long canoes, all deep with the weight of many men, Kioga in the lead. I heard a hearty hail—a voice not heard in long and anxious years. "How are you, Kirk?" James Munro cried, by way of greeting.

And then from behind him we heard one astonished word, "*Dad!*" And a beautiful young white woman—Beth La Salle—waved frantically, unable to speak further.

La Salle rushed forth, thigh-deep into the river, and clasped her in his arms.

Elsewhere in those canoes, quick sharp eyes gazed from face to face among us, then darted to the blockhouse on the bank. Eyes in the heads of bare-torsoed, red-skinned men—known for Indians at a glance, red men of Nato'wa, beholding with intensest curiosity these strange white-skinned newcomers.

In one canoe, behind Kioga, a curious figure sat, an old black hat crushed shapeless on his head. More homely face was never seen: crooked, hooked nose, mismated eyes, long, sadly drooping moustache, a neck so lean and skinny that the head sat on it like an apple on a crooked stick—Flashpan, the lost *Narwhal's* ex-cook, and the tireless miner after gold.

Upon his shoulder perched a long-tailed thick-haired monkey. Before him crouched a malemute, as shaggy as a wolf.

Just behind him sat a black-eyed swarthy lad, naked as the Indians, not over twelve years old, taking the newcomers in with quick observant eyes—Tokala, runaway from a civilized Indian reservation.

And in the next canoe sat James Munro, the scientist-explorer. In deerskin shirt fringed on the sleeves, bareheaded, he seemed not to have aged a day.

The canoe in which he sat had not touched bank when out he sprang to seize my hand and clap me on the back. "Stan Kirk! God only knows how you came here, but you're a welcome sight. I know now how *Crusoe* must have felt when he saw men from home."

Seen thus at closer range, Munro had a noticeable limp. "A Shoni spear can give a nasty wound," he explained. "It happened when they stormed our fort. But that's enough of me. How are things home at the museum?"

"All well," I told him. "But what is this about the People of the Tusk?"

"You must have discovered my notes," he answered with eyes that kindled suddenly. And now the man had subtly changed. He was the scholar, standing on the threshold of some fresh discovery. "I have a carved tusk, which tells a baffling history. Strange people, somewhere north of here. A mighty culture, oldest on the earth. A racial drama now unfolding stranger than any you have ever read or written of. But more about that later."

Meanwhile, Cap'n Scott and his crew met these men of the wilderness and were getting acquainted by the light of crackling aromatic hardwood, above which fresh-caught fish were sizzling.

Tokala, the lithe and handsome boy, acknowledged introductions with a grave reserve, for he was Indian. Now and then a ripple of purest Shoni glided from his tongue as he spoke to a dusky-skinned girl, fair of face and form, Heladi, the beloved of Dan La Salle. A knife was at Tokala's belt. Nato'wa and its ancient ways had claimed him.

"How well you look," said La Salle, surveying Beth with enthusiasm. "I'd never think you'd known any hardship."

" 'Tis love, sir," ventured Flashpan banteringly, with a knowing smile. "Love makes her look like that. 'Affection lights a brighter flame than ever blazed by art.' "

"And who may you be?" asked forthright Scott, taking notice of the little miner for the first time.

Flashpan struck another pose. "Aloysius Butterberry, citizen of the world—known to his friends as Flashpan," was the quick reply. "First to sink a pick fer gold in new Nato'wy. Miner, master barber, gunsmith, locksmith, blacksmith, cook on twenty ships in seven seas, an' hero o' the siege o' Teskatuna. Now does that answer, sir, or do ye wish me to enumerate my many other qualities?" And with the question Flashpan regarded him with open guileless gaze. "It's glad I am to meet white men of yore good nature, Cap'n Scott, and gladder still to welcome all of ye into our midst."

Scott put forth his hand in instant cordiality, a grin upon his face.

But now Beth's father's voice was heard, a trace of his anxiety sounding in it. "I had supposed my son Dan would be with you. No doubt he is to follow?"

There was a sudden silence, broken by the Snow Hawk's quiet voice: "I'm going out to meet him."

La Salle's face lengthened as his eyes met Kioga's. "To meet him—or to search for him?" was his question.

Kioga, seeing that evasion must only multiply La Salle's anxiety, gave him the facts. "You're not to worry," he concluded. "There are a dozen things which could have delayed him. I'll find him—depend on me."

"I shall not find that difficult to do," La Salle responded. "Good luck."

Outside the blockhouse it was a brilliant night. The Indians, intolerant of walls and roof, had built an outside fire, and they made room for us about it. And while Kioga gave his instructions to the warriors, we watched the strange firelit scene—or turned away to behold the long fingers of the ghostly aurora flickering across the dark sky.

A bed of brown-red embers formed, the while Kioga still talked with his warriors. Then, so quietly that some of us did not know he had gone, Kioga took his leave, to search for Dan La Salle.

Small blue tongues licked up and down the resinous remnants of the firelogs. No one broke the brooding stillness of the midnight hour. The howl of far-off wolves came muted from the distance. As if touched off by that, there came the sound of taut bowstrings vibrating. A warrior began the prayer-chant of his tribe. The Shoni voices rose in easy harmony—an ancient chant composed before their first ancestors wandered from Nato'wa, to settle in America and become the tribes found by the earliest white men.

It was this sound—a prayer-chant rising on behalf of his success—which followed Kioga out into the mazes of the gloomy forest. . . .

About the breakfast fire on the following morning James Munro revealed to us the import of Kioga's final talk with the Indians and himself the night before:

A month ago, content no longer with their bark canoes, which provided small security against weather and possible attack by savage men, the Snow Hawk's band had set to work. Equipped with tools, all earlier hammered from crude metal on Flashpan's forge in Fort Teskatuna, they had begun construction of a stancher river boat more suited to their needs.

Upriver logs had been felled. With ax and iron wedges the men had hewn and split, trimming the resultant planks with cunning hands. Of good hard wood a keel had been shaped. Where holes were needed, they had been burned through with heated irons. A rudder and tiller had been cut but not assembled. A stout sapling formed a mast; and from deerskin, cut and sewn together, a sail had taken shape. All the joints were caulked with pine pitch. In this state of near-completion the vessel now lay hidden in a cove nearby. Today we were to fetch her from that hiding place and tow her near the blockhouse where the final work could be done to make her fit for use.

This was achieved without delay, and many hands made swift work of what remained yet to be done upon the vessel. Our labors were a partial antidote for the depression caused by the absence of Kioga and Dan. As we worked, guns in the blockhouse covered our movements, against the possibility of Indian attack.

At last the hardwood deck was caulked, the mast firm-seated, the rudder hung astern, the bilge bailed out. A generous supply of powder and ball were stored forward; rifles and pistols were placed in convenient racks, and one of the fort's small guns bolted to the foredeck beam. Stout oars were included.

A strange craft indeed, lacking paint and much else that goes into the manufacture of a modern vessel, but she was stout and formidable withal. We splashed her peak with river water, and called her *Amazon*—a name which time and events would more than justify.

CHAPTER 5

Knowing the impulsive and adventurous nature of Dan La Salle, and realizing all too well the nature of the human foes who haunted this part of the Shoni forest, the Snow Hawk found slight difficulty picking up Dan's trail and reading into it, by natural inference, a fair approximation of what had happened.

He could imagine young La Salle, who had until that hour been so active in the company of Kioga and the forest men, chafing at the inaction of a hidden camp in the forest, the while all waited for Kioga to return with badly needed arms. He could imagine the young white man looking to his own crude rifle and checking the single-shot pistol thrust through his belt, to find it in good working order. Their food was none too plentiful—of that Dan would have thought as well.

No doubt, as at this moment while Kioga circled round that abandoned camping place, a fox had barked softly in a thicket. Owls had chuckled in the trees nearby. From somewhere near Dan had caught the sleepy gobble of a wild turkey from its roost and raised his rifle, hopeful of an opportunity to kill it. The call had been repeated; it seemed a little farther off. The bird had remained invisible.

Again Dan heard the bird and stealthily moved out among the sable shadows of the trees then waited silently. The guttural call came, just ahead. Dan stalked it, putting into service all the woodland lore he recently had learned. The sound receded; it must be roosting farther away than he had thought. He moved forward once more.

Minutes passed. Dan moved again, on moccasins that made no sound, his only light that from the moon, oft hidden by deep banks of clouds. The voice was still—perhaps the bird had detected him.

Dan moved to one side, amid the thickets, circled widely, ears attentive to catch the slightest sound; then slowly, on a level with his eyes, a human head appeared among the lower foliage.

Down either cheek a wavy ochre line was painted. Two bars of white were daubed upon the forehead. A feather painted red for wounds and trimmed for bravery, fell across one shoulder from a twist of raven braid, identifying a Shoni brave. The eyes, black as the shadows in the forest, were fixed upon him, cold and glittering.

Dan jerked his rifle to his shoulder. With his movement came a sound behind him. Before his finger hooked the trigger Dan quivered from a heavy blow, rocked dazed upon his feet, then fell.

Two pairs of eyes that gleamed with satisfaction met across his prone body. Rawhide thongs fell round his wrists and were jerked up cruelly tight. Silently the Indians picked him up and hurried toward the river nearby. . . . Such was the tale the trail unfolded to the eyes of one trained to translate the signs which ended at the river bank. Among the reeds a small canoe had lain, and into it Dan had been put.

To determine which direction the canoe had taken when it left the bank, Kioga drew upon his knowledge of the river and the habits of the Shoni natives, Since Dan's direction had been consistently upstream from the white men's camp, to have gone down the river would have left them open to discovery from the bank. With deep respect for the sharp marksmanship of the white men, they would not have chanced this risk.

Upriver then, Kioga hastened, running on the narrow beaten animal trails which twisted everywhere along the river's course. Parting the thickets at a point some miles above the blockhouse, Kioga waited, reasonably certain that his speed had exceeded that possible to a small canoe moving against the currents. And presently, moving toward a midstream island, he glimpsed a light canoe, two warriors at the paddles, with another person propped against the thwart. The one propped up was Dan.

Wanting a canoe, Kioga thought to take instantly to the currents. But to swim across directly would make him stand out to watchful eyes as the single object moving against the stream. Instead he turned upstream a little way, swam strongly out into mid-river, then let the eddies bear him down upon the island bank.

Amid the reedy thicket that rimmed the shore he writhed along to gain deeper cover, then quickly found the Indian camp, pitched near the island bank. The warriors were Shoni; markings on their cheeks and brows attested that at once. Numbering two score and more, they quite surrounded the young white captive, now conscious in their midst. Dan maintained an air of scorn, a fact which Kioga noted with approval, for any sign of fear would have doomed him to the ingenious tortures which so amused the Shoni.

Kioga's mind fixed on means of achieving the white man's rescue. An attempt made at this time of day could only end in failure, give warning to the enemy, with likely injury to Dan at the first alarm. On the other hand, to wait for nightfall might be to see the warriors depart before that time. A better idea sprang into mind. And Kioga melted away as he had come, slipped silently into the water again, and let it bear him down toward the blockhouse.

Tense with suspense, the little garrison received him anxiously. In quick sentences, economical of words, he told what he had seen, making no further attempt to minimize the danger, and quickly sketched his plan of action thus:

"Bring out the *Amazon*. We'll come upon them unexpectedly, and with a show of force and strength. Sometimes that is effective with the Shoni. But speed will count. Move quickly!"

Munro told off six men, myself among them. The *Amazon* moved from her berth nearby and out upon the river. And aided by just enough wind to fill her sail, the crude craft moved grimly upstream, toward where the Indians had bivouacked.

"We'll throw a scare into 'em," threatened Flashpan, looking to the falconet up on the forward deck. "They ain't a Injun livin' who can stand ag'in what I got here."

Nearing the island, we who accompanied Kioga, had our first view of the Indian camp. Upon a sandy spit a dozen good canoes were drawn up in a line. On shore the ever-present abattis of spearlike branches stood raised against the forest prowlers.

Around the fires half a hundred naked red men squatted, plumes waving, pipes sending up their incense to form a picturesque group as from a painted scene of long ago.

Then suddenly a warrior pointed. As one man the hostiles leaped afoot, to gaze in wonderment at the awesome craft bearing slowly in upon them, sunlight glowing redly upon her sail.

But Flashpan left them not long in wonderment. Leaping to the bow, he shook a hairy fist and sent a shout across the intervening space: "Whoopee, redskins! Ye asked fer trouble, and here we be."

Too late Kioga sought to restrain the little miner's enthusiasm. The Indians, realizing the identity of their unexpected visitors, sent back sharp greetings in return. The twanging of many bows foretold the deadly skitter of arrows across the waters, while several thudded viciously into our planking.

Raising his head above the forward bulwark, Kioga warned the natives gathered on the bank: "Put down your arms, warriors, and give up the white captive—or we destroy you!"

The savages sent forth a wild defiant yell, followed by another storm of arrows. Kioga turned to Flashpan with a nod, and the old miner turned to his falconet. While Munro held the tiller steady the moustached gunner blew hard upon his smoking match and lit the priming powder. Came then a flash, a belch of flame and acrid smoke, then rolling thunder.

A pair of iron balls, held together by links of chain, flew spinning furiously toward the shore. With a rending and tearing of bark and framework, the row of canoes on the spit flew into fragments. Not one by one, but all at once, as if a bomb had struck them! No single craft escaped the missile which, crashing through the flimsy craft, ended its career by smashing down half of the abattis and splintering a rock behind the Indians with a startling shower of fire.

The *Amazon* had spoken. While the echoes of her voice recoiled from cliff to cliff, the Indians stood frozen to the earth, beholding the settling ruins of their many craft. Then as with a single mind they wheeled and scattered into the depths of the island's jungle.

Of Dan we had as yet seen no trace; but wading swiftly ashore and giving chase to one of the fleeing warriors, Kioga overtook, disarmed and pulled him violently down, throttling him.

"Where is the white man?" demanded the Snow Hawk, releasing his grip that the other might answer.

"Where you will never find him," was the sullen answer.

Kioga increased the pressure on the other's throat, but then relaxed. Not even death can part the lips of a Shoni brave who does not wish to speak. There was a better way, Kioga drew his knife. The savage watched like a cornered wolf.

"Come, now, *ehi,*" he said. "Where have they gone? Speak

quickly, or I will crop you short-haired like a white man, and when you go back home all the women will make a mock of you."

Stubbornly the savage kept his silence. Kioga seized one of the glistening braids, proudest possession of the native warrior, and put the edge of his knife against it. The warrior writhed, but could not break that iron strength which held him down.

"Who will know you spoke?" the Snow Hawk said persuasively. "I do not wish to make you a laughingstock for all the tribe. Quick—where is the white man?"

Eyes upon the knife, the savage yielded sullenly. "Twelve warriors took him earlier upriver."

"What will they do with him?"

"By torture they will make him tell where the white men have concealed the black dust and the sticks which kill."

Kioga knew he meant firearms and powder, with which Munro's party had held mastery over their Indian foes. "They waste their time," he told the savage, permitting him to rise. "We have moved all elsewhere. But you have told me what I wished to know. Go, then—and think well of the Snow Hawk."

The other started. "I am of the Wacipi, who dwell far in the mountains, *Ai,* I know you now! Why do you linger with the whites, when all our tribes are at each other's throats? It was not so when you ruled us as chief-of-war. Why do you not come back and reunite the tribes?"

"Blood speaks to blood," Kioga answered. "Long though I dwelt among the Shoni, the whites are still my kind. I must remain with them."

"Come back," the other pleaded. "A thousand Shoni maidens all slim and lovely as the moon, would welcome you."

"There is a white-skinned woman I have chosen," the Snow Hawk answered. "It cannot be, warrior."

"Then luck to you," the other said regretfully. Kioga watched him disappear, knowing that but for Beth La Salle, he would have chosen the exciting life of a Shoni savage, to any other on earth. . . .

The Snow Hawk returned to the *Amazon* with news of what the Shoni warrior had told him. "They have the start of us by several hours. To go back for our own canoes would take much time. But with the oars and half a breeze, it may be we can overtake them."

"Let's git a-goin', then," said Flashpan, breaking out the

oars. Thus pursuit began, the clumsy *Amazon* against the Shoni greyhounds of the river. A stronger wind blew up behind us. What with that and our strenuous efforts at the oars, the crude craft forged onward—when suddenly with a jar, she heeled, and lost all way, brought up upon a bar.

Clearly only war-canoe could overtake war-canoe, particularly in shallow-upriver waters. Reluctantly Flashpan put the tiller over. By dint of mighty efforts on the part of all, the little vessel was refloated, and under oars moved once again into her berth beside the blockhouse.

In haste we made the change from *Amazon* to Shoni longboat, and set forth eagerly afresh, recruiting several of Kioga's red-skinned allies as extra paddlers. Few craft are swifter than the Shoni war-canoes. Pressed onward by its brawny paddlers, the racing longboat left a bubbling wake behind, and keen eyes watched ahead for traces of the craft which bore the captive Dan.

Arriving at the junction of two rivers, there was no way of knowing which route the enemy, still unseen ahead, had taken. While those aboard the pursuing craft debated, from a point somewhere nearby there came a short owl's hoot, followed by the *yap-yap* of a fox—the signal used between Kioga and his Shoni friends.

The Snow Hawk cocked an attentive ear, raised a hand for silence, and dipped quietly, turning the canoe toward the bank. On the instant Flashpan, Munro and the others leveled ready rifles.

Kioga laid his paddle down without a word, and in its stead took up a war-bow. Once more the signal cry now came, and on the shore a movement in the thicket drew the black stares of our rifles. For of the band to whom that special signal had been made known, all were here present in the war-canoe.

"Who is it? Speak!" Kioga challenged in the Shoni.

There was no audible reply. But as all watched the thicket, suddenly a slim figure stood boldly forth. The tension eased. "Tokala!" came Flashpan's voice. "What'n tarnation be ye doin' in the woods alone?"

Tokala's eyes were on Kioga while he answered, in a swift flow of liquid Shoni. "They do not want Tokala in the camp of Captain Scott. I am too small, they think, to do a grown man's work—I who served the guns of Teskatuna!"

Kioga's face remained impassive.

"What do you, here?"

"I bring you word of Dan."

"Speak, quickly, then."

"He passed here not an hour ago. Twelve warriors guard him."

"Where did they go?"

"I heard them speak of the Empty Lodges."

Kioga's face expressed a sudden understanding. "Abandoned caves up near the Tamasili—the Mountains-that-have-no-tops," he said to James Munro in explanation. "I know them well. I often hid there when a boy. What lies beyond those northern mountains no one knows. Their peaks are always in the clouds."

Tokala watched the Snow Hawk sharply, although he took no step toward the canoe. For all that he was preoccupied with gravest fears for Dan, the Snow Hawk still found time to read Tokala's thoughts. The boy had sought, successfully, to make amends for certain small mischiefs of which he had been guilty of late. Kioga said no word, but moved a little back and made a gesture.

Needful of no further urging, Tokala sprang eagerly into the craft, admitted to a place of honor in the band. The long canoe moved on again, its goal the Empty Lodges.

To reach this goal we now must face the swift white waters of the river's upper reaches, and by main strength prevail against the ripping currents lashing at our craft. From far astern I saw the bare backs of the paddlers gleaming bright with sweat, and in the bow the splendid torso of Kioga, like some perfect sculpture by Cellini come to life. . . .

Cunningly the Snow Hawk took advantage of each factor in our favor in that long-drawn contest with the boiling waters. Now angling across the stiff unyielding breakers of a mill-race; now changing cautiously from one channel to another; now paddling furiously, now thrusting deep their river spears in poling on their craft; and again riding easily against the direction of the stream by hugging shore to gain help from the counter-currents; so by water-wisdom, strength and dogged persistence we left the danger well behind and came at last in sound and sight of Tamasili—the so-called topless mountains, in which a thousand streams both large and small take their rise as cataracts which ultimately swell the mighty rivers of southeasterly Nato'wa.

Amid the swirling mists of waterfall which thundered to our right we put the craft against a lesser fall which veiled an overhanging cliff. An instant there the war-canoe rebelled, as if her every instinct were opposed to passage through that seemingly solid wall of liquid.

Then with the combined goad of all our poles she surged ahead. The thick fine spray enveloped her; a sudden torrent all but swamped her under. Another mighty effort from each man, and she was through the water-wall, the whirlpools of the falls behind. In the cavern lake deep under and behind the fall, an utter stillness rose about the craft as she moved ahead. Far astern already, the light shone through the fall as through a stained-glass window. But forward was velvet darkness, and a deep oppressive stillness.

Suddenly a spark appeared ahead, and then upon the gleaming walls the reddish flicker of a fire. Close above the rocky roof hung low, and far ahead the hidden lake stretched out its dark and silent surface. Upon a ledge above the water level we now could see the forms of men.

Without a sound Kioga drew the craft against the wall of this deep under-mountain cavern: and bidding us await him there, was suddenly no longer with us, but on a hidden path known only to himself, and moving like a stalking panther toward that distant fire.

In his persecuted boyhood, oft the Snow Hawk had hidden and wandered through this honeycomb of ancient chambers, occupied in olden times by some long-forgotten race of cliff-men. Now calling on his memory of its winding paths, he found a way which brought him presently within the sound of human voices. He turned his head to listen, caught the gutturals of a Shoni dialect, and then the clear voice of Dan La Salle.

The words held grim significance. "I wouldn't tell you if I knew. Go on, you copperhead, pull out the nail!"

The Shoni, then were seeking to wring from Dan by torture the secret of the arms and powder-cache! There fell a silence during which Kioga crept in view of the dreadful proceedings. Dan was by the rock wall, his tight-thonged hands bleeding. Before him in a semi-circle sat his red tormentors; and as Kioga watched, one of the warriors held a flaming stick against Dan's arm, already seared from previous torture.

Observing Dan with practised eye, Kioga saw him near collapse. The Snow Hawk looked about for the sentry, and saw him standing a little apart from the others, but like them, intent on the torture. Upon the sentry Kioga glued his eyes, inching forward flat against the wall. Dan screamed in sudden agony. Derisive laughter from the warriors echoed.

Anticipating it, Kioga struck with suddenness, a deadly, short hammer blow upon the sentry's temple.

The man sagged flat against the wall, the laughter of the warriors covering the sound of fist on bone. Ere he could fall, Kioga drew him out of view, and in a flash possessed his blanket. Draped therein and muffled to the eyes, he moved into the firelight, complaining gutturally of the chill.

The torturers took no notice as he bent above the mooring rope of their own canoe, cast it free and watched it drift well beyond reach. They did not see the lightning glance which played upon Dan's face, nor the lowering of the wrap by which Kioga revealed himself to the captive for one short instant.

But none could overlook the vehemence of the sentry who suddenly advanced upon the captive, brandishing a knife before his face.

"Stand back, Ogoya," said a tall warrior, laying hand upon Kioga's blanketed shoulder heavily. The supposed sentry flung it off, as if in anger, and answered gruffly: "Why do you play with him? Thus, with my knife—and thus—I'll mark him for a coward."

The bonds about Dan's wrists, cut through, were loosening. Aware of rescue, Dan feigned fresh agony. Kioga, whirling of a sudden, obliterated both light and fire with the blanket.

Plunged into darkness, the startled Shoni had not risen to their feet before the Snow Hawk swept all the embers from the stone into the water. Then bearing Dan in arms, he softly backed away, leaving the Shoni to hurl themselves upon each other.

Pursuit would follow, he knew, as soon as the enemy could pull themselves together and realize that Dan was gone. Nor was Dan fit for fighting after his frightful ordeal. To us who waited on his arrival, the Snow Hawk said as much, and lowering Dan to our canoe, gave orders that the Indians return as they had come, with the injured man, to await us two hours' journey down the river. We would rejoin them there later, after having led the enemy off on a false scent. Thus casually Kioga bade his warriors farewell, realizing as little as the rest of us who stayed with him, what length of time and strange events would intervene before we saw those warriors again.

The first hubbub amid the Shoni warriors had died. At any moment now we might expect pursuit. Kioga led the way by what sixth sense I do not know, for none of us could see an inch before our noses. We followed like blind men, guided only by a hold upon the Snow Hawk's leather rope, which stretched from man to man and formed a kind of guide and safety line.

At last Kioga called a halt. We heard the rasp of firesticks, smelled smoke and saw flame. We stood upon a ledge two feet above the water level. Lighted by Kioga's torch, taken from the remains of an old fire, we saw a wall in which were niches cut into the rock.

"The entrance to the Empty Lodges," Kioga said. "The Shoni think the place is haunted by the spirits of the dead."

"So do I," muttered Flashpan; and though he spoke half jestingly, the stillness of the place had gripped the miner as it had the others, now climbing up the niches on Kioga's heels. A rough-hewn stair was also climbed. We gathered on a sloping platform just above. It seemed we could progress no farther.

But while Munro held up the torch, Kioga leaped catlike upward, seized a hand-grip, and vanished overhead. An instant later the coil of his rope snaked downward. Hollowly, as in a well, his voice now came, bidding the others take hold and so be drawn aloft.

Upon a second platform there was ample room for all, and off its inner edge a cavelike hole led toward the bowels of the mountain. Kioga led the way with torch ablaze. The others followed through a tunnel which now was large and spacious, and again almost too narrow for a man to squeeze through. Nor was the passage straight, but tortuous with sudden dips and turns, whose complicated convolutions confused the sense of place and direction, and with frequent passages leading off in darkness.

Our moccasined feet trod with scarce a sound along this polished hidden route. It needed scant imagination to suggest what must befall the one who lost his way in these submountain fissures, probably formed in ancient times by gas forced out from the center of the earth.

Again the tunnel narrowed, then opened up abruptly upon a cavern whose distant walls the torchlight could not reach. Nor was its ceiling visible. But in the range of light, dim traces still remained to indicate its use by other men, for under foot were bits of charcoal and half-burned wood, of which Kioga presently had built a fire.

"Dan and our warriors are safe," he said. "The Shoni will never follow us hither, but we had better wait a few hours here to give them time to quit the caverns. Munro, at least, will find it interesting."

The scientist looked up. "What's in your mind?"

"Back farther in the caves are chambers which once were used by other men. I don't know who they were. Unlike the Shoni, whom you call Indians, these were blue-eyed men, although I think their skins were coppery."

Munro took that up instantly. "How do you know their eyes were blue?"

"Drawings on the wall portray it unmistakably."

"Never heerd of blue-eyed Injins," offered Flashpan.

"Among the Mandans of America white men found them," Munro answered. "Some lay it to contact with Scandinavians. Others call it some queer form of albinism and so dispose of a racial riddle without really solving it. These drawings may throw new light on the Mandans. Let's look them over."

Kioga led the way. We climbed a narrow path which ascended one side of the vaulted chamber, proceeded along a twisting byway, to pause before a flat, smooth wall. In colors well-preserved and striking to the eye, some primitive artist had drawn strange pictures on the rock.

A moment Dr. Munro eyed them, with a deep absorption, then turned to me, subdued excitement flashing from his eyes.

"Another link," he said, then realizing that his words were meaningless to me, withdrew a fold of snowy birchbark from an inner pocket of his hunting shirt. Used in lieu of paper, one side of this record was covered with peculiar hieroglyphs. "You remember my note about the People of the Tusk?"

I nodded, well recalling too the tusk itself, which Munro had among his effects back at the blockhouse—the largest tusk I had ever seen, not excepting any which are displayed in Africa or India.

"This is my copy of the carvings on it," Munro went on. "Notice those drawings on the wall—how similar they are. It may be that among them I can find the meaning of these hieroglyphs."

Munro began his study with the absorption of the scientist at work, and in a little while grew jubilant.

"For months," he said, spreading his notes before us, "I sought some key by which to read those signs. The ones which oftenest recur are what I call the symbols of the dove and the horn, which look like this." Munro then scratched these rough figures on the stone:

"The other signs, in order of their frequency, are thirteen in number and look like this." Then to the first Munro added these remaining picture-signs:

"Therefore, here is a writing consisting of fifteen signs, not representing letters, buy syllables and sounds. In our own alphabet we have twenty-six letters, capable of infinite combination. Our numerals convey ideas of sum and quantity to any figure. In these inscriptions from the tusk, however, the fifteen signs double in number by being reversed or inverted. The language of the tusk may be more perfectly expressed than our own, with tones, inflections and shadings of which our writing is incapable."

Kioga, who had never realized the significance of his discovery, heard the words with deepest interest, as did we.

"Egyptian hieroglyphs were first deciphered by Champollion, from a Greek translation on the Rosetta Stone. His discovery moved the date of written history back in time thousands of years. I hope to do as much for the people whose writing is here," declared Munro, his eyes alight with scientific fervor.

"The writing on the tusk ran not lengthwise line after line, as does our own, but spirally, round and round the tusk, from tip to butt. I quickly found that out. But the clue which put me on the trail is on this wall. Can you not also see how several of these signs resemble Indian pictography?"

We could not but agree with him. Munro continued:

"One sign in particular—the symbol of the dove, a branch between its mandibles, occurs most frequently. . . . What tribe does that suggest to you, Kirk?"

"The Mandans," I recollected suddenly. "Whose beliefs resembled Christian Scripture."

"Exactly!" Munro agreed. "The only blue-eyed Indians in North America. With that clue before me, and having a knowledge of the Mandan tongue, I could perhaps go ahead, keying the Mandan syllables to the signs as written on the tusk and on this wall."

And while we watched, Munro concluded his translation, which as later perfected read:

And honor to our kings, descendants of the mighty line of Ru the Merciful, who ruled six thousand suns ago. Preserved be their monuments and citadels, preserved their herds and sacred to the labors of our kings.

Rise up, O Sacred One, and bear this favored prince who goeth forth to learn what is beyond, whereof to bring us tidings. For know that seven centuries ago, our wise men read the heavenly bodies and calculated that the earth was round and had many times the compass of our kingdoms.

O shade of Ru, behold this prince, his princess, his slaves and all his retinue; watch over them, that all may soon return to Mandha. And if this be, we people of the sons of Ru shall sacrifice an hundred slaves to thee.

"What does it mean?" I asked when Munro had done.

"It means that somewhere in Nato'wa there was a tribe of blue-eyed, copper-skinned men who spoke and wrote a language similar to Mandan."

"But what about the tusk? How did they come by that?"

"They probably found it, just as today the tusks of mammoths are found on the Ivory Isles of Siberia. The mammoth became extinct here in the Arctic, you know."

So spoke a scientist whose learning was of the outer world. The Snow Hawk, listening, knew things about Nato'wa as yet unknown to modern science. Munro did not especially notice his odd preoccupation, but would recall it later. "We're on the trail of prehistoric man," he went on enthusiastically. "A race who at one time were masters of an unknown kingdom, prisoners of their environment. Centuries ago the people whose artist drew these pictures on the wall set forth upon a strange migration to the outside world. Some were successful, and reached America—as the Mandans. The great remainder somewhere met with tragedy —and where more likely than in these very caverns?"

Flashpan glanced about uneasily. Tokala's eyes grew great with apprehension of the silent dark beyond the fire. Kioga sat expressionless, but presently rose.

"Come, we will run the clues all down before we leave."

Once more we moved, still deeper into the caverns. . . . Kioga, in the lead, paused suddenly. A darker chamber loomed ahead. The torchlight, threw into dim relief a scene weird and unnerving.

The cavern was filled with whitened skeletons of men. Among them Munro picked a way gingerly. The still remains lay all about as if they had been overtaken by some lightning-swift catastrophe. Some lay at stretch, as if the end had come while they slept, others had crouched before a fire in a circle. The embers of the ancient blaze were undisturbed. Upon the long-dead coals the strange utensils of the band still were perched; in them could be seen the shriveled dry remains of that supper, so tragically interrupted centuries ago.

Kioga glanced among these dead indifferently, as one to whom death and its evidences were a commonplace.

Not so Munro, who found on a large round metal jar the signs he sought to link these dead with those who had been mentioned in his translation. Without a word he pointed out a duplication of the dove, the horn and others of the picture alphabet.

By now the Snow Hawk's interest was aroused, and glancing round among the bones, he saw that some wore round about their upper arm-bones broad copper bracelets, each of seven links, each ornamented with a sign; and pairs of these skeletons were shackled together at the wrist.

The great majority were grouped about two skeletons of smaller size, one of a young girl, the other of a youth. The girl had worn a clasping golden circlet; etched with pictures in the manner of the tusk and jar. The youth wore on his breast an oval plaque, of gold inlaid with copper, the whole depending from a fine-worked silver chain. The plaque was also filled with carvings. The better to decipher them, the scientist removed the plaque and hung it on Tokala's breast.

Awhile Munro studied. Then, "*'Behold this prince, his princess, his slaves and all his retinue,'*" he quoted. "*'Watch over them, that all may soon return.'* Here is the tragic ending to a bold adventure."

Tokala stood up straight and tall, the better to do justice to the regal ornament he wore. Observing him, James Munro laughed. "It does become you, son. I hardly think the poor dead prince will ever miss it."

"You mean," Tokala said, with shining eyes, "that I may wear it?"

"Why not?" the scientist replied. "But keep it covered with your shirt, to preserve the etchings. We won't disturb the circlet on the princess' neck." He turned away, glancing about as if in search of something else.

Kioga chanced to find what Munro sought, beyond the farther entrance to the chamber. A mighty skeleton lay there, the dry bones of some enormous animal, too great for passage through the door which had given entrance to the prince and all his retinue. Other slaves lay near the bones. Still attached to the giant skeleton, were moldering remains of what had been a splendid caparison, held together in decay only by the delicate warp threads of imperishable copper-gold with which it had been worked. The great saddle, formed of wood inlaid with ivory and horn, fell to pieces at a touch.

A close comparison flashed into mind. Once, in the jungles of the Far East I had seen the like—the bones of a great bull elephant. Munro was triumphant at his discovery. "So ends the mystery of 'the Sacred One'!" he exclaimed. "And if anything were needed as a proof of what it was, here it is." He held aloft an implement of bronze some four feet long, equipped at one end with a hook beneath a sharpened point—unmistakably a goad.

I had not grasped Munro's implication on the instant. He was patient. "Recall the words of the translation—'*Rise up, O Sacred One, and bear this favored prince.*' This, I should say, is the Sacred One."

"An elephant—no, a mammoth," I declared.

"The mammoth was an elephant," said the scientist, "and now our picture is complete. Upon this brute—sacred because it probably was the last of its kind alive—the youthful prince set forth to find a world which he knew nothing of. There lies the prince, last of his line. Here lies the last of living mammoths, the elephant of the Arctic. Kirk, you're looking at one of the greatest finds in the history of the North."

"Scalp me," muttered Flashpan, "if I don't wish we'd move along back where we come from! They may be dead, these fellers, but they give me the willies just th' same."

"A little longer, Flashpan," said Munro. "See if we can't find some traces of where they came from."

Flashpan shook his head uneasily. "The curse o' death is on this place. No good will come o' tryin' to seek out a dead race. But I would rather go than wait behind with these fer comp'ny. Lead on, Kioga. I'll stick with ye."

Again we moved ahead seeking to unravel the mystery of these folk who had fallen victim to some unknown form of death. Further researches added nothing to what we had already found. Our advance blocked by a solid wall, we must perforce return.

Outside these Empty Lodges, the Shoni hostiles likely had abandoned us. We now turned back as we had come. As we descended through one of the lower chambers, the

Snow Hawk paused and stepped abruptly back. His torch threw light upon the steps before him, which we had earlier ascended.

Black water rimmed the way up which we had come.

Munro drew sudden breath, and every man knew instantly that he was trapped, retreat—as he had come—cut off.

"Perhaps we're on the wrong trail," suggested the scientist.

Kioga shook his head. "I know the way. This is the trail. The waters of the river have come up—perhaps a cloudburst in the mountains swelled them. . . . A bursting subterranean spring could have done the same. If that is so—" He paused.

Munro was quick to see his meaning. "If it is, we may never be able to pass back as we came here."

"We must go forward, now," Kioga agreed, "because, although we have water, we have no food."

He bent, cupped water in a palm and put it not to lips but to nostrils, then flung it back and dried his hands. "Unfit to drink. Poison, most likely."

The needs of men ofttimes assail them suddenly. Until this moment, absorbed in our researches, we had thought little of food and water. But with the realization that neither food nor drink were now available, we suddenly grew hungry and knew thirst.

I thought of the statistics I had heard. A man may live for weeks without food, but only for days without water. Thank heaven, that at least we had fresh air to breathe. The thought had scarcely come when Tokala clutched Kioga's arm, then sagged, and would have gone down had not the Snow Hawk caught him.

"My head's a-swimmin'," muttered Flashpan.

Kioga sniffed the air suspiciously, then flung at Munro: "Gas—or sulphur."

Munro stood rooted, smelling the air with an expression which cannot be described. His words betrayed his thoughts with dread suggestiveness. "Good God—not even air! This was how those people died."

Asphyxiation, death for lack of oxygen, dark in which no torch could burn to light the end—the thought of it was full of a terror that grew by leaps and bounds. One knew in such a moment the thoughts of men who, while at labor in the ocean depths, have found their air lines cut; of men entombed in mines whose shorings have collapsed; of men in sunken submarines whose every breath brought nearer the inevitable end.

"Quick!" came Kioga's voice like cooling spray on our quivering nerves. "Follow me." Tokala hung limply in his arms, breathing heavily as Kioga bore him upward. Close on his heels Munro followed heavily, and after him Flashpan and I, our breath all catching in our throats.

Now for a little time the air was free of taint, for we moved faster than the vaporous thief of life which came behind. A rocky tube led downward to some unknown place. The Snow Hawk paused, confronted with a fateful choice—to return where the wall had barred us back; or down this other path which led he knew not whither. How temptingly that unknown pathway beckoned!

The Snow Hawk turned the other way. He who in time of danger acted with a courage bordering on the reckless, now favored a course which seemed bereft of reason and good judgment.

Back at the wall, Tokala revived sufficiently to stand alone. While once again we faced that barrier which seemed impassable, Kioga gave his reasons for returning.

"The men whose bones we found came by this route. The brute which accompanied them could never have passed through that unknown passageway below. Either they came through solid rock, or else—" He paused, deep in a speculation known to him alone.

His quick eye scanned the rock before us as if to pierce it through. While Munro held a torch, Kioga went on hands and knees, feeling with his fingers along the base of the wall. The others watched, conscious of the thickening air.

Now with his knife Kioga scraped at the rock, then introduced one of our rifles crowbar fashion into a crack he thus uncovered. Upon the butt he threw his weight, and in the fitful light a rough rectangular block was seen to shift the fraction of an inch. Inch by inch the block moved under leverage until Flashpan and I could add our labor to Kioga's, and strain against the stone.

The air was now rank and oppressive. Munro sank with a gasp, and Flashpan held up the torch he dropped. The little miner's face was wet with sweat and ghastly in the light, when he too lost his strength. With what energy still remained in me, I then wedged the light between two stones, powerless to aid Kioga further, and conscious of a terrifying physical nausea and weakness.

The Snow Hawk turned to scan us swiftly, saw Tokala's dark head nodding heavily and Munro lapsing into stupor. Hope for the others now depended entirely upon him. The great block stood well out from the wall. Kioga bent and caught the corners. All the power of his mighty frame was in the several successive jerks he gave it. The block moved forward—then seemed jammed.

Kioga gasped for breath. Even he now felt the choke of slow asphyxiation. He rallied, tugged anew. The muscles on his back tensed up like cables, and on his arms the veins stood starkly out. If ever lives hung on one man's strength, ours did in that long moment.

Now Kioga drew upon his last resources, putting every ounce of force remaining in him into one tremendous effort. It seemed we heard his joints crack with the strain. Then came a heavy *thud,* and instantly a rush of air—musty and of a peculiar odor, but like an ocean breeze to us who stifled in a fog of sulphurous gases.

A black rectangle showed in the wall, and through this aperture Kioga lifted Tokala, took great draughts of fresher air into his lungs, and then returned to help the rest of us through.

When all were safe beyond, Kioga returned, filled the opening with stones—fallen from the roof—which lay here and there, and filled in the cracks with earth and small stones, the better to seal out the fumes which had so nearly overwhelmed us.

That done, he turned, and by the dim light of the torch saw that he stood at one end of a lofty vault in which the air, though stale, was fit to breathe and proving revivifying to his companions. Upon the floor he glimpsed a cup-shaped empty vessel. In it was a length of strawlike cord, and instantly he caught its close resemblance to an ancient lamp. Presently he came upon a little jug, sealed at the mouth with hardened clay, which gurgled when he shook it. Cutting through the seal, Kioga smelled a fragrant scent and saw oil on his fingers. He poured oil from the jug into the lamp and lit the wick—only just in time, for the torch was sputtering out.

Now by the light of the newfound lamp Kioga pursued his search, a definite hope and object in mind. For if men had come through here, however long ago, their steps could be retraced to some outer place where man could see the stars and feel the breeze of freedom again.

He did not at once find exit from this vault, but in his search came on great urns and jars, likewise tightly stopped with covers of clay. Within these tight-sealed urns was water, curiously flavored, and dry hard kernels as of wheat, or some like grain. Of these urns he took one each back to the others of us.

In the dim light of the lamp we ground the kernels in our teeth and washed them down with economical drafts of water. Thirst and appetites appeased, we gained new strength to seek the second exit from this vault. But deep in the shadows at one side we made disheartening discovery: A cave-in had destroyed the exit.

Attacking the broken rock, we finally emerged into a tunnel measuring certainly not less than fifteen feet from floor to roof. Upon the walls were deep marks, as of tools. Here too were skeletons of men, apparently trapped while laboring. The tunnel extended only a hundred feet, ending in broken rock beyond our powers to penetrate.

But in the wall close to the tunnel roof there was a blacker recess in the wall. Bounding up, Kioga found a hold and drew himself aloft. Here was a ledge quite wide enough to stand upon, and just beyond it, unmistakably, an inner chamber.

Kioga moved ahead into a second room, smaller than the first. Upon the floor lay skeletons again, two large, one small. Unmoved by these dry relics of the dead, the Snow Hawk glanced about. This room had the appearance of a dwelling, for contrasting with the catacombs that had been left behind, doors opened off on every side.

Kioga called this information down to Munro, then chose a door at random. Of heavy lumber, spongy with decay, it fell through at a shove, into another chamber whose entrance proved to be near the roof above the level of his head. So for an hour he moved upward as in the compartments of an ant-hill. And in each one only relics of the dead remained. Since all were supplied with grain and water in sealed jars, since all were likewise closed by heavy blocks, Kioga knew that this was means of sepulture, and that the dead so buried in these rock-walled rooms had been supplied with food and drink against the needs of the hereafter: And Munro concurred when Kioga brought back news of it.

Further progress found us rising far above the level of the first chambers. It was as if we climbed some cruder ancient counterpart of a modern skyscraper, save that there were no lights, nor lifts to carry us aloft.

By Munro's calculations we had come over twelve miles underground from our point of entry, and had climbed somewhat more than five hundred feet since entering the chambers of the dead.

"Which ought to bring us out somewhere beyond the Mountains-that-have-no-tops," the scientist added.

The chamber which we next encountered proved empty, save for a store of jugs, jars and baskets exceeding any we had seen before, all filled with grain and water. But here was something we had not encountered before—a strong door, of some richly paneled wood. A moment Kioga stood before it.

We knew his thoughts, and felt them too. The vast proportions and imposing solidity of that portal suggested something unusual to come. The bar was made to be raised from either side by means of a copper chain. Kioga raised the bar, and the barrier creaked open. We hesitated on the brink of the unknown, then stepped across the threshold, as if into another world.

Unlike the rough undecorated walls below, here every inch of space was hewn and carved with wondrous artistry. Arching pillars everywhere were cut into the hard volcanic rock, of which the walls were formed. In niches in the walls fine vases rested; the furnishings were massive carven chairs and tables. The very floors were overlaid with gleaming wood, incised with figures of men and animals, with everywhere the sacred symbol of the mammoth predominant.

We sought for dead in vain. None were visible, as in the catacombs below. On entering this room, we had come a step above the civilization of the lower chambers. The departed, it presently appeared, all rested in great etched copper coffins.

"They left their dead to occupy the dwellings they had used in life, then sealed up the rooms and never entered them again," said Munro. "Then up above the one-time dwelling they occupied another home, which upon death was given up in favor of yet another dwelling higher up."

The words were true. We literally moved upward through successive layers of some strange civilization. Happily the custom of entombing grain, oil and water with the dead prevailed. Lacking food and water and light, we would have perished in the lower catacombs, days before our climbing had brought us to this huge burial-chamber wherein the exit was choked with broken rubble.

Again we ate of dead men's food, then lay to rest preparatory to the morrow's search for exit. And yet "tomorrow" was merely the term we now employed to indicate the periods between our sleep. There was no other way of ascertaining, the time of day or night save by this roughest kind of calculation.

At least our sleep had heretofore been deep, down in these silent tombs of the speechless dead. Tonight our slumbers were interrupted as by the sound of rolling thunder. Kioga was the first afoot, and had one ear against the rocky wall, seeking to orient this first outer sound which we had heard since entering the lower catacombs.

There was a pause enduring perhaps five minutes. Then again that rolling rumble muttered through the silence. Thunder, yet not thunder—too quickly begun, too quickly ended. Silence once again; followed by the heavy *tramp-tramp-tramp* as of an army on the march, and soon thereafter rumblings anew.

Munro stood stiff and tense. Flashpan listened at the wall beside Kioga. Munro's eyes leaped to mine, in sudden comprehension.

"Those sounds are made by men—by living men!" he cried.

We counted twenty such disturbances, too regularly timed to have been volcanic rumblings. Then suddenly the noises ceased. Instead there came a heavy intermittent *thud-thud-thud,* as of some mighty battering-ram against a castle gate, continuing for hours at a stretch, until this also finally ceased and silence held its sway again.

Disturbed by these impacts, rubble began to flow through the larger opening. Clearing it aside as quickly as it came chuting in, we saw an exit forming. Up this the Snow Hawk went and called back hollowly that we should follow.

Obeying him, we seized his rope and clambered up. In the chamber at this newer level, light streamed through a heavy quartz-like glass which lined the chambers at one side—the first daylight which we had seen in no one knew how many days. By it we now glimpsed that which made us catch our breath.

We stood at one end of a regal chamber. The floors were

lined with silken skins of tiger, snow-leopard, bear and many more. The walls were hung with richly gleaming draperies. The furnishings were of a highly polished wood, carved in the shapes of birds and animals and ornamented thick with gold and copper appliqué.

Along the walls hung weapons, cunningly devised; great maces, war-axes, bronze knives and daggers, light but sturdy bows of horn and bone, with curious cords of twisted hair, and bronze-tipped arrows in square cases at their sides.

Of these Kioga appropriated a dagger, long bronze sword and bow with arrows. The others armed themselves with half-swords, axes or such other weapons as seized their fancy, for by this time each man had realized that we were almost face to face, not with the age-old dead alone, but with a race of living men, for this was patently a very recent entombment.

Among the shadows of one corner a shape took form, lying upon a platform raised above the level of a man's chest. Upon it a figure stretched, covered to the waist with robes embroidered heavily with golden-yellow figures. Before this dim, reclining figure, stood a small figure of a mammoth of stone. Upon its back were bowls of food and drink. Against the dais rested axe and shield of copper-bronze.

A shock awaited those who looked upon the figure's face. The eyes were closed. Undoubtedly the man was dead. But in the cheeks was color; in the jet-black hair the gloss of life remained. The veins stood out, even as in life, upon his hands, crossed on the breast. An expression of majesty was on the hawklike face, so lifelike that it seemed at any moment he must rise demanding what this motley group of intruders was doing in his mortuary chamber.

Tokala backed unwittingly into the chamber just beyond the platform. He turned, took one swift glance about the other interior, then wheeled and fled into Kioga's arms. His show of fear threw apprehension into ourselves, until the Snow Hawk thrust him gently to one side and entered the other chamber.

The reason of Tokala's fears was plain: this was a sacrificial chamber. Here lay the slaves and household attendants of the dead king in the other room. Like him, each one seemed merely to sleep. Three maidens, garbed in robes of cloth and gold, lay nearest to the door. Four youths came next, still linked together wrist to wrist as in life, no doubt the ruler's favored slaves. Ten maturer warriors were next ranged in a semicircle, weapons in their hands, as if defending the dead king. Then came a row of women, sumptuously clothed in richest robes, their thick dark hair filled with innumerable golden ornaments.

Other evidence proved this a very recent burial; for in the sacrificial bowls, the wheatlike kernels were not yet dried out. The meat, besides, had not the juiceless hardness of that found in the lower catacombs, but yielded a decided flavor, as of coarse and grainy beef.

Now Kioga paused before a door of intricately chased bronze. He laid a hand upon its polished grip and twisted. The mechanism worked without a sound. The door swung inward, slowly, due to its heavy weight. There came a rush of air, pure, clear and wonderfully sweet. As one, we all moved toward that open door, gazing out upon a vast expanse of star-shot sky, the moon agleam in bright relief against it, like some highly polished silver medal.

Beyond the door we glimpsed a kind of platform. Out we strode to feast our eyes upon a night-time sky which we had not seen for long uncounted days. It was the northern sky we saw, for we had emerged upon the north side of a mountain range, whose peaks rose towering at our backs.

Munro had calculated rightly. The mountains which the Shoni called the Topless Peaks were now behind, and ranging out of view to east and west. The platform on which we stood was near the apex of the cliff-tombs, which below us, tier under tier, ran deep into the earth.

Slanting irregularly earthward down the sloping wall below, there was a stair, hewn from the solid stone. From the platform no way of gaining it could be perceived. Undismayed by its apparent inaccessibility, the Snow Hawk tied his rope about one of the stone pillars, dropped the other end over and clinging easily, slid downward to reconnoiter the wall beneath.

He soon returned with information that the stair which we had seen could be reached. By a similar use of the rope, whose bight he passed beneath our armpits, the Snow Hawk lowered each man upon the stair whose landing he had discovered. Himself following, he then retrieved the rope and passing it among us, like a safety line, led the way downward toward those lights still flickering far below.

Frequently along the stair there were broad platforms, before the tombs carved into the rock. At each of these we paused to look down, each time a little nearer to amazing discovery. But long before we reached the bottom, the lights became obscured. Clouds and a heavy mist blotted out the moon, now shedding but a vague gray glow to light our way.

In this poor light there suddenly was heard upon the stair below the sound of human voices, chanting. Armed only with the weapons found in the chambers of the dead, uncertain of the force which now approached and of the kind of greeting to be expected, we took quick cover on the nearest platform, in the shadow of a portico at the entrance of a cliff-tomb.

A moment passed. The voices grew louder. A glow appeared ahead. Then round a bend there came a strange procession. Two muscular figures, unshod and almost naked, and bearing smoky torches, led the way. Immediately behind, five dark-skinned warriors followed, in helms of simple unworked metal. These men were girt about the loins with skins, and from their belts depended daggers and small long-handled axes. Each one bore on his shoulder a kind of mace. Their features were regular and strong, but their expression was hidden in the semi-darkness.

Next came two other slaves with heavy pads upon their naked shoulders. Upon these pads there rested long curving wooden handles, attached to an ornately carved and decorated palanquin, supported on its other end by two more slaves, who raised their portion by means of handles built lower on the conveyance. Thus, though the ascent was at an angle of more than thirty degrees, the equipage rode quite level, its seat facing outward from the wall.

Five other warriors, equipped as the first, were succeeded by two more torch-bearers. Although the procession moved with regal dignity and the low and musical chanting continued, to our complete surprise the planquin was occupied by no one. Continuing upward, the odd procession passed from view.

Withdrawing from his hiding place, Kioga led us downward once again. The mist was heavier. The glow from down below was much diffused and nothing there was visible. The descent, too, became blinder, for at this point the stair ran downward through a crevice in solid rock, walled in on either side. With danger of a fall removed, Kioga coiled in his rope that linked us man to man, that each might be free to use his weapons should the need arise.

Thus cautiously the final descent was made, when almost at a last turn in the stair we paused to listen. The quiet, hitherto conspicuous, was broken by a sudden bedlam of shrill yells, mingled with a curious hoarse chorus of sound.

Urged by curiosity, we reached the platform which marked the bottom of the rocky stair, and from this point of vantage gazed out dumbstruck upon a scene of confusion, color and activity unequaled anywhere on earth.

Upon our left a high cliff towered, the base of the mountain of which the rock tombs were a part. A great hole made a black half-circle, its flat side resting on the ground. Out from this tunnel there emerged majestically a double row of stately brutes, chained one behind the other, hauling mightily against their heavy breast-straps.

At sight of them I felt a thrill run through me. Low in the quarters, high in the shoulders, bearing each before it a curving pair of polished curving tusks, I recognized those lumbering great-bodied forms. No naturalist could fail to know the monstrous head, the muscular, thick, prehensile trunk, the thin wide fanlike ears, the entire beast clothed with a mat of coarse dark hair. They were, beyond a doubt, a species long believed extinct—mammoths, elephants of the Arctic, trained to the service of men in this, their ancient range and last stronghold, the polar north.

Upon each shaggy head a naked figure sat, a goad in hand. These mighty creatures, numbering in all fully fifty beasts, dragged from the mountain side great flat-bottomed sledges, piled high with blocks of stone. No sooner had a sledge emerged than from all sides a swarm of naked unshod men rushed, hastily uncoupling the vehicle from the chains.

The mammoths, thus detached from their load, returned hitched to an empty sledge, into the tunnel, trumpeting in unison as when they had emerged.

Now from the outskirts of that human milling herd a dozen smaller beasts moved in. Upon them sat men garbed in white and orange shirts, each one of whom possessed a long, thick-handled whip. Now we saw that which explained the status of the naked shoeless men. For as they hauled and struggled with the sledge, the long whips sang forth and cracked among their sweating bodies.

Sometimes a man went down beneath the press of other

slaves. Rarely did he rise, for at this sign of weariness, several of the shaggy mounts were guided to the spot, and the whips laid cruelly on until the luckless creature lay out still and silent, whereafter the mighty beasts were driven roughshod over him, the other slaves then following.

Although we did not know it then, these fallen slaves would not be wasted.

The stone, it now appeared, was being hauled by human labor to some destination beyond view from our platform. Scarce had one load been borne away when another appeared, dragged in the same manner from the tunnel, to the accompaniment of the same bedlam of outcries. Another swarm of slaves rushed forth in numbers evidencing the cheapness of their toil. When again the field was clear we saw two of the herd men return, cast ropes about the feet of the fallen slaves and drag them by the score out of sight, indifferent to the moans of those who still had life left in them.

Absorbed in this spectacle, combining grandeur, novelty and callous cruelty, we stared aghast and speechless, when suddenly the Snow Hawk turned, and gave a shout of warning.

The alarm came too late. Descending on us swiftly were the band who earlier had gone up the stair. They swept upon us, pinning Munro, Flashpan, Tokala and myself before we could offer more than a feeble resistance, and thrust us into the hands of the barefoot slaves who had borne the palanquin.

Kioga was not so easily taken. Armed with the thin bronze blade he received the first upon its point and ran him through. In falling, the warrior's weight wrenched the sword from Kioga's grasp, whereat he seized the club the other dropped and swung it in a mighty arc, to crush the second attacker in his tracks. Another fell, his skull cracked open like a melon, and those who followed him drew back, before a well-aimed missile from above had laid the Snow Hawk limp and motionless on the platform.

By now the melee about us had gained attention from below and presently we were the center of a yelling mob whose movement bore us down into the clearing. Now through that howling press the herd-men cleared a way, trampling all who stood before them.

And thus, securely bound and dragged along without

resistance in their path, we passed beyond the clearing toward a nearby city now dimly visible in the moonlight.

We hardly dared conjecture our fate; judging from the threatening mob surrounding us, short shrift would be our lot.

CHAPTER 6

South of the barrier called the Topless Peaks, two hours down the river with the wounded Dan La Salle, Kias the Shoni had obeyed implicitly Kioga's order to await him, while two of his red-skinned warriors attended Dan's hurts.

When several hours had passed above the stipulated length of time, Kias dispatched Dan in one of the canoes back to the white men's stronghold down the river, and waited yet a little longer for the absent Snow Hawk and his companions.

As yet Kias was not definitely apprehensive of misfortune to the one-time chief of the Shoni tribesmen. But when the band of warriors who had kidnaped Dan emerged from the mists about the waterfall and passed on southward out of view, and when two additional hours brought no sign of Kioga's return, Kias and his warriors went back as they had come, re-entering the subterranean river in search of him.

Examining the trail, the skilled red trackers traced the men they sought to the point where they had taken the downward-leading pathway, which now was filled with water welling from it in a steady stream. Kias quickly grasped the meaning of that circumstance: From somewhere underground a spring had found its way.

His friends had passed through here before the waters came, and either had been drowned upon the rising of the spring or had climbed upward beyond the flooded area, to higher ground—which Kias knew existed, for in boyhood explorations he and Kioga had more than once scouted within these intriguing Empty Lodges.

Knowledge of a trail past this dip sustained Kias in the hope Kioga and his party might be safe beyond the inundated pathway. And with these tidings Kias and his companions returned to the blockhouse. Before the gathering of intent listeners here, Kias told of his attempts to dive and swim below the level of the passage in the effort to find trace of his vanished chief. He showed his bruised and bleeding hands and those of his warriors in evidence of attempts to pierce the stone by digging into the mountainside.

"Hands were not made for breaking rock," said young La Salle. "But in the caves downriver, we have enough gunpowder to blast through fifty feet of it."

His thought brought forth an instant chorus of assent, with every man eager to join those detailed to the attempt. But Scott, on whom command had devolved in the absence of Kioga and Munro, checked their enthusiasm with wiser counsel.

"Ye'll bear in mind that half a dozen men will be enough, with Indians to paddle and defend them in case of need. Do not forget that when they find them, as I hope they do, we'll want to be away from this accursed land o' dismal night and murderin' savages. And it's a ship we'll need for that, my lads. There's labor and to spare for every man-jack of us, if that ship's to be built. Let them who know this forest and its ways go up the river. The rest of us can better set to work on the shipbuilding."

This plan was agreed upon; and with no time to lose, La Salle, with Kias, his warriors and two of Scott's crew, set forth. Arriving at the powder-cache, they loaded most of the supply into the canoes; then bending to their paddles, repassed the forest camp and, cheered on by all, proceeded toward the cliffs and the Empty Lodges.

Not an hour had they been absent when, coming from the forest on silent feet, two warrior-scouts brought to the blockhouse tidings of the enemy. The marauding crew of the *Pirate* were now engaged in extensive mining operations in their search for gold. Their camp upon the seacoast had been enlarged, completed and fortified with light arms from the ship. Excepting those who stood guard at these coastal headquarters, most of the men had scattered, pairing off to pan the creeks and streams just inland from the coast, in hope of finding yellow dust. But there were two, Mioka added meaningly in broken English, who would never find it. Before the men remaining in the blockhouse he tossed two dripping scalps.

"Ho, Shoni," muttered Scott at last, "ye've broke the ice. We'll be in for it now, or I'm a Chinaman. They've made friends with some of the Indians, who'll gladly retaliate. Ye should've thought of that."

But though retaliation must now be expected, Scott was of

no mind to let it interfere with his plans. Arming his men the heavier, and guided by the scout Mioka, he set forth toward the coast, leaving six Indians familiar with the white man's firearms, with Beth La Salle and her father at the well-stocked, easily defended blockhouse.

Traveling by canoe as far as possible to avoid the thickets with their swarming savage denizens, Scott and his men debarked to travel overland and reach the coastal cliffs, beyond which, in the brilliant Arctic moonlight, the reefs showed black and terrible in a tossing lace of foam. Along the rugged shore below the cliffs, they sought some likely place, accessible to tide and timber equally, on which to lay a keel.

But wherever deep water could be had near shore, the neighboring cliffs were bare of trees; and where the timber grew most plentiful, the water shoaled away to reefs and bars not suited to a launching. Seeking farther for a location which combined the necessary features, they neared the spot on which the *Bearcat* had met her end, well out amid the reefs.

What with an ebb-tide running, the poor bones of Scott's dead ship were exposed to view, and on the instant her former skipper had an inspiration.

"We've got eight hours free and clear before the tide comes in again. She's sitting high and dry enough. I have a mind to salvage what we can before she's a total loss. 'Tis worth a try."

Close on his heels they followed, bounding from reef to reef and skirting salt pools as they went. An hour brought them to the looming iron hulk, of which the sea had made a pile of scrap bearing slight resemblance to the fine old whaler she had once been.

Yet out of her they took a precious lot of articles which still remained among her ruins: lances used for cutting-in; cutting-spades, flensing knives and other implements of the whaling trade; odd blocks and tackles; her full equipment of harpoons, complete with cast-iron bomb points; and her store of carpenter's and blacksmith's tools, of which they stood in greatest need.

From a bin below deck a hundred fathoms of salt-encrusted whale rope was broken out; and as much again of foreline, commonly carried out behind the shot harpoons. The whaling gun, breech-loading, with a bore of three and a half inches, mounted at the bow, they next unbolted and lowered by means of block and tackle upon one of the

Bearcat's several torn-off plates. To these ropes were affixed. All hands fell to, and on Scott's order, "Haul away!" slowly and laboriously dragged the gun toward shore, returning to do likewise with the other salvaged objects before the tidal waters swirled behind them.

Equipped with tools and some of the materials most necessary to their project, they found at last a site combining lumber with deep water. And after a much-needed rest they fell to work, felling, hewing, splitting and hammering with sounds not heard before along that savage uninhabited coast.

The work of Scott and his men had little of the hopelessness attending that of young La Salle, upriver. Even before arrival at the fall which hid the caves, the river was seen to be in a swift and swollen stage, because of unseasonable lateness of the temperate autumn, which had caused melting of the glacial ice miles above, atop the barrier range.

The week or two during which they had counted on being able to work before the coming of the late fall rains thus passed without affording them the hoped for respite. Hardly had the glacial flow shown signs of subsiding, when the regular seasonal downpour began, raising the water yet another several feet, precluding even an approach to the task they had set themselves; and back to the blockhouse they must go, defeated.

Six weeks these late rains continued, with swollen streams persisting yet another two; whereafter once again Dan and his Indians set forth—to find the elements still in league against them; for carried by the torrents down the mountainside, ton upon ton of rock, eroded earth and rubble had covered all approaches to the caves, altering even the landscape almost beyond recognition.

Attacking this with a persistence which recognized no obstacles as insurmountable, they presently were checked afresh by sudden cold, which clamped the icy lock of winter on their labors. An hour of paddling back amid the keen-edged skin-ice forming on the river, completed their defeat by skiving through their thin bark craft, compelling them to go afoot the return distance to their base.

Impatiently had Beth La Salle awaited the news that Kioga had been found. But when the hours lengthened into days and no word came, not one of her companions at the blockhouse but observed the slow collapse of all her hopes. Not given easily to admit defeat, yet conscious of a growing sense of dread, the girl sought means to occupy her mind and beguile those dragging hours.

The simple tasks of cooking meals and seeing to the comfort of the men in the blockhouse had grown mechanical, providing labor for her hands without employment for her mind. To fill that lack she turned almost in desperation to keeping a daily chronicle of events that touched her life and the lives of those sharing this wilderness exile with her.

She wrote with clearness and with a gift for observation which found no detail too small to be of interest to herself, and to one who would later draw upon her facts. Her journal tells of the deep discouragement which ensued when Dan returned reporting failure; of how men sat before the blockhouse fire pondering on the gravity of their situation. Momentarily leaderless, deprived of him upon whose knowledge of the channels through the reefs to sea they all had counted, with winter drawing on, with hostile redmen lurking ever near intent on lifting the scalp from anyone who ventured between the blockhouse and the shipbuilding, and with wild-beasts howling through the night beyond their walls, small wonder that they found no cause to welcome each new day.

And we, the objects of their searching, in company of Kioga, were not far from being in the straits they feared.

CHAPTER 7

As the city proper neared ahead, the noise and din decreased so that we now could hear the language of the people, who lined the route on which we marched. It was a smooth and flowing tongue, most pleasing to the ear. One cry was oft repeated: *"Wai! Yamala Wai!"* and mingled with it was the constant *"Uh-uh! Ya! Uh!"* of the mammoth-drivers to their shaggy heavy-footed mounts.

I glimpsed the Snow Hawk being hurried up beside us; and to my vast relief, although there was an ugly bruise upon his temple, he seemed not seriously hurt. His captors held him warily, closely surrounding him on every side. His gaze leaped here and there amid the motley throng on either side.

Even the mammoth-drivers now spoke in subdued tones as we neared a splendid edifice built in the solid cliff. The work of its construction was all on a gigantic scale, its pillars and capitals artistically executed, the more effective in that the frontal work was executed in contrasting colored stone.

But we were given little time in which to admire our surroundings. Our captors hurried us between two rows of observers, now utterly silent as if in awe, and into the imposing edifice whose great bronze doors were guarded by five rows of warriors armed to the teeth. Their ranks extended well into the splendid hall which opened out beyond. The walls were hung with gleaming spears and swords of many shapes, which covered carved reliefs of animals and men, extending up and clear across the lofty vault. Great oil flares threw their light upon the interior.

The floors were also carved with war-like scenes in low relief, bisected by a bare path for the common feet of such as those who led us toward the far end of the room. Some fifty feet before their destination our captors paused, removed their footgear and our own, and on bare feet approached a kind of elevated throne, across which, from arm to arm, there hung a golden chain. The throne was quite unoccupied—as that palanquin had been, moving up the cliff-side stair. To either side were lesser seats, built lower than the central throne. In each of these there sat a man, and these men scanned minutely our group, which stood before them.

In dress they were magnificent, wearing robes of fur, clasped at the shoulder with golden buckles having silver tongues. Upon their feet were sandals of soft white skin, thickly soled as with a coarse cowhide. Each on his breast displayed the tattooed figure of a hawk, the symbol of the ruling class. Their skins were copper brown, their features regular, if not precisely handsome. But of most interest to every one of us, many of their eyes were pale light blue. And at least one displayed an overbearing arrogance.

Gazing at us as if we were dirt beneath his sandaled feet, the nearest to that lofty central throne, conspicuous for the malevolence of his countenance, shot quick staccato sentences at our captors. In deferential, almost whispered tones, an answer came, with gestures clearly telling how we had been captured.

The questioner deigned to rise, and moved toward us. Slowly up and down he strode, examining each one of us, our features and attire. A sullen sneer about his lips, he neared Kioga. For one long moment he sought to stare the Snow Hawk out of countenance, but in vain; his cold eyes wavered on their own account, and concentrated on a lesser prey. He neared Tokala, found the boy's eyes on him as with fascination, and in a fit of cruelty, took him by the ear and twisted until the smarting tears were in Tokala's eyes.

Events transpired with a suddenness that caught the Snow Hawk's captors off their guard. Kioga's sinewy hand closed round the tormentor's neck, raised him bodily from the floor and shook him as a terrier would a rat, before the guards were pinning him anew.

It was an act of angry impulse on Kioga's part, and what mercy he might otherwise have expected was by it sacrificed. His victim's thin lips were compressed, forcing color from them. Pallor drained his face. Fury, due to the frustrated indulgence of a whim, which never until this moment had been subjected to a check, raged in the man transparently.

Never had the Snow Hawk in all his life of many close passages with death been nearer to destruction than in that moment when the noble whipped forth his dagger and raised it high, the hatred blazing in his eyes. Then suddenly he paused, smiled thinly and stood back, with a quick order to the Snow Hawk's captors, who took him from our midst.

A further parley then ensued; whereafter each of the assembled nobles scrutinized us carefully, then conferred, seemed to agree, and waved us scornfully from their presence.

This time what little care we earlier had been accorded was now dispensed with. Spears pricked us from behind if we so much as stumbled. On passing through the mob anew, the same respectful silence reigned; but in proportion as we left the great hall behind, the babel broke forth afresh and questing hands made free with us, tearing our clothing.

Thus it chanced that by a withered crone Tokala's shirt was ripped away, revealing the golden plaque that still hung about his neck upon its chain of beaten metal.

The ancient crone stood rooted, her wrinkled face a study in amazement. Her beady eyes seemed filled with sudden terror. A wild shrill screech escaped her, as she pointed to the plaque upon Tokala's chest. Another then took up that unintelligible cry; and in a moment it had spread like wildfire throughout all the mob which ringed us in.

In front of wondering Tokala the crone had thrown herself upon her knees; and as we watched, in equal wonder, others followed suit. The word spread round. A hush fell on the people. Sight of that golden plaque had wrought the change.

Munro, quick to interpret its significance, turned to me and hazarded an explanation, quoting from the carved tusk, so long absent from our thoughts: "*'Behold this prince and all his retinue.'* Apparently they think Tokala is an incarnation of the boy-prince who left the kingdom centuries ago. Let's hope they do."

"Aye," muttered Flashpan fervently, "let's hope hard and do a lot o' prayin' on the side. But look thar! Who's that a-comin' down the street?"

Our glances followed his. Upon a stately mammoth, draped with richly woven trappings, there sat the light and slender figure of a man garbed as had been those nobles in the great hall from which we came. But there the likeness ended, for on this face the hint of gentleness was seen, despite the flashing eye and sharp imperious gaze.

He controlled his beast with admirable skill, guiding it through the almost solid press with ease, and injury to none. Attracted by the earlier outcry and subsequent hush, he slowly neared Tokala, glimpsed the plaque upon the Indian boy's breast, and paled like the rest.

But his was a pallor not of fear but of almost overpowering amazement. A quick command brought the ponderous mammoth down upon its knees. Uttering words we could not comprehend, the rider stretched forth a hand, which Tokala had presence of mind enough to seize, mounting up beside the other.

Gesturing toward ourselves, Tokala looked at the other inquiringly; whereat the mounted personage, evidently one of great authority, rapped out an order to our captors, who followed in the wake his risen animal created.

From that time on, we suffered no further indignity from the mob, who followed us until we paused before a high black granite wall extending outward from the cliff; heavy grated gates swung open at a signal from the master of the mammoth.

We passed within. The gates closed heavily behind, shutting out the sounds of rabble on the streets. Within, there was a lighted court. Unshod slaves ran to receive the master, at whose signal the brute sank down upon its knees, affording easy dismounting for Tokala and his benefactor, who led the way toward what now appeared to be a dwelling sculptured from the solid rock.

Tall and splendid the structure rose, magnificently carved from *stone* whose veinings had a hundred hues. Six fluted columns held the ornamented lintel up, and on its face were bas-reliefs of tigers, mighty stags and other creatures of the wilderness, with at the center an enormous carven mammoth.

Within the great bronze door there was a chamber, covered on the floor with gleaming skins reflecting red lights from a blaze in a great fireplace. To either side of this a slave stood silent with folded arms, ready for the commands of the master.

At a clap of his hands strange food was brought and set before us in ornate vessels. Golden goblets brimming with a pungent liquor were proffered first to Tokala, then to each of us. As we supped, our host beheld us with intense interest, and sought unsuccessfully to make us comprehend his language.

But suddenly a gesture accompanied his words. Munro's attention centered on the other's moving hands; in return he also gestured. The other watched him closely, seemed puzzled for a time, then smiled and made new signs with his slender hands. Thus slowly and experimentally for a time, but with growing facility, the two engaged in halting sign-talk.

Presently the gestures swiftened, and though each one of us, Tokala not excepted, knew Indian sign-talk, the meaning of this code evaded us.

When he had conferred for half an hour, Munro turned to us, between signals. "We understand each other," he said. "He uses what appears to be a very ancient form of sign-language. It takes some mental juggling, but I grasp about a fourth of all he says."

Of all the strange things we learned while in this hidden kingdom, not least of them was this, that that curious manual talk, in use among the many-tongued American tribes, traced back its origin not to the primitive but to this semibarbarous race, our present captors.

More animatedly now, Munro and our strange host pursued researches into one another's minds. As they progressed, Munro translated intermittently, so that we too might share in that slow and silent discourse. Gradually we learned much about our benefactor and his people.

His name was Mahri (as nearly as may be written from his pronunciation), indirect descendant of the line of Ru the Merciful, who ruled in ancient times. His land was called M'Anda; his people called themselves T'emaho, or People of the Tusk. Mahri was of a noble line, the second highest caste in M'Anda, and one-time owners of many estates and slaves, but now by reason of the late king's recent death, prudently deprived, by enemies in the present barbaric court, of many powers, until the question of the succession should be resolved.

A slave here interrupted the discussion by accidentally spilling a drop of beverage upon the master's robe. At once Mahri raised up his hand. His twisted quirt whistled through the air, slashing upon the slave's bare back Once, twice and yet again, the coarse thongs fell upon flesh that writhed and crawled beneath its cruel red welts. The lot of one who is a slave among the T'emaho is not enviable.

Without change of expression, as if the sufferings of a fellow man were incomprehensible to him, Mahri turned back to Munro. Indicating Tokala, the noble suddenly put a question, of which we caught the gist:

"Long did the people of M'Anda await his return who left our kingdom centuries ago to seek the outer world. Long have our priests predicted the return of him whose rule was interrupted by that journey in the long ago. Now he is come, about his neck the plaque of the last of the line of Ru. How came you to meet our prince and bring him back to us?"

These signs were conveyed with utmost solemnity. But as Mahri waited for an answer, his eyes were preternaturally keen and piercing, as if he would have plumbed the depths of Munro's mind.

What answer of the scientist would best preserve this immunity from harm which Tokala's presence had won for us? Could the subtlest of falsehoods deceive the watchful Mahri?' How much of the people's superstition did he subscribe to, and how far agree with the priests whose prediction he had quoted? These were the questions, of course, in Munro's mind.

He attempted no deceit, however, but recounted the manner of our arrival according to the facts. The keen-eyed Mahri watched the movements of his hands in silence. When Munro had done, the other's eyes were closed, and veiled in a singular expression. The hand with which he received a goblet trembled, then grew steady once again, and for a time it was as if he brooded gloomily. But presently his hands were signaling again; varying expressions passed across his mobile features; at what his hands said, Munro too became thoughtful. Mahri's hands were presently at rest. Munro then turned, acquainting us with much that Mahri had just told him.

"He seems to share the general superstition that Tokala is resurrected from the dead; but he says that unless we can maintain that belief among the people, we're almost certain to be destroyed in one way or another. He wishes to help us, and will do all in his power to teach us the customs and the language, on the condition that we do nothing to destroy the people's faith in Tokala.

"They deify their kings, dead and living. Their old king has just been entombed. The question of the succession occupies the nobles and the multitudes at this moment, and an internal war is possible. Tokala's return as the long-departed Ru of other days will resolve all the difficulties, for by their way of reckoning, the young prince never served out his reign, and is merely returning to what is rightfully his own. Mahri undertakes to instruct Tokala in the part he is to play as puppet king. And since his life as well as our own hangs upon it, I don't see how we can afford to refuse."

"King o' the T'emaho, hey?" murmured Flashpan thoughtfully. "Why should anyone refuse to be a king?"

"It has its risks," said Munro soberly. "For should the people learn the facts of how we came here, not even superstition would save us from treatment appropriate to violators of the sacred tombs."

"Aye, there ye're right," muttered the little miner, adding: "But I'd feel a good deal braver if we knew what happened to Kioga. Meanwhile, if we can stick together, mebbe T'kala when he's High Muck-a-muck, can make 'em trot him out."

Tokala, on his part, heard what was said with something more than interest. Bright for his fourteen years, and full of quick intelligence, it seemed that by this chance, by this acting of a kind of play, he might redeem the fallen fortunes of the elder men about him. It promised a risk of peril and strange intrigue which stirred his blood; and it touched his pride to realize that he held in his younger hands the safety of his elders. But most of all did it suggest that somehow he might influence the safe return of him who was the idol of us all—the Snow Hawk.

With glowing eyes he faced Munro, and in a tense voice said: "Please, Doctor, let me do it. With Mahri helping me, I know I can!"

The scientist beheld him, eager and full of confidence, and was moved to confidence himself. He turned to Mahri, waiting taut and silent, and signaled. This time we recognized the signs. They said: "It is agreed."

The face of Mahri lighted up with pleasure. Observing him, we shared a common thought among us: What certainty could there be that, having established Tokala as king, Mahri might not then, through fear of what we knew, seek to be rid of us who shared the secret of his uncertainty about Tokala? For none of us was quite his dupe where that uncertainty was concerned.

But for the time at least our fortunes were improved. The noble clapped his hands and issued orders. From rooms beyond, the slaves brought garb more suited to our residence among the T'emaho than the deerskin rags which were all that remained upon our backs. Each one received a cloak of heavy wool-like material, a belt of plaited leather for his dagger and curved short sword, and a close-fitting undersuit of leather extending down to heavy-soled sandals of buckskin.

Tokala, as befitted one about to be presented as the boy-king of the realm, was given into the keeping of Mahri's domestic slaves, to be prepared for his eventual presentment before the nobles.

Then having drunk and dined sufficiently, we were conducted with all marks of respect to an upper sleeping chamber in the sumptuous cliff-dwelling. . . . Ere retiring, our talk was of the Snow Hawk, whose fate had not ceased to occupy us since earlier in the day we saw him borne away under guard of the warriors.

CHAPTER 8

The Snow Hawk slept that night upon a harder couch than his more fortunate companions. Hurried from their presence between a score of watchful guards, his journey, if not so far as theirs, was equally of interest.

He saw no mobs of people, though the murmur of their presence came to him before his captors chose a route that led between the cliffs on one side, and a towering wall on the other which seemed to gird the entire city, toward the outer limits of this populous center. Against the cliffs, rising higher than the eye could look, the dwellings of the people rose, some connected by visible steep stairways, others dependent on some hidden routes for their accessibility one with another.

The cries of hawkers could be heard from the rising stairs above. From openings in the cliffs roped nets were let down here and there, and raised again with products in them from the back-baskets of the hawkers down below. Again the sellers tossed bundled stuffs aloft unerringly, and in return received white objects, caught in waiting hands.

One of these less deftly thrown rolled at the feet of Kioga's guards. It was a square of ivory, carved on either side, the legal tender of the city. The warrior possessed it, refusing it to the protesting hawker, who let it go, hatred mingling with fear upon his face.

Long before his guardians reached their destination, Kioga was fully himself again, light upon his feet, his leopard muscles all responsive once more, and every sense alert to observe his route, his captors, the sights about and his chances of escape. Of this, however, he gave no sign, allowing them to lead him docilely.

From time to time he glimpsed a pair of mammoths being ridden through the streets by barefoot men, no doubt toward that mighty excavation in the mountain. Often, too, a gang of slaves walked past in silence, driven by an overseer who plied the whip unnecessarily.

Then suddenly he stood before the village wall, a splendid man-raised defense of ponderous blocks that rose full eighty feet above the level of the street, pierced at intervals with gated doorways, through one of which he and his escort passed. Beyond, he glimpsed a long, steep slope, leading downward to a broad river, on which he dimly saw strangely shaped craft. Across the river was a valley, cleared along the stream, but thick with forests farther in, and dominated by mountains in the distance. A short way down the slope there squatted a smaller building, likewise of stone, to which his guards now led him.

Entering in their company he beheld several warriors, heavily armed. At a word from Kioga's captors these raised a heavy bronze trap door, exposing a black, rectangle. Without a word the Snow Hawk was hurled through bodily. The metal trap clanged shut above.

Rescued from a heavy fall only by his great agility, Kioga brought up on all fours against a floor of damp cold stone. Vermin scurried to the corners, startled by his fall.

Rising to his feet, with every nerve on the *qui-vive,* Kioga sought to pierce the darkness with his eyes, which presently discerned the nature of his prison. It was a dungeon, having doors on either side. In one there was an open grate through which the Snow Hawk peered. And as he looked, a thin and ghastly corpselike face appeared and stared into his own. Spidery hands attached to bare and pipestem arms reached forth between the grate.

Another would have drawn back in fear or loathing; Kioga waited, enduring the other's touch, which harmed him not, but sought his hands and held them tremblingly. Here was a human soul in need of sympathy, and though Kioga knew nothing of the language of the people he had been thrown among, he said, in his own native Shoni tongue: "*Pohau*. Peace to you, brother!"

The skinny hands drew back to grip the bars convulsively. A startled gasp escaped the other captive's lips. Then in a labored whisper came an answer in the last language Kioga would have thought to hear in this strange hermit kingdom —his own. "*Ai-i! Pohau!* Give me your hand. How sweet it is to hear my mother tongue again! Who are you, brother?"

The Snow Hawk saw tears in the other's blinking eyes

and answered; "I am Kioga of the Shoni, who dwell beyond the mountain barrier to the south of here. Who are you?"

"I am Mingo of the tribe which is forgotten. This is my home."

"What mean you, brother?"

"For forty-seven suns, year after year, I have dwelt below the ground. Three generations of my captors have come and gone, and you have seen the fourth above."

"How can this be?" the Snow Hawk asked.

"My mother was a royal slave. For twenty years I was a favorite with the rulers. I fell from favor and was put to labor with the other slaves. I sickened and was thrust in here, to be forgotten."

"How do you speak the Shoni tongue?"

"My mother taught me, so that if I should escape, I might know my people when I heard them speak."

"You also speak the tongue of those who dwell near by?"

"Like one of them," said Mingo. "But tell me, brother, how came you hither from the outer world?"

Kioga told him briefly, observing that as he did a host of other naked figures gathered one by one about old Mingo, slaves just like himself. When the Snow Hawk had done, the other counseled him.

"Give no offense to those who guard the gates above. Wait patiently until they come again. Themselves are slaves, though of a higher order, permitted to bear weapons. Until they come, here is to eat and drink—the half of all I have." And with the words, the old man thrust through the grate a bowl of water and a strip of coarse smoked meat.

Unappetizing though it smelled, Kioga took it with a word of thanks, and not to give offense, made show of eating it, drank from the bowl and then returned it, saying: "I'll share with thee one day."

"But hark!" said the other guardedly. "They come!" His voice was stilled. A rustle followed as those within that prison moved back from the grated door.

A glow of stronger light came from above, revealing a ladder, down which two warriors came, the first to stand on guard, his short keen sword in readiness, while the other stripped Kioga of his every garment, head to heels, tossing him in their stead a single piece of figured cloth to wrap about his loins.

Expecting now to be imprisoned with the other slaves, Kioga saw one of the warriors take from his waist a ring of keys, with one of which he unlocked an opposite door and waved Kioga toward it.

The Snow Hawk entered, heard the door slam shut behind him, and the grating of the lock. The gloomy vault in which he stood was empty, save for himself. At one end was another door, at its side three slits, not thicker than his arm, forming an aperture beyond which there was light. Looking out, he saw a square enclosure, open to the sky.

Leaning on the door, to his surprise he felt it move outward. Taking advantage of this seeming way to escape, he pushed it wide, stepped quickly forth, and found himself within a deep doorway. Two steps brought him to its threshold, affording view into the enclosure.

At its either end, down near the stones, there were two low black orifices cut in the walls, the nature of which he could not immediately ascertain. At its far side, some ten feet up there was a rail—and over it there gazed one he had already learned to hate, the noble whose dagger had threatened Kioga earlier, in the hall of the nobles. Beside him stood his armed retainers, each wearing a long stout whip, thonged about a wrist—a whip the like of which had often kept Kioga's foes at bay among the perils of his native forests.

A laugh told him he was seen. Drawing back instinctively, he caught a sound behind, and wheeling, saw his door of exit swinging shut behind. A touch assured him he might not return as he had come. The door formed a trap through which one might enter, but not retreat. Advancing once again, on his reappearance a fresh guffaw greeted him.

The situation dawned upon Kioga. He was to be the toy with which the noble played, taking amusement from his reaction to the baiting. Aware of that, Kioga withdrew behind a mask of stoicism, which changed not one iota when the long whips slashed across his naked torso, which presently showed red weals from neck to waist.

Disappointed in his hopes of a cringing prey, bounding about to escape the whips, the noble on the balcony rapped out an order. Hearing a clangor at one end of the enclosure, Kioga turned to see two gaunt lean shapes slink forth. He knew them for long-hungry wolves, unfed until the ribs showed through their shaggy coats; and had he felt or showed the slightest fear, they had been springing snarling at his throat, for brutes detect fear-scent with infallible instinct.

Sensing in its place his grim defiance, they sought to circle and come at him from opposite sides, a maneuver which Kioga thwarted by taking a position back to wall, crouched to receive the first which dared to spring.

Upon the balcony, observing him with gleaming eyes, the noble's next order raised the second trap, whence issued yet another two such starving brutes, who joined their fellows in that ever-narrowing ring of menace.

Now from above again the whips licked forth, seeking to distract the victim, that the wolves might take him off his guard. But now, because Kioga moved into the shelter of the doorway, the hissing thongs could not quite reach; and one of Kioga's persecutors in his eagerness to please the noble leaned far out to stretch his range. The lash curled out and down—and, reaching forth, Kioga seized its end before the wielder could retract it, and jerked his persecutor off precarious balance and tumbling down to share his danger.

Sprawled on the stones, the warrior's first instinct, born of fear, was instantly to cover up his throat from the baiting pack who swarmed snapping ravenously about him; his struggles threw his heavy short-sword halfway from the scabbard; instantly Kioga whipped it fully forth and smote the brute whose fangs were nearest to the other's neck.

The tempered weapon clove the fierce head almost from the shoulders, and with the smell of blood its hungry companions turned rending fangs upon the fallen wolf.

The warrior rose and glimpsed his companions up above proffering him assistance in the form of loops made in their whips on which to seize and so be drawn aloft. He also saw the noble, white with rage, compelling them to desist; and never did a slave more bitterly recognize his own low value; for rather than interrupt the unexpectedly entertaining turn which matters had taken, the master chose to see his property torn limb from limb.

And such the warrior's fate had been indeed, but for the deadly execution Kioga wrought, felling two more of the brutes with swift blows, driving the one remaining back to its kennel snarling.

Balked of his expected entertainment, the noble on the balcony heaped epithets upon his warrior-slave below. His handsome countenance, the lips drawn back in semblance of a snarl, looked furiously down upon the luckless one, the native beauty of the features marred by lines of cruelty.

Beholding his abusiveness to one whose only fault was

overeagerness, Kioga felt a sudden rancor needing spilling. Slashing the thong which bound the lash to the warrior's wrist, he took it up. His arm shot forth; the thong sang up. Its striking tip struck hard and true, diagonally across the noble's face from jaw to temple. He tottered back, clapped both hands to his bleeding mouth, and for the moment disappeared, attended by the others of his horrified slaves, beyond view from the lower enclosure.

Turning to his companion in the pit, Kioga, saw the man staring at him, almost in unbelief of what had just occurred, and rightly interpreted his expression as that of one who never had conceived defiance to that authority inhering in the upper classes, represented by the noble. The other flashed a glance up toward the balcony. Again the Snow Hawk read him: This time he saw that last extreme of fear which, though he had done naught deserving censure, bespoke the utter degradation of his state, which allowed him not even to dare protest injustice.

Now in a kind of panic, the other signaled Kioga to follow, and ran to the door through which the Snow Hawk had entered the enclosure. With a key he turned the bolts, threw wide the door and entered, Kioga at his heels. The door which led back to Kioga's earlier prison yielded to another key, and locking this behind them, the noble's fleeing guard now let them into that dungeon from which the old man Mingo had spoken.

Scarce had they entered, when a human swarm had gathered round them, hearing in a hush the swiftly told account of the warrior-slave who was but a step or two above them in their state of bondage. As the account progressed, Kioga saw their eyes turn wonderingly upon himself who had marred the noble's features with a slave-whip.

Mingo pushed through the press, speaking first to Kioga's companion of the day, then to the Snow Hawk in the Shoni tongue: "Hast made a deadly enemy, warrior! Him you struck was of the ruling caste, who one day may be king. Of all who own slaves, he is the cruelest. But though you have an enemy in him, among the slaves you have already many friends. For never in my memory has one slave dared to aid another as did you."

"I wish that I might speak with them. Teach, me their language," said Kioga.

"You know the language of the hands?" the other asked.

"Yes, but what of that?"

"They use it too, who dwell in M'Anda. Behold!" And with the words old Mingo uttered a sentence in the other tongue, then gestured its equivalent. Thus, as his friends had done, Kioga found sign-language useful in his learning of the new tongue, and in a little time was master of their simpler phrases. These, added to the movements of the sign-talk, enabled him to understand and have his own expressions comprehended.

Now from old Mingo he derived much knowledge of the people and their land and customs, concerning which the other kept himself informed by closely questioning each newcomer who was thrown among the other slaves.

Slavery among the T'emaho was hereditary. The slaves consisted of three classes, each separate and distinct; household, field and military, the latter made up of the most reliable and trustworthy. A fourth degree, possessing not even the distinction of a name, comprised all those who, by offenses to their masters, had fallen to the lowest possible estate—the pariah class who inhabited these and other prison catacombs.

A slave might raise himself to leadership among his class, or advance into another class by special effort or manifest fitness. But there opportunity ended, for among the T'emaho manumission, or the liberation of slaves, was almost a thing unheard of. One born a slave or made a slave by the edict of the nobles must remain a slave forever, and all his children to eternity.

"Are they not men?" Kioga asked his aged informer. "Why do they not rise and strike their masters down?"

"*S-s-t!* What do you say?" the other whispered, looking fearfully about. "Let no one hear you utter such a thought! The penalty for rising, or urging another slave to rise, is worse than death. And he who informs the nobles of the danger of a rising in the pens, is richly rewarded for his watchfulness—so attempts are few."

Old Mingo paused to indicate a figure at one side.

"There is one who forgot the spy, and lives to be an example."

Kioga saw a man who squatted in the shadows, a grim reminder to all observers of the penalties of inciting others to violence. One arm and the opposite leg had been stricken off. Glancing round among these crowding naked figures, lowest of the slave classes, the Snow Hawk observed many hideous mutilations on faces and bodies, each in punishment of some crime committed, identifying men, so long as they might live, as dangerous plotters. Some had had their ears removed, others both hands and their tongues as well, that by no means might they communicate with their fellows, in hatching other schemes.

Now Mingo told of the recent king whose death had left the throne of M'Anda vacant, and of the rivalry among the distant city rulers to fill his place. For when a king has died among the T'emaho and left no heir, a vote by all the highest nobles decides who shall occupy the empty throne. At such a time the more hopeful among the lowest slaves dare look for some improvement in their condition; while others crave no more than to be led forth into the baiting arenas, quickly to end their worthless lives in combat with each other, or with fierce brutes whose fangs give quick release from lives which immutable slavery has made burdensome.

On the occasion of the present preparations to elect a new ruler, a high excitement was prevailing, because of the progress, made under the dead king's direction, in tunneling toward the outside world. At any time the last rock might be pierced and egress realized. To this end, a mighty host had been assembled, waiting to bear the banners of the new-selected king into the vast unknown—the world beyond the southern mountains.

Kioga listened intently to old Mingo's accounts of his far travels in the M'Anda kingdom. But in the silence following, his thoughts were busy with conjecture as to the fate of his companions.

In company of Mingo, the Snow Hawk explored the far recesses of the slave dungeons, extending for several hundred yards in rambling catacombs, ill-lighted by oil pots hanging from brackets here and there suspended from the walls, and ventilated overhead by grates of metal, across which free men marched back and forth from the walled city to the river, indifferent to the wretched captives within sound of their voices down below.

But though his mind played incessantly upon devices for escape, of this Kioga breathed no word to Mingo or any other of the slaves about him. No man must be his confidant; a lone hand he must play in plotting for his liberty, lest in the hope of lessening their own miseries, the slaves themselves betray him to the minions of the nobles.

Counting upon being summoned forth to answer for his

defiance of authority in the baiting pit, the Snow Hawk overlooked the state of high excitement in the kingless kingdom, which would postpone that reckoning for many days. But in the interim, instructed by old Mingo, the Snow Hawk went far toward mastering the language of the realm.

Once every day the guardians of the entrance came and to the slaves tossed chunks of mammoth meat from two great baskets, as to so many wolves locked in a den. Like wolves the half-starved slaves fell fighting on the meat, snatching each all that he could obtain and retiring to devour it, before another and more powerful might deprive him of his share.

Reduced already to the level of human beasts, a three-day interval of neglect, during which no food was brought, degraded the unhappy prisoners to that last degree wherein they glared upon each other, obsessed by a fierce temptation.

One night the terror broke. A wild scream broke the stillness after midnight. A scuffle ensued. One slave more recently confined, and consequently less emaciated than his fellows, was set upon by a dozen of the others. Breaking away, he darted through the passageways, his weaker assailants shuffling more slowly on his heels. Cornered in a blind passage he fought in silence, but went down overwhelmed by numbers. . . .

Another day brought no cessation of the horror. A second victim fled this human pack. Chance brought him near the cell apart, which Mingo long had occupied and now shared with Kioga, and into it he fled, with a distraught plea: "Hide me, in the name of Ru the Merciful!"

Kioga flashed a glance at Mingo, who muttered: " 'Tis death for both of us to do so."

"Better death than this," returned Kioga, planting himself across the entrance as the pursuit came dimly into view. Then to the slaves ranged threatfully in a half-circle before the cell of sanctuary: "Whom seek you, brothers?" he asked as best he could in their own tongue.

"Him you harbor, the one who came but yesterday," answered one.

"What will you do with him?" the Snow Hawk demanded, wishing to make them name the crime which they intended, the better to dissuade them from its accomplishment. There was a silence, born of the shame which even famished men may experience when called upon to speak of the unspeakable. But finally one among them, a tall, lean-featured fellow with a madman's eyes, made answer:

"Do you not hunger like ourselves? Are all to die because the guards have brought no meat?"

"Better die than live by eating fellowmen," Kioga countered.

"Then die!" was the muttered answer as the other hurled himself suddenly upon the Snow Hawk, thinking to take him unawares. Desperate though he was, and doubly strengthened by his desperation, Kioga threw him swiftly back, carrying down three others in his fall.

Sounds of the attack, and of its swift repulse, had the effect of drawing others to the scene. The night wore on. Each hour found the famished horde drawn slightly closer about the cell the Snow Hawk guarded with a strength, which, like their own, was gradually failing. As yet no individual slave had dared repeat the earlier assault, lest, being similarly repulsed, the others might in their great extremity fall upon himself.

But the dark was full of whispers: ". . . Look now! He has relaxed. . . . Now, at him!" Now and again the hungry slaves feigned a combined attack, each one of which fell short before that alert indomitable figure at the entrance.

Upon the threshold, behind which ancient Mingo trembled with the slave who had been marked for death, Kioga called on his last deep reservoirs of strength, girded himself, and waited grimly.

The thought of all his friends of civilization was with him in that hour; of those who had accompanied him upon this unexpected journey to the land of a strange barbaric people; but most of all he thought of Beth La Salle, to whom, if he fell in this blackness underground, no word would ever come to tell her of his ignominious end.

CHAPTER 9

Above the fetid chambers of the slave dungeons, the City of the Kings was in a state of great ferment, preparing for the coming of the reigning rulers from the distant cities. In all the fever of a national holiday, it was small wonder that Kioga and the slaves were for the time forgotten, save by ourselves, the foreigners among them, who, in the company of Mahri, waited on the city wall to view the new arrivals.

By Mahri's own statement, seven of these nobles should appear, from all the seven cliffside cities, east and west of the City of the Kings. These cities, it appeared, held under tribute other lesser villages in the mountain wilderness that stretched northward beyond view.

As we waited for the first to arrive, we might behold, across the nearby river, the wide plantations of the noble classes, planted and harvested by slave labor and the labor of the mammoths. But now, save for a few great brutes hauling the last of the harvest down to the river bank, the rolling fields lay idle, and beyond them frowned the forest, rarely invaded by the people, save in hunting the wild mammoths.

Upon the river appeared several curious craft, high in bow and stern, some eighty or a hundred feet in length, having each a mast equipped with two graceful wing-shaped sails, and steered by an elongated oar astern. Upon the bows a plume of smoke rose from a little urn. Occasionally one or another of the crew threw something into the river with an odd singsong cry.

"Tribute to the river-god," said Mahri, and thus we first learned that the people were primarily river worshipers, much grimmer evidence of which we eventually would witness.

The strange river boats drew into berths, cast up their ropes and began the slow unloading of their cargoes. Slaves, piled high with merchandise, labored heavily up the slope toward the city gates. Some bore a freight of fine thick skins; some carried between them long and curving tusks of mammoth ivory; yet others bent beneath a load of gleaming pottery, arranged on wooden shelves like bricks upon a workman's hod; and others still brought fragrant plants and strange and shining fruits unknown to us.

Now from one of the handsome vessels emerged three mammoths, ponderously climbing up the gangways. Their tusks were carved and capped with reddish gold. Upon their trunks and round their heavy ankles long strings of copper bells gave music with their every stride. Each wore a back-blanket decked with rich embroidery, and strapped about its paunchy belly by broad belts burned deep with strange designs. On every ponderous head there was a golden sun-burst, hammered with great artistry. The coarse long hair upon their sides was braided in designs fantastic and bizarre and hung with silver pendants. Their very tails were bound with alternating bands of color, their toenails painted twenty hues.

Such were the sacred mammoths of the first of the M'Anda rulers to arrive, who now appeared, amid the deep full-throated chanting of his crews, and stepping on the backs of prostrate slaves, mounted to the shoulders of his mammoth.

Led by two goad-men at the head of every beast, preceded by the naked criers of the household, the noble family slowly rode toward the city gates and entered to a mighty welcoming blare from curving ivory horns, blown by watchers on the walls.

From wicker baskets hung at the shoulders of their mounts, the visiting nobles scattered handfuls of the ivory coins among the crowding dwellers on every side, largess to flaunt their wealth for all to see. From every side bare brown-skinned children rushed to gather in the ivory, for spending later at the great bazaars, whereat the produce from the distant realms would be hawked for sale by hoarse-voiced vendors.

Slowly the splendid equipage wended its dignified way along the main street of the city, beneath the towering apartments in the cliffs. From every balcony and window floated clouds of colored leaves, gathered in the autumn forests for this supreme occasion. Shouts and cries, the ringing of the household bells of hammered bronze, and hoots of horns were mingled with the frequent brazen trumpetings of the mammoths, to form a frenzied discord, the like of which we of another world had never heard before. But this was only a beginning.

The second ship had just disgorged its passengers. Another noble was entering through the city gates, preceded by a force of soldier-slaves, armed for display and beating on enormous drums, borne each between four warriors. Behind the royal mounts came a second pair of mammoths, each dragging on the now familiar wooden sledge, huge bronze-barred crates.

In one a striped long-haired tiger roared and rushed against the bars. The next contained a giant bear, goaded to a frenzy by the soldiers' pricking spears. In others still strode lean lithe mountain leopards, their shrill screams adding to the din. Close behind them, padding on the street, a troop of snarling wolves next came, separated from each other by wooden rods chained to their metal collars, their fierce jaws muzzled. The slaves, armed with short loaded whips, dragged them along and stirred the laggards harshly with punishing thongs.

"Beasts for the carnivals," shouted Mahri above the howling din. "And here come those they will contend against." He pointed.

Down the road, behind the brutes, came men appearing themselves little less brutish. They were a brawny, surly, scar-featured lot, the pick of those who had survived unnumbered combats. Bare to the waist, their muscles knotted underneath the ugly scars, they passed in silence, the cynosure of every wondering eye, linked to each other ankle to ankle, their chains clinking on the solid pavement, slaves one and all and yet well fed that they might furnish greater amusement for their barbarous masters.

Thus as the hours went, the several arriving nobles entered through the city gates and passed. Of seven who were expected, six had now gone by. There grew a tense expectant hush, as of some great event to come. Men crowded women and children from the first rows along the line of march, and looked impatiently toward the city gates.

Once more the horns vociferated blaring sounds of welcome. Now came the clash of round bronze cymbals, shivering the silence with a brassy ring. A splendid mammoth, tallest of all we yet had seen, passed beneath the stony portal. Upon it, straight and tall, barbarically beautiful, there sat—a woman.

"Loalli, Princess of Ayal," said Mahri in a voice whose

stifled tones drew all our eyes to him at once. If I did not mistake, the look upon his clean-cut features was that of one who loves—nay, worships. And that the object of his ardor was one to kindle fire in the heart of man there was no doubt.

Her age was certainly not more than twenty-two or -three. A bronze band which clung to her head served but to emphasize the smooth perfection of her brows and forehead. Attached to the band a ring rose vertically up behind her nape and head. Round and round this ring the dark coils of her hair were twisted, forming as it were a black frame for her face, whose features were as smooth and regular as those of any European beauty.

Mahri now called her name and in response Loalli glanced up. Below their narrow brows her eyes looked forth, a singular cobalt blue, in striking contrast with their background of dark hair. Her mouth was wide and rippling, the touch of coldness in her gaze belied by a full lower lip. Her delicate ear lobes were pierced by little silver hoops, her firm breasts capped with golden cones.

She must have seen Mahri, leaning far out to gain her attention. And yet that perfect calm repose, in which her facc seemed carved of ivory, remained unaltered by the slightest smile or sign of recognition. Her swift, sure gaze ran over each of us in lightning rapidity. Then she had passed along her way.

Mahri watched her go, his face alternately pale and flushed. He seemed to have forgotten us, himself, and all that was transpiring about him, since the passage of the radiant vision who was Loalli. He had no eyes for the remainder of that following cortège, nor further words of explanations anent the dignitaries who succeeded it.

Below the level of the roadway from the wall, another listened intently to the sounds of the procession, passing hour by hour above the grating overhead. The famished occupants of the slave dungeons, recently remembered by their keepers, had gluttonized upon the food tossed down to them, and now, indifferent or apathetic, had retired to their miserable pallets, there to sleep away their after-gorging stupor.

Not so the Snow Hawk, who saw in their condition the long-awaited opportunity to try his strength upon the grates and bars, which made the dungeons his prison, unnoticed by his fellow slaves.

Throughout most of the catacombs, grates admitting light and air were situated at the center of what formed their ceilings at a height of twelve or fourteen feet; a calculated circumstance, well conceived to make them difficult of access to the imprisoned slaves. But those two chambers just below the road which led toward the City of the Kings were exceptions, perhaps because their grates occupied so prominent a place, in constant view of the guards upon the city walls and all who trod the busy thoroughfare.

The slight difference in the placement of these latter grates was not of a degree to have availed an average man. But to Kioga, whose quick agility and climbing powers were to the average man's as are the gibbon's to the sloth's, that little difference was just enough. For now, by climbing to the niche in which the oil pot was hung, he found a base for yet a further upward spring, enabling him to seize hold of the grating and raise himself to a position permitting him an oblique view of proceedings in the outer world of free men.

Against the hour when even his great holding power should tire, he had borne aloft with him old Mingo's tattered robe, which, tightily twisted, formed a tolerable rope, the end of which he passed above a bar of the grate. Tying both ends of the twisted robe together to create a loop, through which he thrust one thigh, he thus might readily gaze forth for hours with no more discomfort than restricted circulation in the supporting leg.

Perhaps no other dweller in that kingless kingdom had stranger view of the arrival of the suzerain lords from far and near than he whose keen eyes watched intently from below the very feet of those who passed. Across that metal grating, not more than inches up above his head, there passed the naked feet of warrior-slaves, the feet of freemen shod in mammoth leather, the feet of tattered mendicants, enwrapped in strips of rags.

Clearly to his ears came the shoutings of the populace, the greater part of which he now could understand, without the help of Mingo to translate them. From time to time his view was blocked by passage overhead of bull-drawn sledges rumbling with the weight of unseen freights. He heard the roar of caged animals, the rolling beat of drums, the raucous blare of horns, the deep hoarse trumpets of the mammoth teams, the clanking of chains by which they hauled their enormous loads. Now and again a vast round padded foot was set upon the grating, and by its monstrous size he knew a mammoth passed—its hauling chains dragging—to seek another load.

But more than that flashed to his understanding. On one such mighty pressure he felt the grate from which he hung yield suddenly, as bits of dislodged stone were by that heavy weight chipped from the seat in which the grate had once been tightly set.

Forgotten were the sounds and sights above him. If by some device he might enlarge upon the damage to the grating already begun, escape from his prison might yet be achieved. Hope rose in him swiftly, to be as swiftly conquered by reality; for having no place whereon to brace himself in order to exert a pressure which might loosen the grating further, the fact of its unsuspected weakness remained to mock him. Nor was there aught within the catacombs—of this he long since had made sure—which might be raised to serve as platform from which to apply his full strength.

He was conscious of a sudden hubbub close overhead. The bellow of a mammoth bull sent thunder rolling through the slave dungeons, which instantly must rouse the satiated sleepers, and bring them to perceive one of their number engaged in patent efforts at escape.

Working hastily at the knots in Mingo's robe, by which he hung suspended from the grating, Kioga prepared to drop back to the dungeon floor before discovery by the slaves put him in peril of betrayal as one who dared seek to be free. But long suspension had tightened all his knots, delaying their undoing.

He heard the rustling pad of naked feet hurrying nearer through the catacombs; then from above another deep hoarse trumpeting betrayed some punishment inflicted on a mammoth bull. The hubbub in the street was increased and from all sides the shouts of men were adding to the din. Above them sounded the cries of a bull-driver urging on his beast and suddenly Kioga heard a shout:

"Make way! Make way, blundering fool! You block the passage of the high-born ones!"

Then in an instant the Snow Hawk saw and understood. The great hook, fastened to one end of a mammoth's dragging chain had caught upon an angle of the depression in which the grate was sunk, deterring the great beast in its passage. The frantic driver, conscious only of the enormity of his offense in holding up that traffic of barbaric royalty, had not the wit to realize promptly what caused the check to his mount, and only sought to goad him on.

Responding to the brute's great surges, the chain alternately drew taut and slackened, without dislodging that restraining hook.

Inspired by a quick idea, Kioga waited until again the chain went loose, then swiftly seized the hook and drew it under one stout bar. Once more the mammoth surged. The round bar bent. The grate was under fearful strain and now upon it swarmed a host of slaves, shouting at the driver, seeking to make him understand the cause of his restraint.

He either did not hear or did not understand. His cries of *"Uh! Ya-uh!"* redoubled. There was the sound of blows upon the hairy quarters of his mount, whose trumpeting went shrill with pain. Again the goaded monster surged, and with a tearing, cracking sound the grating was rent upward from its fastenings, Kioga clinging to it.

A score of slaves, crowding on and near the grate, were by its sudden yielding hurled to the stones in a confusion of tangled arms and legs. The goaded mammoth, leaning forward on the breast-straps, and thrown off balance by the sudden breaking of the grate, fell to its knees and rolled upon the roadway with his screaming driver, adding to the disorder.

Thus for a moment pandemonium and chaos allied themselves upon the Snow Hawk's side, affording him the necessary instant to detach himself from the grating, and gather his wits, the better to avail himself of this sudden liberty.

He thought at first to bound among the throngs who lined the road on either side and lose himself among them. But close at hand he saw the better way, less fraught with danger of discovery.

No slave among those now rising from the stones was differently garbed than he. All wore the simple cloth about the loins and went barefooted in token of their degradation. Among them there were blue-eyed men and brown, of several degrees of height and build. Following prudent custom among the T'emaho they had been recruited each from a different locality, scarce knowing one another's names. One more or less among them would excite but little curiosity in men who were hereditary slaves, trained to accept and not to question in any matters of their daily life.

Now round Kioga rose the toppled slaves who hastened to

replace the grating, that the nobles still to come might not meet with accident. The Snow Hawk turned to lend his strength. The massive grate was raised upon one edge and poised. In the short instant before it fell back into place he saw, down in the slave dungeons, the upward-gazing faces of those miserable lifelong captives. Among them was the face of aged Mingo, to whom Kioga owed his knowledge of the language of the realm, a deal of its geography and many of its customs.

He had, moreover, come to have a great affection for the old Shoni, denied for so many years his birthright of freedom; yet to speak to him now were to betray the fact of his escape, which otherwise he hoped might pass unnoticed until, perchance, the noble who had felt his whip sent for him. He dared not jeopardize his present precarious liberty. And so, as the slaves, of whose number he no longer counted himself one, let fall the grate, Kioga turned on a sudden impulse toward the fallen mammoth driver, his arm pinned beneath the heavy brute.

The animal itself was now heaving to its knees. Before it could attain its feet Kioga aided the driver to its shoulders, and as if sustaining him, mounted lightly beside him as it rose upon all fours.

Anxious to end the delay to the procession, of which the accident had been a cause, the driver signaled to the brute, which lumbered on its way down toward the river. Intent upon the manner in which he controlled the beast, Kioga made careful mental note of every call and watched the animal's responses.

As they proceeded, the other recovered sufficiently from his accident to say a word of thanks, adding: "When it is learned what I have done this day, it will go ill with me." And when Kioga looked a question: "The slaves might have escaped."

Kioga laughed, as if amused at such a thought. "It could not be," he said. "The damage was too quickly remedied. What slave would dare attempt escape before the eyes of all the city?"

The other seemed encouraged by that logic and scanned Kioga as if endeavoring to place his features. "Whom do you serve?" he asked.

The Snow Hawk's mind worked swiftly, basing his reply upon the knowledge Mingo had imparted to him of the customs of the City of the Kings. "A noble within the walls," he answered. "Sometimes I guard the slaves, whose escape you feared; again I labor on the walls. Always have I hoped to have a mount like this. How cunningly you guide its every movement! Brother, I envy you."

Pleased by the compliment, the other smiled. "It is not difficult. See, when I say *'Uh-ya-uh!'* he hurries. When I prod him thus, below one ear, he turns in that direction; and when I press him on the flank with my goad, he stops. All of the laboring beasts obey such signs. Remain a while with me and I will teach them to you."

Kioga affected hesitation. "Will it not be thought strange that two of us sit here together?"

"Not so," the other answered. "Two is the usual number—one to load and one to drive. My companion of yesterday was flogged to death for running against a noble on the river boat. I am Tahro. What is your name, brother?"

Caught unprepared for such a query, Kioga invented swiftly, again upon the facts he knew from Mingo. "I have no name—a punishment because my mother died when I was born, and so could bear no other children to her owner."

"Then I will call you by the name of him they flogged to death. His name was Akra."

So came Kioga by the name which, before many moons had passed would echo through the realm and be on every lip.

Their shaggy mount drew near the strange ship moored at the dock below the high-walled city. On every side perspiring slaves were lightening her of ivory, of baskets filled with vegetables, of huge cheeses made from mammoth milk, of ornate furniture, or chests crammed full of gold and silver ornaments, and bales of multicolored cloth, woven from mammoth underwool.

Their mount dropped to its knees at signal, and directed by Tahro, the Snow Hawk piled the beast's broad back with merchandise, making all secure with ropes of hair. At signal the mammoth rose, and to its chains another slave made fast a sledge, heaped high with other articles belonging to Tahro's royal owner.

Against the growing chill, the slaves donned woolen overrobes. To Kioga, Tahro flung a similar garment, once the property of his dead companion. The Snow Hawk wrapped its folds about him and prepared to mount beside his newfound friend, when suddenly he saw that from a swollen bundle on the sledge, a dozen weapons had burst forth.

Replacing these securely, he took the opportunity to secrete a foot-long dagger in its sheath beneath his robe—for he had been required to return to its owner the short-sword seized in the baiting pit,—then climbed upon the beast, which lumbered toward the city gates, preceded and followed by others of its giant kind.

Thus, high above the throngs, Kioga passed again into the City of the Kings, alert for any signs of his companions from the outer world, and keenly observant of the sights along the route.

Through all the lesser press, beyond the close-packed nearest rows of watching free men, tattered beggars circulated, with their shrill and nasal cries of *"Wa-o! Wa-o!* Help the poor and wretched! Give an ivory disk."

Below the fine rock dwellings, rising tier on tier in the cliffs which marked the mountain side, troops of agile tumblers leaped and twisted to earn the slighter ivory coins, tossed down from high above.

Two swarthy musicians, blowing fiercely into long and bulbous instruments, created weird ear-torturing cacophony.

An old sly-featured thief, trapped with his greedy fingers in the garments of two prospective victims simultaneously, was chased, but scurrying too swiftly for his wealthy pursuers, took up his trade a little farther on, his cunning fingers reaping endless harvest from the well-sown pockets of the rich and well-to-do.

So, alternately advancing and halting in the jam of excited humanity, the beast which bore Kioga and Tahro came presently to pause anew. The latest pause had coincided with the passage of Loalli, and her extensive retinue, which passed not twenty feet away, affording the Snow Hawk easy view of her.

Loalli's mount, a towering bull, passed close before a row of laborer-beasts, which waited the time when she had passed to go about their tasks. The press was close and unaccustomed noise had made the great animals restive and ill-tempered.

One of their number, ill-managed by its driver, rolled suddenly out of line, attacking with its formidable tusks the brute which bore Loalli. Assailed thus from one side the royal mammoth staggered and fell upon one knee, its shoulder badly gored.

Loalli, leaning forward in the act of addressing one of the slaves who led her mount, was caught off balance and thrown sliding forward from her animal, too suddenly to grasp its ornamental housings. Her drivers, too concerned with punishments to come for failing to foresee this danger, stood for an instant stiff with fear, for her and for themselves.

Kioga, from his mount, was quick to apprehend her peril and from his perch sprang to the ground beside her, seizing as he went Tahro's stout mammoth goad. Scarce had he felt the stones beneath his feet when what he had anticipated suddenly transpired.

The brute which had attacked, incensed now by the sight and smell of blood, swerved round to charge anew. His rush upon the wounded animal must pass across the spot on which Loalli stood, for the instant immobile.

But such a mighty juggernaut, by reason of its very size, is slow in starting, a circumstance which, aided by Kioga's instant grasping of it, preserved Loalli's life. Before the surly bull had more than wheeled, Kioga seized Loalli by her slender waist and tossed her bodily back up atop her mount, now rising to its feet, though gory on the shoulder.

Then spinning, with the heavy goad in hand, he crouched an instant before the onrushing animal.

Loalli's sudden scream behind and up above Kioga expressed her fears for him whose life appeared about to pay the price of hers. Her voice as quickly altered, to express a cry of sharp encouragement and admiration.

For when it seemed that he must be trampled to a senseless cake beneath the bull's vast feet, almost upon him, Kioga suddenly bounded to one side. The goad, first swung for the creature's mighty head, he changed in its fall, sank its hook deep in the foreleg above the foot instead, and pulled with all his strength.

The charging bull, about to throw its weight upon that foot, came down, instead, upon its knee, and with momentum gathered from its rush, rolled on its back, its flying chains dealing havoc among the people closest by. Before it could come up, one of those chains was swiftly lapped about a fore leg and a hind leg. An instant more and the Snow Hawk was upon its head.

The bull, a moment earlier insensate with destroying lust, recognized defeat and mastery. Its rumbling voice gave way to the peculiar nasal trumpeting which is the peace cry of the mammoth.

Glancing up, Kioga found Loalli's eyes full on him, their great dark pupils wide with the excitement of her close escape from injury or death. Her face was for that moment robbed of all its arrogance and for that little space she was no princess of high rank, but a woman who beheld with something more than interest the man who was her rescuer.

Thus for an instant they were face to face. Then she whose pride had scored a noble's greetings smiled upon this man who seemed to her a slave.

But to her great surprise he smiled not in return. He rose, turned swiftly round, sprang up atop his own mount beside the gaping Tahro, gave the signal which sent the animal surging forward and added to it an urging prod which made the mammoth grunt. A crowd moved in between, composed of warriors and slaves and mounted bodyguards.

As he departed, without waiting to receive her thanks, Loalli's face went momentarily blank, before slow color rose into her cheeks, in token of bewilderment and something else besides—the product of that meeting of the eyes which made her pulses quicken still. Then the line of march continued slowly.

Deaf to the cheers—as much for Loalli's rescuer as for her own escape—another watched, upon his face a deathly pallor. A wreath of leaf and flower, intended to have been tossed before her mount, now fell forgotten from his hand. Mahri of the noble blood had seen and noted all. With jealous eyes he saw what she had not yet herself realized. . . . As Mahri turned away, black bitterness was in his heart, and memory of a face he never would forget nor cease detesting.

CHAPTER 10

Publicity was farthest from the state of things which Kioga desired—at least until he might go unrecognized by those who had seen him. Only by remaining unknown might he escape the consequences of the enmity he had aroused among the powerful, for in one momentary glimpse he had seen hatred in the face of one who stared upon him from a balcony and recognized another foe, whose cause for enmity he knew not.

His acquaintance the mammoth driver Tahro, pointing behind, said suddenly: "Loalli sends her slaves to seek you out. Why do you run from honor?"

"Some day perhaps I'll tell you, Tahro. But now I must back to my master's house," Kioga answered, slipping to the ground near where he earlier had made his escape from the slave-keep. "Mayhap we'll meet again."

Tahro touched his outstretched wrist, equivalent of a cordial handshake among the People of the Tusk, and said, "Come to the wharves if ever I can do aught for you. We tie up there until the king is crowned."

Kioga nodded understanding, wrapped his over-robe about him closely, saw to the looseness of his single weapon in its scabbard and turned to mingle with the heterogeneous crowd that lined the highway, listening to ascertain if any of the people had observed a slave escape. Hearing nothing untoward, to make assurance doubly sure, he spoke to another slave.

" 'Tis rumored that a captive slave got away. My master sent me to confirm the truth of that."

" 'Tis empty rumor," came the answer, "I saw it all, and I will vouch that no slave could have done this thing and been unseen."

The questioner persisted. "But hark you, brother, 'tis further said that he who whipped the noble, Semya, was the one who got away."

"And now I call the rumor doubly false," the other said.

"Eh, then would you know him if you saw him?" asked the questioner, drawing back a little to set hand to his hidden weapon.

"Not so," the other said, "but I was talking with a friend who guards the slaves. Semya—may his life be short—sent for that daring one to punish him. They found that he was dead."

"Dead!" The questioner started very suddenly, then recovered his earlier aplomb. "Eh, of course. Of his confinement, not a doubt."

"Not so. Where have you been, not to have heard?" his informer answered, flaunting his superior knowledge proudly. "The other slaves devoured him. The guards forgot to bring them food."

The persistent inquirer paused, digesting this astounding piece of information. "But is it certain? He was as tall as I, and strong besides!"

"Certain as may be. Mingo, the truth-teller, told them he had seen him killed and eaten."

"Ah, cunning Mingo!" muttered the questioner, at which the other sent him a glance of inquiry. "You said? The shouting—I could not hear."

"Poor unhappy fellow," amended the questioner hastily. "To be eaten is indeed sad. But he had his desserts, one who would raise his hand against the highborn. Semya."

"You may think so," the other remarked, glancing about to be sure he was not overheard. "But I would I could have touched that brave slave's hand before he died. I wish"—and his voice dropped lower still—"I wish that he had killed that Semya."

The inquirer looked properly startled. "You wish that? But why?"

"He is my master," said the other and turning, bared his back an instant. The skin was slashed and bruised from neck to hip.

"Do not despair. It may yet come to pass," the stranger in the over-robe remarked and would have added more, when suddenly he glimpsed a band of warrior-slaves striding swiftly toward him. Murmuring hasty thanks to the other for his information, he turned to mingle once more with the crowds, when the foremost of the approaching band called to him a command to halt. "In the name of Loalli, the High-Born!"

Now that Kioga had learned of his own supposed demise, the freedom of action thus made possible could be continued, he realized, only by perpetuating the rumor so cleverly endorsed by crafty Mingo. Therefore to be haled up before the noble beauty, publicly to hear her praises, was an honor to fly away from, lest of the thousands who had seen him earlier in the realm, someone should come to recognize him.

And what with the thronging, craning crowds about, no doubt the Snow Hawk would promptly have eluded those who sought him out, had not a second incident occured which drew eyes from the great parade in his direction.

A wealthy merchant of the city, well-shod in gleaming leather and richly robed, cried out in anger: "*Ho wai!* Stop, scum of all thiefs! *Stop!*"

Scurrying close past Kioga went a familiar form in tattered garb, the nimble-fingered old pocket-picker, plying his light-handed trade anew upon a different corner. Seeking now to hide behind this taller stalwart, who shunned the limelight equally with himself, he but involved them both in greater publicity.

"*Ss-s-st* there! Away!" Kioga growled. "Can you not see that I am sought as well as you?"

"You are a slave and not a thief," the other answered hastily. "They seek to honor you who saved Loalli's life. They seek to cut the throat of me, Ameeg. I hide perforce, but why should you?"

"Must I account to you, sly-handed one? Quick now! Since you will not begone, we'll run together. You have the cunning and know the runways and the hiding places. I have the strength to guard you. So, away!"

And with a mighty surge Kioga cleared a pathway through the crowd, along which Ameeg slyly darted with a speed belying his years. After him, Loalli's minions close at heel, Kioga sprang. The chase led swiftly from the busy thoroughfares and in among the lesser buildings of the city, toward that poor section infested by such as Ameeg, who now doubled on his tracks like a hare seeking to evade pursuing hounds.

But two of these, more subtle than he had expected, lay waiting to ambush the thief along one of the paths, on which he so confidently sought escape, and rose to seize him, as he came near. Squealing in his fear, Ameeg cried shrilly to his companion in the flight:

"It is a trap! Help me, my friend. Help! *Help!*"

One of the pursuit, aware of danger from the rear, wheeled round and raised his blade to strike. But like a flash Kioga disarmed and threw him stunned and helpless to the ground, and with his falling sword engaged the second warrior-slave.

This adversary counted much upon his skill and not at all upon the lightning quickness of the Snow Hawk, whose cut upon the forearm sent his weapon clattering. Before he could recover and snatch out his dagger, Kioga overbore him and rushed on behind Ameeg, overtaking the thief just as the remainder of pursuit swung round the nearest corner.

"*Azik,* but you are strong and quick!" the little brigand panted. "Remain with us and be a thief. We have great need of such an arm as thine."

"First lead me to your burrow," came the Snow Hawk's answer.

As if in answer, Ameeg made a sudden turn into a space between two buildings, thence down a crooked stair into a kind of cellar, and through the cellar to a room down lower still, whose door, invisible to the casual glance, fell open inward at his signal. Into this room Ameeg entered, blown and weary, followed by the Snow Hawk, who heard the pursuit clatter on by.

Seeing only in this tall stranger the foe whom Ameeg fled, a dozen dark-visaged fellows, clad in little more than rags, closed in behind the returning thief, preparing with their shining daggers to make short work of the pursuer. In time, but only just in time to avoid bloodshed, Ameeg intervened:

"Sheathe, brothers, sheathe! He is my friend. Touch wrists with— Eh, but my memory fails with age. What did you call yourself, my friend?"

Kioga had recourse to fresh invention. "My name is Akra. I am a potter from the north, seeking in these parts my brother's slave, who has escaped. The better to cause his return, I dress and act as slave myself." He heaped invention on invention: "The one I seek is broad and strong, the father of two hundred, therefore very valuable. He has a brand upon his neck and two great scars across the face. Has any one of you seen such a man?"

They had not seen such a slave, they said. They were poor laborers more given to industry and toil than wandering idly in the streets. Here in this humble dwelling they had gathered for a day of rest from toil, to play a round of *oka,* the chess-like game, popular with noble and laborer alike. Thus in their turn they lied to him, and watched him furtively to see if he had been deceived.

But what Kioga saw convinced him that those brown uncalloused hands of theirs were far more skilled in wielding dirks than tools, and that the game they played had more to do with plunder than with entertainment. He answered dryly:

"Ameeg was also playing *oka* when interrupted by a merchant whose pocket had been picked."

Perceiving that no good would come of falsehoods, and having earlier betrayed his occupation to this Akra anyway, Ameeg turned to his associate thieves indignantly. "Have you no pride? Will you deny your trade? Are you ashamed of taking such a little from them who possess so much? Ah, bah! That you should lie to this dear friend of mine—you whom I taught to be the nimblest pack of thieves in all the city! Uncover what you took today, that Akra here may share my admiration. Eh-eh"—turning to the Snow Hawk—"no lock is strong enough, no pockets are too tightly sewn for them to pilfer. It is a trade which takes one many years to learn." And Ameeg puffed out his little chest. "But I, Ameeg, am master of the art. Abide with me, friend Akra. You have an honest face; which goeth exceeding well with nimble fingers in our occupation. You'd soon be rich enough to have your own pocket picked!"

Pleased with this fresh thought, the leader of these banditti laughed, and the Snow Hawk laughed with him. "How do you dare betray to me what I might easily betray to others and so endanger you?"

Ameeg glanced at him out of slyly narrowed eyes. "No fool am I, Ameeg. We keep no evidence around. What comes to me is gone forever. And furthermore, I think you need Ameeg, as earlier he needed you." The thief's voice fell lower, and leaning near, so that his henchmen might not overhear, he added: "Escape from Loalli's messengers was not all you sought. A thief I may be, Akra, but I owe my life to you. Therefore I will not betray to anyone that when a grate was torn up from above the slave-keep, there was a slave who came up with it. Ah, it was quick, yes—quicker than the fingers of a cutpurse—but old Ameeg has eagle eyes. Nay, reach not for your weapon, friend." Ameeg there paused to show the dagger which had been Kioga's, now held in his own hand. "I took it from you when you entered. Ten men stand ready to cut your throat at a word from me."

"Then speak it," Kioga answered, knowing his deception pierced and prepared for any eventuality. "See how few shall remain before I am laid out."

Ameeg raised a pacifying hand and handed back the dagger. "*Zik*, you grow hot for nothing! My life is yours, and I do not forget. Look you, friend; you tread on rotten ground. Your face will presently betray you."

"All life is fraught with risks," Kioga answered. "I must accept them as they come."

"Well said; he who would change the world must be a fool," quoth Ameeg wisely. "But *faces* may be changed, and ere you go abroad again, Ameeg will make yours uglier, safe even from the eyes of fair Loalli, who knows a handsome slave at sight."

"You saw her accident?"

"And more," said Ameeg, pursing up his thin slit of a mouth. "And so did a certain high-born one who haunts the gardens when she treads in them, and is in twenty places, just to see her pass and win the smile she gives to—Akra, the slave." Ameeg chuckled long and deeply.

"What mean you, brother?" demanded Kioga uneasily.

"Loalli is a willful wench," the other answered irreverently, "as willful as she's beautiful. And powerful besides, with many slaves to do her bidding. She'll not forget thee, friend, if I am any judge."

Kioga pondered that, thoughtful of Loalli's long, deep, admiring glance. He turned to Ameeg. "To work, then. Make me ugly as a toad if need be. For I must move about with freedom. There is much to do."

Ameeg obeyed. With grease, to which a pigment had been added, he rubbed in shadows underneath the Snow Hawk's eyes, and from the cheekbones to the lower jaw lines, next did the same, to give Kioga's face a haggard look. The jaw itself he made to seem less square and forceful by sparing use of brownish color from another jar. Now round Kioga's head he bound a kind of fillet in the fashion of the middle classes of the country, and under this drew taut the hair back from one temple, thus giving to the nearest eye an odd and upward slant. The Snow Hawk's sound white teeth he easily discolored here and there by application of a kind of stain derived from berries. The nostrils he broadened by inserting bits of wire which did not show nor interfere with breathing. The upper lip was made to bulge and overhang by introduction of a bit of leather, the which, by interfering with enunciation, made even Kioga's speech sound thick and different.

Beholding his strange handiwork, he added little touches here and there, achieving from a handsome manly face, the appearance of its opposite, a hungry-looking sullen expression having something sinister about it. The work of change complete, he held before Kioga a mirror of polished bronze, set with dully gleaming stones—part of the store of objects stolen during this day.

Kioga looked and started, so cleverly had old Ameeg labored. Not even those who were his friends might now identify him from a stranger. " 'Tis magic, Ameeg," the Snow Hawk averred admiringly. "I do not know myself."

"Keep these about you," Ameeg replied, handing Kioga a little packet containing pigments and a smaller mirror. "Be vain. Look often at yourself. Renew my work from time to time, as it is needed. Now listen well to me, for any empty-headed fool could prick your story full of holes. It too must change."

Kioga listened intently as the old thief spoke: "No potter, which you claimed to be, bears arms. You are instead a warrior, serving whoso pays you highest. You keep the same name, Akra, which is a common one with slaves and freemen. You have no relatives; someone might ask their names. You have no home; someone might ask about a neighbor. For the rest, depend upon your wits. If trouble comes, wear this upon your ear, stone outward. My men are everywhere; someone will see and make himself known to you. Help will come." Ameeg gave to Kioga a tiny ear ornament, and he screwed it to the lobe, stone in.

Thus it came about that he who had entered Ameeg's den of thieves as Akra the slave, stood among them now as Akra the mercenary soldier, to all appearances as great a rascal as any of the rest. No longer attempting to conceal their pillage, they spread along a rough table the products of their stealthy activities.

The items for the most part were small enough to have been worn upon the persons of the victims; gold and silver jewelry, with here and there a precious shining stone set in copper-bronze. A pile of ivory coins grew higher as from the secret places on their persons the thieves produced and added each his take.

With glittering eyes Ameeg surveyed the plunder, then scanned his men with swift but searching gaze. "Maro!" he said at last, fixing him of that name with a piercing stare. "Art holding back, dishonorable wretch!"

The one called Maro started as if stung. The eyes of all the others leaped to him with anger in them. Before he could protest, a dozen hands fell on him, stripping him down to bare and dirty skin. Within a little hidden pocket, fashioned in a fold low down upon the lining of his over-robe, four jeweled trinkets came to light, secretly withheld. Discovered in duplicity, Maro turned pale, his long eyes sliding weasel-like from face to face, and reading there the penalty which he must pay. Then with the quickness of his apprehensions, he sprang toward the door, to escape.

He was anticipated by a move on the part of the nearest thief, one Daki, so quick that even Kioga's hawk-keen eyes scarce perceived it. And Maro clutched his chest and sank upon his heels without a sound, stabbed to the heart.

Dishonesty found out and punished, Ameeg now made twelve piles of plunder on the table. Eleven of these he then divided into approximately equal parts, and placed an arbitrary value on them, asking each if he were satisfied until all his cohorts had accepted his figure. The twelfth heap—Maro's take—he added to the share of Daki, who had slain the guilty thief.

Dealing out payment in the ivory disks, Ameeg received the stolen articles in their stead. And the thieves set forth again to seek fresh plunder while the crowds still swarmed.

With them went Kioga, while ringing in his ears were Ameeg's final words of advice: "Listen much; talk little—and remember the earring."

Thanks to Ameeg's skillful handiwork, the Snow Hawk passed easily as a nondescript soldier, albeit having the appearance of a rogue besides. Taking leave of his companions, he turned in the direction the parade of nobles had taken, intent upon finding us, who had been his companions on his entry into the realm of the tyrant kings.

Along his path he came upon a crowd, collecting about a gated wall before the carven dwelling of one who, someone told him, was named Mahri of the noble blood. Who Mahri was, Kioga had no least idea; but rather than make himself conspicuous by betraying ignorance and inquiring, he sought instead to move amid the throng the better to inform himself by listening to the talk of others. But very soon he found himself confronted by several men, suspiciously demanding to know his identity and business.

"I am a warrior, as you might know by looking at me," he answered to the nearest. "My name is Akra, and my strength and weapons are for sale."

"Why does he not seek a warrior's employment at the walls?" demanded one whose eyes were fixed on Kioga mistrustfully. "He means no good, mayhap some harm. Lay hold upon him then! We'll have him up before a wiser one. Let Mahri question him."

CHAPTER 11

Kioga would have been the last to realize how near his meeting with the friends he sought impended, for he knew nothing of the fortunes which had followed us who had been separated from him.

Had Tokala, for example, wearing that plaque of royal inheritance about his neck, come into view less spectacularly, when first seen by the nobles or their priests, the keen edge of a priestly knife would most effectively have put an end to his pretensions, along with his life.

But this return, supposedly of the last of the Ru, had found the people more than willing to accept him. And since an old woman among the people had discovered his supposed royalty and sent the word like wildfire among the crowds, and since the people had displayed such great enthusiasm, summary action by the nobles could not be undertaken without grave risk. Swift to grasp that fact, swifter still to ally himself with one destined to become the popular favorite, was Mahri, under whose roof Tokala had been kept, surrounded by the noble's bodyguards and loyal slaves.

And Mahri, whether or not he doubted the young Tokala's *bona-fides,* had nonetheless perceived the power to be gained by backing a promising pretender publicly, in order to stand near him when he exercised great power as boy-king of the realm.

Nothing, therefore, was left undone to assure the boy's protection: And when a host of men among the joyous populace acclaimed him at the doors of Mahri's fortlike home, Mahri was the first to bid them welcome as a guard of honor, and to see that their enthusiasm was kept high by gifts of food and drink, sent out by slaves in the name of the youth Tokala.

And we of Tokala's party enjoyed a like protection and all the freedom of Mahri's home. Flashpan, quick to put a finger on the cause, explained it thus: "Two words from us, spread to them other muck-a-mucks, would give the ammynition to bring Mahri's cyard-house a-topplin' down round his ears. Mahri holds a dang' good hand an' hopes to fill it with a king—meanin' Tokala. . . . I'd sure like to hev Kioga here 'longside of us to see us through."

"Then let us remind Mahri of him again," I interposed. "For any one of us to go in search of him would be next to impossible with that mob outside the gates."

It chanced that to remind Mahri would be unnecessary, for he joined us in our sumptuous quarters, after the parade of nobles had gone its way into the city proper. Troubled of eye and long of face, he squatted down among us with the air of one who knows not how or where to begin telling evil tidings. At last:

"I fear some ill has befallen him you call Kioga. One of my messengers has been about with open ears. Kioga was taken down beyond the city and thrown among the slaves. Semya, whom you saw among his fellows in the hall of state, went there to play with him—he loves the sight of fear, this Semya. But from the gossip my messenger brings, Kioga seized the whip they used on him and stroked Semya on the face, so sharply that he'll bear the mark for all his life—may it be short! Then Kioga turned back into the slave quarters. Sending for him later, Semya learned that during a hunger riot among the slaves, who were forgotten when the nobles came, Kioga had been slain."

Munro went white; Flashpan's jaw fell slack, his moustaches quivering as he turned to me, who felt as if some mighty prop had been removed from under me. The miner looked back to Munro, sitting speechless, then turned to Mahri with a question: "If he be dead, they have his body somewhere. I'll not believe it till I see the proof."

Longer still grew Mahri's face. "There is no body," he answered. "The slaves were hungry."

And he went on to explain how one Mingo, for decades a captive in the slave-keep, had volunteered the information that he had actually seen Kioga killed.

"Semya himself is tearing his hair in anger," added Mahri. "He had prepared some further entertainment for him who left that mark upon his face."

Who would convey the news to Beth La Salle? Whatever must eventually be told, at least the manner of Kioga's end should always be known only to ourselves. Nor would we break the news to Tokala, whose boyish idol Kioga had ever been, until it could not be avoided longer.

Now more than ever, were we dependent on Mahri; and we were, therefore, constrained to make the best of every opportunity to prolong our present safety until such time as those vast borings in the southern mountains should pierce a way to liberty for us and for the people of this hermit kingdom. With that vast engineering project, labored at for generations, now nearing completion, and the impending elevation of asking, the realm seethed with double excitement.

Now came a clamor from without, the sound of challenge and of answer, the creak of gates that opened, then clanged shut, the tramp of footsteps on the flags. Now on the bronze doors of Mahri's fine dwelling came a heavy knock. A servant looked forth through an opening before throwing wide the door to a little company who entered, in their midst a tall and sullen-looking ruffian, with shoulders on him reminiscent of the Snow Hawk himself.

The leader of the troop which guarded him had made obeisance and was speaking now to Mahri.

"We found him, High-born, loitering in the streets without excuse. He comes from far, he says, to sell his weapons to the highest bidder. But would a warrior not go to the walls and look for other warriors there?"

Mahri's eyes were on the captive a little wearily. That earlier rebuff by Loalli in the city street had both depressed and angered him. The smile bestowed upon a valiant slave had been as salt rubbed in an open wound.

"Is it then a crime to pass my house?" he asked with a trace of impatience.

"We thought—it seemed—" began one of the self-appointed vigilantes lamely. "He meant, perhaps, some harm to the little Ru—else what would he be doing near the dwelling of a noble?"

Now Mahri foresaw that what were rumors today undoubtedly would be realities tomorrow when the hostile nobles came to unite their strength against his young pretender. It would not do, then, to treat this vigilance of the people shabbily. Accordingly he summoned and gave an order to a household slave, who presently returned with young Tokala, splendid in his close-fitting dress of supple leather, that golden plaque conspicuously worn upon his breast.

Before the youth Mahri made a deferential bow and said: "Look well upon these men. For when you shall be ruler over all the nobles, it will be your duty to reward them fittingly."

Drilled in the part he was to play, and already quite familiar with it, Tokala scanned them, and said, with grave simplicity: "I shall remember you. When I am powerful, come to me again."

Listening in amazement, he who called himself Akra the warrior had his first intimation of Mahri's deep intrigues; and with them came instant apprehension of the perils, particularly to Tokala, in the way of their fulfillment. He saw the young Tokala's eyes rest on his face, then rove elsewhere without a sign of recognition.

Kioga had quickly recognized Mahri as he whose eyes had been upon him angrily, following the fall of Loalli's mount. Carefully he had watched, to see if he in turn were recognized and found his disguise unpierced. Seeing Mahri disposed to belittle his importance as a dangerous character, Kioga uttered that which brought the noble's gaze upon him sharply.

He spoke in tones of simulated indignation and appeal: "This is a hostile city to a warrior seeking only to serve an honest master. Arrested now for passing in the street, struck down earlier by that cursed slave who played the hero to Loalli—ah, by my father's bones, better had I stayed in my own country!"

Overlooking the first and last, the noble seized upon that center of Kioga's talk which mentioned Loalli and the slave: "You saw that daring fellow? Which way did he go? Did you recognize his companion?"

Kioga answered in the order of the questions: "I saw him running toward the kennels of the thieves, in company of one who seemed to be a thief."

"That much my servants have discovered. What they did not find out is where he went thereafter."

"They must be lazy," quoth the warrior Akra. "Strange that they could not smell down a common slave within their own home city. Now, with a nose like mine—" He paused and rattled several ivory disks deep in the pocket of his over-robe.

"Think you you might produce this slave?" asked Mahri, leaning nearer and speaking in a lower tone. The warrior Akra shrugged, answering:

"I am a homeless soldier, ragged and poor. Such works required more than mere enthusiasm." Again the disks clicked against each other with a broad suggestiveness.

"You shall have home and money in my service," said Mahri softly. "And if you find this slave for me, rewards yet greater."

"He must be valuable—much hated or much loved," remarked the warrior Akra, with the tolerated boldness of his class.

Mahri's face first flushed, then paled. "Yours to obey, and not to question," he said sharply, "—particularly when the pay is good." He flung a pouch to the other, containing money of the realm. "Find me that slave, and you shall have as much again. *Hé,* Ilo!"

A slave came running as his name was called.

"House this man below, with leave to come and go at will. Give him to wear the badge of those who serve your master," said Mahri, and turned, to find the men who had brought this loiterer staring in amazement at these developments. The noble smiled and ordered yet another slave to serve them refreshments below in return for their vigilance. They filed out, amazed but none the wiser about their captivc's sudden change of fortune and employment in Mahri's services.

Decently lodged in a lower chamber of the splendid dwelling carved in the rocks, Kioga counted the hour well spent which brought him under the same roof, unknown as yet to those whom he had sought with little expectation of finding them so quickly. Akra the slave, of course, would never be brought before the jealous noble by Akra the warrior; but for appearance' sake, he must seem to make an effort to locate the slave whom Mahri desired. And the search should be both long enough and wide enough to familiarize him thoroughly with the City of the Kings.

Ostensibly departing in his search, Kioga went by a roundabout way toward the den of Ameeg the thief. His path led through the narrow crooked streets choked by the dwellings of the middle classes, through some of which a mammoth might scarcely pass. Here dwelt the workers in creaking, strong-smelling leather, makers of rich housings and trappings for the royal mammoths. Here toiled the armorers at their ringing anvils and roaring forges, beating out *kuris,* long as rapiers yet heavier, the common sidearm of every warrior, used to cut or thrust; and *okals,* weapons in the form of clubs, long in the handle and heavy in the ax-like head, for wielding against foot-warriors from mammoth-back. Here too were long keen-bladed spears, with hooks upon one side, for use in foot-warriors' hands to thrust at mounted foes and drag them to the ground.

Upon the stones were ranged two-handed, two-edged swords, broad toward the point for defending the city's walls; and oddly shaped, short-handled throwing blades, sharp at every edge, so thin a man might carry half a dozen, hurling them at need without thought of retrieving.

For forty pieces Kioga bought a *kuri* suited to his height and wrist, slid this into its sheath and buckled it at waist. Ten pieces more brought a vest of copper chain, fair proof against small-arms, with double thickness at the back. Armed now as were the other warriors in the city, he left the place, having seen but half the common weapons of the T'emaho.

Beyond were the marketplaces, filled with cries of price and offer by scolding women and haggling hucksters. Farther still, deep in the concentration of their work, ivory carvers bent above their intricate designs, working in their doorways; just as for uncounted centuries their fathers had carved before them in an art that is the oldest on this earth, the carving of the mammoth tusk.

A crowd of warriors gambled in an open-fronted public place, consoled when they lost, by copious drafts of *lohe*, the beverage-drug favored by the warlike brotherhood. The topic everywhere was the assembling of the nobles for the crowning of her newest king. Debate raged hot between those who foresaw the rise of Semya to that important office, and others who foresaw with equal certainty the crowning of the youth Tokala, whom they referred to as Ru the Last.

"I thought, perchance you came to tell me of some treasure waiting to be stolen," said Ameeg when Kioga had reached the rendezvous of rascals. "Instead you do not speak, but are silent as a stone."

"Ameeg, my friend, you daily risk your neck to pick the pockets in the streets, when at your very feet a mine of gold lies waiting to be had with half the risks. You cut thin purses and overlook the riches of a king."

"Eh, now, what's this?" Ameeg demanded, pricking up his ears at all this talk of riches. "Shall an honest man teach Ameeg what to steal?"

"I do not speak of stealing. Thieving has paid you well, but not as richly as would honesty pursued with equal cunning. You have, you said, men everywhere who are your ears. They must have told you that not later than tomorrow week the young Ru will occupy the highest seat in M'Anda. But have they also said Semya plots his death?"

Ameeg's wide eyes had narrowed suddenly. "What boldness! How come you by the knowledge?"

"No matter how. I say that it is rumored, not that it is true. Now, whoso assists Ru the Last upon the throne will be a favorite when he sits in power. 'Tis said he'll have, of gold ten thousand *kuls*, and of ivory coins a hundred thousand pieces to give away, to mention nothing of slaves and other gifts he will distribute or bestow upon his favorites."

"Ten thousand *kuls!* A hundred thousand pieces!" Ameeg muttered the words like one dazed. "*Azik!* I did not know the realm contained so much. All this is news. How do you come to know what is a secret to Ameeg? Will you tell me that Mahri who protects the youth has told you?"

Kioga showed the insignia of Mahri's household beneath the fold of his robe. Ameeg looked his astonishment, expressing what first came to mind: "An honest man turned thief! You stole the robe."

"Not so," Kioga answered, "I am in Mahri's warrior service."

"You are in Mahri's ser—" Ameeg blew out his sunken cheeks without completing it. "What do you here, then?" he asked uneasily.

"I seek that slave, sought also by Loalli, who was last seen in company of Ameeg, the famous thief."

"You seek yourself!" cried Ameeg, between amazement and amusement. "Ah, that is capital. And shall you find yourself, think you?"

Kioga laughed. "Mayhap I shall, if the reward be great enough! But that can wait. As you can see, Ameeg, 'twere better that you be an honest man for a little time. They watch the entrances to your street. They watch the men known to consort with you. And why? Because that slave they seek is thought to be in hiding here."

"Why did I begin with you, friend Akra? You bring me naught but trouble."

"Use me, Ameeg, and you shall gain a hundred times what I have cost you. Help me to protect the young boy-king; ally your men upon my side; and when all is done, you shall be pointed out as the thief who rose to high nobility in the service of the Ru."

Ameeg's keen eyes were on Kioga sharply. "You have a great ambition, you who were a slave."

"I crave my liberty," Kioga answered, and in this told nothing but the simple truth. "And if you toil with me—"

"I will," Ameeg said, on a sudden. "You have a long head, Akra. And since you will not join Ameeg as a thief, Ameeg will join with you as an honest man and answer for his own. What is to do?"

"First," said the Snow Hawk, "accept this purse as token of what is to come." He threw the purse received from Mahri—and lacking only the fifty pieces expended for his warrior's outfit—before Ameeg, who snatched it up, emptied it, and counted avidly. "Half of the price I am to have if I produce Akra the slave. This is to pay you for having harbored him. Now in the second place, contrive to place one of your men in every noble's household, to listen and report all plots against the little Ru."

" 'Twill not be easy," responded Ameeg, with a frown.

"To make a king was never easy," said Kioga simply.

Upon the realm of M'Anda the endless northern night had fallen. Yet in the sheltered hermit kingdom of the T'emaho there was no long-continued frigid cold, save on the higher mountains. A piercing chill came with the rains, of which this was the season, but robes of mammoth underwool sufficed to warm the people. A little snow fell now and then, but swiftly disappeared, unable to exist on ground so close to sources of inner-earth heat.

Along the mountainsides, across the valley of the nearby river, steam spouts were as countless pale ghosts in the darkness, where thermal springs ran boiling hot beneath a cloud of heated vapors. The river, swollen by the rains, and having sources far in glacial mountains, alone was bitterly cold, and on its surface mists collected, enveloping the city now and then in dense gray fog, which hung like hanks of white wool in the streets, obscuring everything ten feet ahead.

The warmth of Mahri's dwelling was most welcome; and seeking him at once Kioga told of this day's developments. The other looked at him in approval.

"Well done, well done indeed! I have for some time suspected Semya. But saw you nothing of the slave I sent you for?"

"I pressed him very close, I am confident," Kioga answered, "but until now I have not quite come up with him."

"The search must wait. And we will deal with Semya. First I have another task for you. Go to my stables; select my tallest mammoth. Go then down among the slaves within the mountainside. Seek out an overseer named Tali. Bring news from him how many days must pass before the tunnel is cut through. When that is known, I can know how to proceed."

So to the noble's stable Kioga went, choosing from its stall a tall but active animal, equipped with blanket and pad for riding. Then mounting to its high broad back, he passed out leisurely into the city proper, slaves and freemen afoot making way for him.

He passed between the crowded dwellings of the middle classes, able from his lofty perch to glance into the upper stories and see the people at their household tasks of weaving cloth of mammoth-wool and plaiting cords and ropes of bull hide.

He rode along the ancient wall toward the east, upon that route by which he and his friends had first approached the hall of state; and presently he saw the entrance of that monumental feat of M'Anda's engineers, the work on which they based their hope of spreading all their tribes about the outer world.

His stately mammoth strode like some mighty rolling ship above that sea of humanity which was the army of toiling slaves, contending with the loads of rock drawn rumbling from the mountainside. He came without accident through the sweating, yelling press and entered the vaulted tunnel.

Generations of slaves had labored and died in the achievement of the present advanced state of the excavating operations, so Mingo had informed him. Observing as he passed along the endless twisting vault, he could well believe it. Two separate roads of thirty feet in width had been constructed. Along the one his mammoth trod, the armies of slaves and their laborer brutes passed inward toward the bowels of the mountain. Along the other, in an opposite direction, went the thundering sledges laden with another several tons of stone each. Thus down uncounted decades had the piercing of the mountain been accomplished.

Where it had been deemed necessary, great trees, hewn in the forests of the middle kingdom, had been employed to shore up rock which threatened caving in. As Kioga proceeded ever deeper toward the far end of the manmade tube, the heat became excessive. Now and then there passed him in an opposite direction a sledge containing dead—slaves who had succumbed while digging in this overheated, overcrowded and almost airless tunnel. Frequent passages leading off to either side and blocked with stone and rubble were borings which had collapsed, entombing countless laborers at their toil.

In one place the carcass of a mammoth bull lay waiting to be hauled away and put to use; for among the People of the Tusk, the mammoth was as the buffalo to the plains tribes of America in the long ago. All measurements of length were based upon the mammoth's tail—about a yard; of weight, upon that of a mammoth's grinding tooth, about a pound. His shoulder skin was toughest leather for their shields and footgear. His hair and wool were woven into rope and garments. His ivory was used in art and industry; his belly formed a water bag; his meat was eaten after his death. The drums the people beat were of taut intestine from the mammoth; his bones were handles for their weapons; his very ribs were set on wooden stands and beaten with sticks to give forth weird hollow music. . . .

Thus, sometimes bending low upon his mammoth's back to dodge the overhanging cornices of rock above, the Snow Hawk neared the far end of the tube, and nearing, sensed the high excitement of the toilers and their overseers. For never in their history had the People of the Tusk so deeply pierced the barrier which hemmed them in their prison-kingdom. Always had some catastrophe come to rob them of the toil of centuries, of which those blocked-up openings were grim examples.

Shouting down inquiry to a slave for Tali, he was directed to the solid wall, the most advanced point of these heroic burrowings. A tall and surly fellow responded to the name, desisting from his hectoring of the sweating slaves to answer the question Kioga brought from Mahri.

"The middle of another moon should see it almost done," he said. "We work according to the calculations of the priests. But even they could not foresee the death rate of the slaves. Tell my lord that if their ranks be not refilled, it may take longer. They die like flies—three hundred in a single moon. Tell him, too, that once again the roof has cracked and must fall in, unless they send us forty trunks of heaviest timber to strengthen it. We wait on that, and on fresh men to replace our dead."

Another litter passed, a body on it, wet and dripping. A slave came rushing to the overseer. "Again the water comes! We shall be drowned like mice!"

Tali reached for his whip. "What if you are? Back to your toil," he answered gruffly; and as the slave obeyed: "Fear makes them bold."

"Fear of what?"

"Today the rising water from a stream somewhere in the mountain. Yesterday a caving of the ceiling. Before, it was the coming of the gas. Tomorrow it will be fear of the whip—I'll see to that!"

"I do not envy you, brother," Kioga said. "Living all your days amid such danger! What shall you do, what shall become of you and all these slaves, if what they fear comes true? Catastrophe has come before."

Tali the overseer laughed to cover an uneasiness of many weeks. "It almost came a moon ago. We raised the timbers just in time."

"You miss a deal, amid this sweat and filth. The nobles came but yesterday. They crown a new king soon. There will be revelry and rejoicing. The streets are filled with the wealthy, and slave girls from the distant cities may be purchased very cheaply."

"Poh!" growled the other on a note of envy. "These things for you, one of the lucky ones. For me, no end of this." He gestured to the dusty, evil-smelling tunnel, lighted by the smoking torches and racketing with the sound of wielded tools, and human shouts, and mammoth trumpetings, the clank of chains and rumblings of the wheelless carts. "What slave girl could I bring to this?"

"Then go and seek one in the outer realm."

"My head would sit upon a pole in punishment."

"A hard life, yours," said Kioga sympathetically. "Does Mahri know of such privation?"

"Tell him when you go forth, and I will be your friend for life. Say that I would wish reprieve, just long enough to cheer his elevation to the kingly seat."

"It shall be done, friend Tali," Kioga answered, and having laid down the groundwork of acquaintanceship with one who knew the details of the excavation, he set forth on his return.

Less easy in his mind than when he had left the house,

Kioga slowly made his way back to Mahri, informing him of the state of excavations in the tunnel.

"Well done, warrior," Mahri commented. "And now I have another mission for you." Mahri's long face was more animated now than usual, as in Kioga's hands he placed a hardwood box, carved with great skill, with clasps and hinges made of cold-wrought gold. "Within there is a collar, two pendants and a jeweled buckle, fashioned by my goldsmith and fit to deck the person of a queen. Bear you them with my respects to fair Loalli, who occupies the nearest dwelling to the Hall of State."

"I am a warrior, high-born," muttered Kioga, "not gifted in conveying tender sentiments. Why do you not send a household slave, with cunning tongue and winning smile, on such a mission?"

The noble laughed, displaying all his teeth. "You are a modest fellow, Akra, truly. Your gifts are greater than you know. And only you can tell Loalli of our search for that fine slave who saved her life. Away, then. Lose no time."

The warrior Akra showed odd interest in Mahri's words. "Then did I hunt that slave to be a gift to Loalli?"

"So let her think," said Mahri, "if you observe it pleases her."

CHAPTER 12

Now it came to pass that in a corner of noble Mahri's stables, three heads were put together.

One was that of Tengri, chief of those freemen who worked for Mahri and overseer of all the slaves in Mahri's household service. That he should be ignored in this selection of a fresh employee struck heavily at the foremost trait of this officious underling of royalty, his vanity.

"He comes and goes, this rascal Akra," said Tengri, with a display of fierce contempt. "Who knows who he is or whence he comes, or whether he is not a spy?"

"Coming or going, spy or not, he always has a bag of money," commented one of Tengri's subordinates.

"Money of which we are deprived that he may roll in richness," cried Tengri. "But there's a way to put him in his place. Have I the need to tell you how?"

The others slapped their hilts by way of answer. Thus did it come about that as Kioga mounted the city wall and strode along, on his way to Loalli's house, three silent shadows fell in behind him, pausing when he paused, and hiding to await a favorable chance to do away with him.

The Snow Hawk paused to glance along this wall, which antedated the Great Wall of China by two thousand years, noting where the sentries were stationed and by what mechanism the gates were controlled. And he paused near the highest point along the wall to sweep the river below with one long speculative gaze, leaning far out the better to see the view.

It was the moment awaited by his stealthy followers, who sprang from their concealment. Apprised by keen and well-trained senses of their movement, Kioga whirled, but not before the first one was upon him, dirk agleam and plunging toward his breast.

Well for Kioga that he wore that vest of copper chain. Although the hard-driven weapon pierced, it did no more than prick the flesh. Before the assassin could withdraw and strike again, he took a hooking blow upon the jaw which laid him out.

Almost before he fell, the second of Kioga's three assailants darted in, but checked abruptly, just in time to avoid impaling himself upon the point of the *kuri,* whipped like lightning from the Snow Hawk's scabbard. Falling back a step in turn, the other's blade came out, and quick to bolster it, the *kuri* of his companion flickered into action, passing not an inch below Kioga's chin in a slash which must have cut his throat agape had it gone true.

Not knowing who his foes might be, the Snow Hawk found them nonetheless of practiced skill in wielding their keen *kuris,* a weapon strange to him but recently possessed of one. Against their superior knowledge of its usage, he pitted now his greater strength and pantherish agility, in spite of which the point of one passed through his guard to graze his shoulder.

That instant wit which hitherto had operated to reduce odds, suggested instantly a move more useful than a return lunge. His hand protected by a twist of his own over-robe, he seized and held the *kuri* which had touched him, then passed his metal quickly through the other's forearm, from wrist to elbow, before his opponent could divine his intention.

The action left him wide for the thrust of the third shadow, delivered with more vigor than accuracy. Passing close beneath Kioga's armpit, the weapon struck the stone behind him and broke off near the hilt, the blade then ringing at his feet; and with that, the enemy grappled—which gave immediate advantage to Kioga, far the stronger.

He hurled the man back with great force, himself sustaining but little more damage than the disarrangement of his hair. A blow upon the knee apprised him of some treachery by his first assailant, the which he foiled by setting heel upon the hand which sought to cripple him by stabbing—and with that aim prevented, by causing him to fall.

To disengage himself in readiness for further assault by the others Kioga seized him by the scruff and flung him to one side. Groping for the wall, the man encountered only air, and with a yell fell headlong down the steep side of the wall, his voice stopped by a heavy thud below.

So far had matters gone, when Kioga turned to find the others staring at him in astonishment. At one quick word from one to another, they turned and fled along the wall, and with the familiarity of city dwellers clambered down its rough inner side and were lost to view.

Accounting it an adventure ended to his credit, Kioga suddenly realized what had made them stare. The rapid action had undone some of Ameeg's disguise. Although he had sustained but little physical injury, the armor which until now had served him was pierced. Someone—he knew not who—had knowledge of his imposture.

That knowledge, if conveyed to Semya, must instantly dispel the myth of his death in the slave dungeons and betray him to the noble as the slave who had struck back and left that lifelong wheal upon his face. Made known to jealous Mahri, it must equally result in his unmasking and exposure as the slave who had saved Loalli from trampling beneath a mammoth's feet. The face of Akra the warrior seemed now about to become a greater liability than it had been an asset. . . .

But at the gates of Loalli's sculptured dwelling—once the private palace of the king, set like a lustrous gem deep in the rock that formed the cliffside—Kioga put away the thought of Mahri and Semya, aware that he would need all of his wits in dealing with Loalli.

A warrior callenged him at the gate, but a female slave opened to his heavy knock, admitting him who came with gifts from Mahri into an inner court. At her command a second inner door moved open, revealing an antechamber hung with heavy drapes and sweet with smoke of incense rising in a slender column from an urn of gleaming gold.

Before a covered doorway there sat four female slaves, who rose to block the doorway on Kioga's entrance. Each wore a buckle at the belt, bearing the hawk's head emblematic of Loalli's service. Each wore a woman's dagger at the girdle, which supported a clinging skirt, split to the knee on either side. Each walked in open sandals; and each above the waist was bare. For as his shoelessness proclaimed a man a slave, so those enslaved among the other sex could wear no upper garment, indoors, save the plain golden collar and the ornaments in hair and ears.

Between them passed the one who had admitted Mahri's messenger, a returning presently to stand aside and signal him to wait. Time passed, but presently a gong was sounded musically. The slave girls drew aside, parting as they did so the hangings of the doorway which they guarded; and at a gesture from them Kioga passed between the heavy curtains, which rustled to behind him.

Upon that threshold to Loalli's chamber Kioga checked, taking in the splendors of the noble lady's household.

She sat upon a long carved chair, raised well above the level of her surroundings, backed with heavy cushions and soft with rich brocades, and dappled skins of animals.

Before her knelt two chamber slaves, themselves famed for their beauty. Each tapped, with pairs of little mallets, the keys of a small instrument not unlike a xylophone, which in response gave out a pleasing wavering music in a minor key. In time to this the slave girls improvised short stanzas on the beauty of their mistress.

Perceiving that her visitor stood waiting, she waved them silent and fixed her gaze upon Kioga, who bore it watchfully, more apprehensive now of recognition than at any other time since assuming his false identity. Belatedly he thought to make obeisance, and rising, drew near.

"You come from Mahri's household, I am told," Loalli said, her eyes upon him steadily.

"I bring these gifts, with Mahri's compliments," Kioga answered, holding forth the carven box, which Loalli took, a little puzzled frown upon her brow. To his dismay, she was apparently more interested in the bearer than in the tokens he brought. But now she dropped her eyes, the long black lashes covering their expression, the while she unclasped the cover of the box and raised it, to behold the pendants, collar and jeweled buckle.

"You bring some message, doubtless, with the gifts?"

"A message of regret that Mahri may not also send the slave who saved Loalli from the great bull's charge."

Her eyes flashed suddenly, then were veiled again by dusky lashes. "He seeks him, then?" she asked.

"Throughout the city, every hour," came his answer.

"And he is still unfound?"

"As if the earth had swallowed him."

"As well for him," Loalli said. "Think you that Mahri would send him to me? Do you not know that he would brand and disfigure one whom I had smiled upon? Know you not the heart behind that smiling face?"

"I have not served him long; and should a warrior fear disfigurement?" Kioga answered cautiously.

"So, you have not served him long? Well, you shall learn the truth of what I say. . . . But look you—" her voice changed, echoing the interest she earlier had displayed in Mahri's messenger. "Doubtless you are brave, judged by that graze upon your shoulder. How came you by it, warrior?"

"A thief delivered it," he answered with a ready wit.

"Ameeg, perchance?" she inquired; and at the words Kioga felt his heart bound in him, though his face betrayed no hint of that. But she continued, not waiting for him to reply: "He is the greatest thief found in the City of the Kings, and quick to wield a knife. Yet never mind. I will not question one who bears the gifts of Mahri. Since you have brought them, warrior, 'tis fitting that you put them on."

"I with my warrior's blood-stained hands to touch the sacred person of a High-born?" he answered, loath to approach so near, in fear she might scrutinize him still more closely, with those clear eyes which had detected already, instinct told him, some part of the falsity of his identity.

She showed insistence. "Come now, when I command! Put this pendant round my neck."

Since to delay afresh would be to rouse suspicion further, Kioga took the pendant from the box, spread its chain and placed it round her neck. To do so, he must come within short inches of her. And coming thus close he heard her whisper: "You fear Loalli, when there is naught to fear. I know you, slave who saved my life, and I am not ungrateful. Return tonight, unseen, when I will leave instructions to admit you. Now we are overheard. One of my slaves, I know not which, is faithless."

A protest formed upon his lips. She cut it short. "Obey—or would you be betrayed to Semya and to Mahri?"

That was an implied threat he dared not challenge. "My master will be pleased that you accept his gifts," he said aloud, to which she answered for the benefit of other ears:

"Convey my thanks, both for the gifts and for the messenger. . . . *Io,* Sari! Sing again to me."

The minor music of the *tara* and the slave girl's sweet voice followed Kioga from Loalli's presence. Upon the street again he breathed more freely, although still conscious that in the lovely noble lay potential peril. This and the encounter on the wall caused him a grave anxiety. The robe of anonymity which he had worn was wearing thin, and with it his security. He said as much to Ameeg, entering his den in search of the old thief's shrewd counsel.

Ameeg puffed out his wrinkled cheeks, in thoughtful

mood. "Then shall I give you yet another face with paint and stain?"

"Eh, no! To play two people is more than enough."

"For you to say," Ameeg replied. "But go with care, and tread softly. That Mahri is subtle as a fox, and Semya—"

"Of Mahri I am sure—almost," declared Kioga. "But what will come of seeing Loalli again? She's subtler than he."

"A woman," said Ameeg contemptuously, "with a woman's weaknesses. So that you play upon them rightly, all will yet be well. And when another moon is gone, we shall divide those ivory pieces and those *kuls* of gold." With that thought Ameeg rubbed his palms together; and leaving him to anticipate, Kioga returned to the mansion of Mahri to make report.

Kioga's noble employer was abroad however; and the Snow Hawk, grateful for the respite, went back to Ameeg's lair, refreshed himself with food and drink, then slept awhile before his nocturnal visit to the dwelling of Loalli, and the meeting he feared but could not well avoid.

This time he was admitted instantly, and without benefit of light, led by rear stair-galleries upward to a chamber overlooking the City of the Kings. He heard the door drawn shut behind him, and awaited her arrival with an undefined but distinct uneasiness.

The night was clear, with stars low-hanging in the sky, a full moon rolling on the horizon like a solid silver wheel. High up along the cliff in which this splendid edifice was carved, appearing small as ants and equally numerous, the enslaved toilers of the noble households were at work upon a portrait memorial head of the deceased Ru, larger than the Egyptian bust of Khafre, builder of the second pyramid of Gizeh.

Again the cheapness of human life was emphasized, for as he watched a little while, three workers, roped together, hurtled sickeningly to the ground and a death which put an end to their earthly toil. Along the precipice, as far as he could see, were these gigantic portrait heads, measuring three hundred feet from chin to crown, cut in high relief against the solid rock.

He glimpsed the nightly ritual of the dead king's palanquin being borne empty aloft to an imposing structure highest in the realm, which topped the tombs of the rulers and waited to receive its occupant, whose tomb it would become in its turn. From the distance came that selfsame chant which he had heard, in company of his friends, on the occasion of their emergence into the hermit kingdom. He wondered whether with all their efforts, this boy whom Mahri sponsored would ever ride on that conveyance.

Came then Loalli, rustling through the darkness, preceded by her fragrance. She saw him there and came to stand beside him, gazing forth awhile in silence. He waited until she would speak. At last:

"You wonder why I summon you by dark, like any common wench, who walks the streets below and smiles upon the warriors," she said, her voice pitched low as if she feared someone might overhear. "It is because I know whence you came into our kingdom; because I know you are not one of us; and because I fear for you and those who entered with you."

If this were said by way of threat, Kioga had a ready answer. "Knowing that, why have you not informed the nobles?"

"Because your lives would pay for desecrating the royal tombs. And one of them does not need informing. He suspects but aids you to advance himself."

"Then would you see his choice upon the throne, and make no opposition?"

Loalli seemed to hesitate, then answered indirectly. "Down all the history of the T'emaho, our people have suffered that a dozen tyrant nobles might domineer each other. Internal wars are never-ending. If so be that Mahri's choice could change all that, mayhap I would give him support. Do rulers elsewhere on the earth stab one another in the back?"

"Whole peoples dwell in constant enmity enduring centuries," Kioga answered. "It is so in many countries."

"We are a nation of great people," Loalli told him slowly, "doers of great works, whose history goes back eight thousand snows; a history written down in blood and fighting and the sacrifice of countless lives. If I were queen, this would not be."

Kioga pondered that, too well aware that in this business which was begun to set a boy upon the throne, all that might yet come to be achieved would be undone the instant the laborers holed through the excavation to the outer world. For on the first report of that, Mahri's hopes would crash to earth with the flight of the pretender he was sponsoring. A splendid people would then be left in chaos, just at a moment when the toil of centuries seemed ready to be realized. He took no pride in this deception which he and his companions practiced to preserve their lives; but now he glimpsed a way to make amends. In this Loalli, young and beautiful, and of them all the only noble with a thought for a people's welfare, he saw the most desirable successor to the throne.

"Why should you not be queen?" he asked her quietly.

Loalli started, then turned to face him. "Because I stand alone, not seldom wooed, but still not won by any eligible noble. Our law demands that to be queen, a high-born woman must have a consort."

"But surely of the several nobles there is one, perchance my master Mahri—"

She answered scornfully, interrupting him. "Not Mahri, nor the highest of the others stirs my blood a beat beyond its wonted pulse."

"But somewhere, someone in the land there must be—" He checked there, conscious that continuing might give offense. But she resumed where he left off.

"Someone, yes!" she answered swiftly. "One who until a little while ago I never saw before. One who rose up before me like a meteor."

"Well, then—" began Kioga in perplexity.

"Not well," she murmured, moving to his side before the railing, "when I must search for him who will not come to me, and speak where he does not."

"*Ei*, then, is the man created out of stone, which cannot speak?" he asked incredulously.

"Not so," Loalli returned. "He is of flesh and blood, yet seemingly bound about with bronze which will not pierce." She gazed up at him. "All that I am could easily be his," she whispered. "Behold me, warrior. Look not away. Am I not good to look upon?" No man with red blood in his veins could have beheld Loalli and denied that.

"Aye," Kioga answered. "Very good to look upon."

And now she set aside all pretense; her next words came so swiftly that he understood with difficulty:

"I said his armor would not pierce. Oh, has he not two eyes, and wits to understand? Does he not see that all this kingdom might be his, his to command; that all our people stand in need of rulers who will free these slaves; that glory, riches and vast power await the man who takes Loalli for a wife? Has he no eyes or thoughts for what goes on among the nobles, who think but of themselves and see no duty to their people?"

Her hands went to his arms, as if impulsively, then slid up

to his shoulders, gripping hard the while she looked up to his face almost entreatingly.

"I ask. But you do not reply," she whispered, leaning toward him. "Oh heart of flint! Am I a woman, young and full of beauty, or just a lifeless stone which hangs about thy neck?"

Her hands were closing the circle of her arms about his neck. "You see at last!" she murmured softly, "*Ei,* then, will you take the night to answer me?"

Her quickened breath was on his lips, her splendid eyes on him. And Kioga, like Loalli, was of savage upbringing. . . . But suddenly Loalli started, drew swiftly back, and with her head averted, seemed to listen.

"I heard a sound. The nobles' spies are everywhere. Go now! Remember all that I have said." She led him quickly to the door above the rear stone stairway leading downward. "Do not return before my messenger informs you all is well." She stood aside to let him pass; and with sensations as of one escaping, he came upon the street.

He had not gone above a hundred paces, when a barefoot slave approached him on the run. He recognized the man as one of those who served the noble Mahri and heard the order which he bore: "Repair at once to Mahri's house. He bade me neither eat nor sleep till you were found."

The Snow Hawk gave the man a coin, paused in a side lane to survey himself in Ameeg's mirror, and confident that the countenance he saw still bore little resemblance to his own, presented himself before the noble—whose face, as always, was a mask as he demanded a report or Loalli's reception of his gifts.

One of the household slaves confirmed Kioga's story that he had once presented himself to report. And he excused his failure sooner to return by a brief account of the attack upon him. Loalli, he reported further, had seemed delighted with the gifts, though apparently disappointed that they had not been offered by Mahri in person. Mahri made little comment, but seemed preoccupied. And after a moment, he ordered:

"Prepare to make a journey. Reports have come that in the northern cities the slaves have risen in revolt and journey now upon the City of the Kings to seek revenge upon their owners for fancied wrongs. A strong bull awaits you at the fourth gate, outside the city wall. Mount and go thence. Move among the people quietly. Discover who has hatched the plot; and when you find him"—Mahri produced a long and wicked-looking knifelike weapon—"plant this in his heart. It bears my seal, that all may know I am informed of every traitor in the realm." As Mahri spoke the words, his long eyes brooded on the face of this servitor. Beneath his false exterior Kioga bore the scrutiny watchfully, unable to read the noble's mind, but sensible of some suspicion in it as he nodded a dismissal.

Departing from the house, Kioga turned toward the city gates. First he would search for one who knew the currents of activity among the slave class throughout all M'Anda. Tahro—who had dubbed him Akra and taught him the signs by which to guide a mammoth—Tahro would be able to inform him of the truth or error of Mahri's rumor.

Along the river wharves he sought his friend among the slaves, and found no trace of him. But in his search a crumb of information came before him from a laborer on the river boats. Another slave, named Mingo, had vanished from the dungeons. There could not be a doubt, said Kioga's informant, that he had escaped, since, had this famous old slave died in his prison, word would certainly have gone about to that effect.

Thus disappointed in his search, Kioga went to the appointed place outside the wall, found waiting there a tall rangy bull, provided for his use by Mahri; saw to its girths and mounted up.

Since to its nature his mission was intended to be secret, he could not now avail himself of boat transportation across the river, since on the wharves there would be eyes to note his crossing. Under cover of a thick night fog which hid the moon, he therefore put his reluctant mount to the swim through the chilly currents.

He was not gone the quarter of an hour when behind him at the city wall the shrunken, active figure of Ameeg the thief appeared, seeking with anxious eyes the tall form of the Snow Hawk, known to him as Akra. Grave tidings must have been the burden which weighted Ameeg down until he seemed to bear the world upon his narrow shoulders. As he turned back to the city proper, his chin was on his chest, and his steps were slower. The street fogs then enveloped him as they had enveloped Kioga, now far out across the river on his strongly swimming mount.

CHAPTER 13

We who had by now become somewhat accustomed to Kioga's loss, thought daily of escape; and of some means of notifying our friends beyond the mountain barrier that we were safe and still alive.

But those tall ramparts which had held back an entire race of men from an outer world they knew existed just as effectively imprisoned us.

The great doors of the tomb rooms, through which we had come, all locked inside. Thus on the last day the resurrected dead might let themselves out for judgment, so the T'emaho believe. And beyond them was the water-trap, impassable.

Such small smoke signals as we might contrive would quickly dissipate among the high winds of the mountains. Such sounds as we could make would by no stretch of the imagination be audible through rock miles thick. No carrier pigeon, no message-hawk that flies, could overpass those half-airless altitudes, save by the freak of wind or storm. No missile we had power to launch, could carry in its shell a message to our friends; and even had we such a thing, the odds against their finding it were staggering.

Yet our captivity was not without its compensations. For my own part, the charm of this strange City of the Kings was on me. Its gleaming houses and temples carved in the rising reddish cliffs, one atop another, all white as marble in the moonlight; the fine mansions of the wealthy classes whose walls of solid rock, richly veined and multi-hued, threw back the torchlight from the streets—all cling in memory.

Up from the streets there rose the gay songs of the weapon-smiths, timed to the metallic beats of hammers on their busy ringing anvils; the deep sad chant of slaves by day or night at labor everywhere; the chiming of the household bells, of water-gongs which rang the hour from the inner courts; the intermittent signals of the watchers on the city walls, street hawkers calling musically; the trumpetings from the mammoth pens afar, like horns on New Year's Eve; the smells of roasting mammoth meat, of tanning leather; of smoke from coal veins that had burned deep in the mountains for a thousand years—to this hour I recall the scents and sounds of M'Anda as they were, and as they doubtless are tonight.

But of us all who were the captives of a strange environment, I think Tokala found the situation most bewildering at the start. As Mahri's choice to occupy a throne, he, a simple Indian youth, was being groomed to play a king.

Slaves waited on him hand and foot, saw to his every comfort, leaping to his service if he but raised a finger. The people brought him gifts from everywhere throughout the realm. Small weapons suited to his age hung at his belt. Upon his shoulder was a leather pad, and on the pad a young hawk perched, trained to bear messages from any point to Mahri's home.

Daily Tokala rode upon the streets in his palanquin, borne on the shoulders of strong carrier-slaves who are the coolies of that northern realm. No move he made was supervised, and he might come and go at will anywhere within the walls of Mahri's dwelling. But everywhere he went outside them, a company of skilled sword-and-dagger-men must follow at a little distance, in order that his safety be assured; and to explore beyond alone was not permitted. The ragged urchins in the street had liberties that he, a king-to-be, did not enjoy.

Wherefore the wish to roam outside grew in him, until his life was one great plot to outwit his several protecting shadows and go alone into the fascinating byways of the city. Especially he wished to track down the hornlike blasts betokening the mammoth pens; and learn what had been done with all the beasts and slaves whose entry he had witnessed recently. But Mahri's walls were guarded, the gates studiously tended. No exit or entry was possible save before the eyes of those who would prevent his leaving. Betraying nothing of his discontent, Tokala considered and rejected several plans of freedom until he glimpsed at last the means of an excursion and a safe return, with none the wiser. Down in the tackle room where the equipment for the mammoth mounts were stored, he found a length of serviceable rope, the which he smuggled to the upper floor beneath his cloak. With fingers that had learned their cunning from Kioga, he made quick knots to form a noose and cast it from the topmost balcony of Mahri's dwelling to that of one adjoining, until the loop fell true. Then making fast his own end to the balcony, he hastily withdrew as an attendant's voice sounded from within. Now at the earliest opportunity he might go abroad.

A chance came that night, when Mahri's household was asleep, excepting those who stood on guard down at the lofty gates. Hand over hand Tokala passed agilely across the rope, finding foothold on a decorative ledge between the dwellings. Mounting the far balcony, he flashed a glance below, but he had not been seen. Without mishap he entered the neighboring house, found it unoccupied, and passed downward by its inside stair of stone.

A small front window gave a view out on the street, where the customary crowd camped on Mahri's doorstep. Peering forth, Tokala chose a moment when no one seemed looking his way and slipped out, mingling with the crowd of older folk and urchins, who, unlike a king-to-be, roamed where they would at any hour of the long northern night.

But now, by reason of his rich apparel, Tokala must beware discovery. Slipping through the streets, he came upon a boy of his own age, clad in a tattered skin, and neared him with a sign for silence. Anticipating some adventure, the other beckoned to a shadowy side lane into which Tokala entered at his heels.

"What is thy name?" the stranger asked.

"Tokala," was the answer. "What is thine?"

"Jemmu," said the other with a friendly smile.

"You shiver," said Tokala suddenly.

" 'Tis cold, but I am used to it," Jemmu replied. "The sons of slaves are born to suffer."

"Thy father is a slave?"

"He tends the mammoth pens by night."

"The mammoth pens!" The words came from Tokala sharply, who saw adventure for the grasping. "And may you enter there with him?"

"With him or by myself—I and my friends," said Jemmu with a superior air.

"If you will take me there, I'll give you—I'll give my fine thick robe," Tokala offered eagerly.

"For that I'll take thee also where the tigers and the wolves are kept and starved before the carnivals."

Excitement burned in Tokala's eyes as he made the exchange, donning Jemmu's tattered robe in place of his. And

Jemmu's eyes were also bright with pride of new possession. Together they passed through the twisting lanes and alleyways.

The deep hoarse trumpeting of the mighty beasts grew in volume as they neared, until at last they stood beside a wall of stone. Now Jemmu led the way. All eyes, Tokala followed through a gate which opened into the pens.

Tokala's eyes went wider still at what he saw within. Crowds of the towering animals moved about the great enclosure. No lean gaunt toil-scarred creatures these, but fat, well-cared-for brutes, their heavy coats all brushed and groomed until they gleamed. An active barefoot man who waved was Jemmu's father, and in among the herd moved several feed-boys, fearless pygmies, surrounded by the tall forms of their charges.

Now by a ladder put there for that purpose Jemmu climbed down into the pens. After him, with apprehensive glances, came Tokala.

Jemmu was known to the herd. But long prehensile trunks reached toward the young stranger, scenting him and gently shoving him about as if to satisfy themselves of his apparent harmlessness. Then one gigantic trunk curled round his waist and gently lifted him in air.

Jemmu looked on expectantly. A dozen other mammoths, drinking at the troughs, now turned, and as if driven by a single impulse, raised their dripping trunks and hosed Tokala thoroughly until there was no dry spot on his body. Next, the beast who held him gently dipped him in the trough and set him lightly back upon the ground. Nor was his odd baptism ended yet.

The mammoth young, no higher than his chest, now solemnly came forth and gave a perfect imitation of their parents; spraying him anew. Jemmu, seated on a calf's low back, laughed heartily. "It is their way of saying that they like you," he declared and laughed afresh.

"Then they must like you also," retorted Tokala, as suddenly one of the older cows sent forth a heavy jet that toppled Jemmu from his perch.

Discomfited and streaming, Jemmu rose. " 'Tis time we visited the dens," he muttered uncomfortably, leading the way past his father's fire, where they dried off, and partook of some simple fare.

The dens, Tokala found, were near an open theater set just inside the city wall. The urchin Jemmu, who knew all the guards and slaves, inveigled an admission to the old and unused slave dungeons, where the beasts were quartered underground.

A heavy smell of predatory animals was in their nostrils. The quaking roar of tigers and the terrifying growls of bears and howling wolves reechoed in the passages, mingling with the ear-splitting screams of hunting eagles and the shrieks of lesser hawks used in the chase.

Each barred grating which they passed reflected gleaming pairs of eyes, bright and hot as incandescent disks; white fangs flashed and grated on the bars, seeking to be at their throats. Answering Tokala's question, Jemmu said: "They are not fed. They must be fierce and hungry for the battles when the king is crowned."

"Battles?" echoed Tokala.

"The combats of the animals with slaves who have turned thieves, and freemen whom the nobles do not like. Some slaves who survive will be made freemen. The rest will die. That night the beasts will snore. Their bellies will be full."

"And why is this? 'Tis cruel!" Tokala cried.

"Cruel or not, when kings are made, there must be sport for them and for the nobles."

"And does the king-to-be know this?"

"No doubt. Nobles are born cruel. But why are you so quiet—art afraid?" demanded Jemmu.

"Yes," Tokala answered quietly, "for I have friends among the slaves, who soon shall be my subjects."

Jemmu started suddenly. "What say you—*subjects?* Who are you anyway, Tokala?"

"I am Tokala today. Tomorrow I'll be king," he answered.

His newfound friend and guide drew back dumbfounded. Tokala did not give him time to speak. "Listen, Jemmu, listen well. When I am king, I shall forbid such things. I'll free all who are enslaved. Think quickly—do you know who is to die?"

"I do," said Jemmu faintly, all but overcome; "one is my older brother."

"They are here in these dungeons?"

"Not far away."

"Then lead me to them, Jemmu, we shall give the nobles a surprise. Look, now—how many friends have you among the city boys?"

"A score at least."

"All brave and stout of heart?"

"None bolder than the sons of slaves!"

" 'Tis good. We shall have use for them."

They had arrived before the cell of those condemned to sport before the king's and nobles' eyes. There was no guard. A small grating was the only opening, through which no man could crawl. The single entrance was through the rooms in which the beasts were quartered. No slave would seek escape that way.

Tokala rapped upon the grating. A haggard face appeared—that of a condemned slave. "What do you want?"

"How many are you in that dungeon?"

"Two score and three. Do you bring food? We starve."

"You shall be fed. The king-to-be commands it."

"The king-to-be?" A gust of grim sardonic laughter rippled through the prison dungeon. "Since when do M'Anda's nobles bethink themselves so kindly of their slaves?"

"When I am king, all men shall be freemen," repeated Tokala solemnly, exposing as he spoke that golden breast-plaque below his inner shirt, the symbol of high birth which was known to every soul in all the realm.

The man behind the grate fell back. Another took his place. "The little Ru!" he cried. "The boy-king comes to visit the condemned!" A shout of incredulity arose. Face replaced face behind the grating, until each man had looked upon Tokala and the badge of royalty on his breast. The hum of disbelief died down. A bitter and reproachful voice spoke forth. "You come to mock us, who must die to make you laugh. We thirst and hunger, yet you talk of food and freedom!"

"Food shall be brought, and drink. When I am king, my first act shall be to forbid these fights of beasts and men. Now I must go. I move less freely than the slaves of Mahri who guard me. Do not lose hope. Come, Jemmu!"

"Save us, and we shall give our lifeblood drop by drop to serve you!" cried the voice, and all the others shouted their approval, as Jemmu and Tokala departed.

Still dazed by knowledge that his friend was of the royal house, Jemmu was mute. Together they came through the streets, pausing near the house that neighbored Mahri's. Tokala pointed out a window near the level of the street.

"In two hours come and bring your friends. Let one by one come near that window and take what is put through."

Parting from Jemmu, Tokala threw his ragged garb aside and returned as he had come, passing softly back to Mahri's house by way of his rope bridge—and none too soon: a soft gong announced the breakfast hour; the household was astir. A slave came with a golden tray and shining service, bearing steaming food and drink of which Tokala partook hungrily.

His first adventure was unsuspected, even by myself and Munro who, with Flashpan, occupied the chamber which adjoined his own.

At the first opportunity Tokala wandered as if idly to the commissary cellars. Working swiftly, he shifted mammoth cheeses, wickered jugs of *lohe,* jars of pickled sweets and long strings of dried vegetables near the window at street level.

Glancing forth, he saw the form of Jemmu loitering there on the pretense of play with others who were with him. Tokala thrust a jug out through the opening. Jemmu chanced to pass and slipped away with it. Others came, each to depart with food and weapons, destined to refresh and arm the starving slaves who were to face the fierce beasts of the carnivals.

Tokala heard his name called from above and hastily emerged, some sweetmeats in hand, as if caught in the act of pilfering the cellar stores. His slave attendant laughed indulgently, conducting him above. Tokala also laughed, within him, finding cause for secret amusement.

This was to be the day of coronation. Events moved swiftly for Tokala now. His body was anointed with a scented ungent. His hair was dressed and brushed until it shone, and gold and ivory ornaments were bound in it. Today, as Mahri's puppet, he would mount the throne.

I could detect excitement but no apprehension in the boy. Munro and Flashpan were both moved to comment on his good bearing. We all could hear, down in the streets, the mounting voice of gathered multitudes, assembling on the line of march between the house of Mahri and the hall of state.

Mahri betrayed signs of his high excitement. Tokala's crowning would mean for him a power which as a lesser noble he never could have hoped to wield. Possessed of that, he might yet win the heart of sable-haired Loalli, whose hand and favor meant more to him than any other conquest in the realm.

What with the tumult in the streets and preparation for our long slow march, we gave but little thought to rival nobles' plottings, rumblings of unrest among the slaves, or contact with the outside world.

But ever in the minds of us who had intruded on this hermit kingdom there were thoughts of Kioga and of our friends beyond the mountain barriers, whose lofty ramparts held us prisoners.

CHAPTER 14

Mounted upon a great riding mammoth provided by his employer, Kioga set out one foggy night and crossed the river, landing in a thicket of giant reeds. The Snow Hawk was about to push forward along the trail when his keen ear caught the murmur of voices ahead. Dismounting, he crept forward—then halted and held his breath to catch the words which carried clearly down the misty wind.

"He was to come this way," said one voice guardedly.

"What does he look like? Suppose we should mistake another for him?"

"There is a scar upon his cheek which runs from jaw to temple. One eye is partly closed. He answers to the name of Akra."

"Will he suspect?"

"We will not give him time."

"I do not like this sticking in the back."

"Nor I; but who dares thwart the noble Semya?"

Waiting to hear no more, Kioga crept back to his mount. In some way Semya knew of his mission. The false front of Akra, the mercenary warrior, could therefore only serve to betray him to the enemy waiting to waylay him. And so, working hastily with the solvent Ameeg had supplied him, he removed all traces of his disguise. Then remounting the great beast, he pushed boldly on again.

A moment later, on three sides, he saw the loom of other mounts converging on his path, one blocking it, two others ranging up to crowd his beast on either side, while on the ground three robe-wrapped figures waited. Lanterns, burning oil, were now uncovered, throwing orange light upon the group. A challenge greeted him.

"Who are you, warrior?"

"My name is Vardo," said Kioga.

"So?" a muffled voice said suspiciously, adding: "Dismount for questioning."

Kioga did as bidden, and as he lightly touched the ground, flung back his overrobe in such a manner that it covered his own naked *kuri*. The three dismounted men approached him swiftly. "Be sure of him," warned one of those who watched from mammoth-back; and in response, the nearest of the three rushed in and with his blade thrust for the Snow Hawk's middle.

Kioga took the thrust upon his ready *kuri*, parrying the other's weapon up. The contact brought them face to face; and by the flickering lights, the eyes of his attacker showed astonishment. "A moment! Wait!" he warned the other two, about to lend him aid. "I see no scar, no drooping lid. We have mistaken you, my friend. It was another we awaited."

"Well for you that you found that out in time," Kioga said heatedly. "I am on Semya's business. Were I to tell him that you sought my life, it would go ill with all of you, my friends."

The men fell back, chagrined. "On Semya's business, even as ourselves! We were in wait for one whose face is scarred to—"

"Quiet, hollow-skull," one of the others checked the speaker sharply.

"Hollow-skulls, the pack of you," Kioga interrupted with fine scorn. "Too full from swigging *lohe* for attending to a noble's orders! The one you seek has passed the while you dallied in the public places. Oh, I would not be you—when Semya finds that you have let him slip between your palms!"

There was a silence, growing from the consternation which these words had implanted. "The fog—we came at the appointed hour—" This from their leader, stammering in his deep confusion.

"The fog has penetrated to your wits," Kioga answered swiftly. "You talk when action is required. Upon your bulls and after him! He cannot yet be out of reach."

The words set spur to their own thoughts. Unhindered now, Kioga remounted, and in their company gave swift pursuit to the figment of his own creation. Hard as they rode—and a mammoth's long slow pace devours distance—they did not travel far, as crows would fly. Within an hour after leaving the river bank behind them they were already in the high foothills surrounded by deep forest, and compelled to follow climbing roads and twisting trails whose hairpin turns might bring them hours later in view of the same road on which they had earlier passed.

The road, Kioga noted with appreciative eyes, was yet another testimony to the skill of M'Anda's engineers, and the ceaseless labor of the slaves and toiling mammoths, being sound and level to the outer shoulders. Where slides of rock and earth had torn these, they had been rebuilt, and shrewdly braced with strong sustaining timbers from the forests on the slopes; and on more hazardous turns and steep approaches rock walls had been erected.

Hour on hour the pace continued. Hard though they be pressed, mammoths show a seeming disregard of weariness up to a certain point—beyond which neither goading nor entreaties will move them forward until they have recovered energy by rest and feeding. With this in view each beast, before the ordinary journey through the peaks, is loaded up more heavily with fodder than with any other single item.

It is the special duty of the cultivator slaves to grow and harvest several varieties of moss, grass, sedges and wild thyme, which form the mammoth's chief food. These slaves, who have no other duties whatsoever, then dry and mix the several plant-stuffs and add thereto a concentrated vegetable substance, used throughout the realm by man and beast alike as a stimulant—as races elsewhere in the world use tea, *maté,* or coffee. The nourishing plant mixture then is pressed by weights into the form of solid mattresses, ingeniously bound with cords in such a way that a simple rip releases just the proper ration for a working beast, leaving the remainder intact.

A portion of the annual harvest is by wetting and compression molded into solid blocks, for storage in marked places on the roads, so that at any time the traveler on his great ship of the mountains may help himself to fuel-food for his mammoth by simply taking out of storage this bricked fodder and beating it loose and ready for consumption.

The dried-out stuff is so disposed upon the mammoth's back that it may first serve as a hard cushion for the rider; which cushion, being drawn upon at every feeding time, ultimately is consumed, until naught but a heavy pad remains between the rider and his mount.

Unfortunately the mammoths of Kioga's party had not been so equipped for a long trip. Along the way, between two roadway stations of supply, one of the bulls threw up its trunk and checked, refusing to take another forward step. All other methods failing, its driver had recourse to deep and subtle means by which these mahouts of the M'Anda kingdoms swear. In loving tones he now bespoke the beast:

"O thou sweet-smelling herb! Thy tail is as a lovely maiden's braid; thy tusks are like the sickles of the bright new moon; thy trunk drips melted honey; thine eyes are soft as dusk in summertime; thy feet tread as petals fall. Condescend, O Powerful, to move one after one until we reach that yonder height, where thou shalt banquet full on scented plants. . . . What, no response? Then shall I tickle thee with my sharp goad, O byblow of a misbegotten bull? One little forward step! What, shall entreaty fail? Epitome of laziness! Here is to quicken thee, O giant stench!"

But neither cajolery nor blows can sway a mammoth with its mind made up; and since they were in haste, regretfully they left the beast behind, roped to a rock. Its driver mounted up behind Kioga, and on they went until another bull refused to move. This time a station of supply was near; and pausing to refresh their animals, Kioga and the warriors threw themselves to rest beside a quickly kindled fire near the road.

They had not been long seated when from the upper heights a train of laden bulls descended, accompanied by slaves and warriors afoot. A score of animals, each laden to capacity, moved down the road toward the City of the Kings. Greetings passed between their drivers and Kioga's companions of the road, and presently a pair dropped out to gossip for an hour with men so lately from the capital city.

Semya, by their account, had formed alliance with several other lesser nobles dominant among the mountain cities, gaining their support in mammoths, men and arms. None of the soldiery knew in what cause they had been enlisted, save that it paid them double wages for the period of a full moon. Beasts, warriors and weapons were to gain admittance to the City of the Kings, ostensibly to honor the new king. But secret orders bade them be in readiness for anything, armed fully at all times. Among the warriors there was speculation on the reason for such mystery; but to Kioga it was all too clear.

Shrewd Semya planned a *coup* of one kind or another at the capital, but whether before or after the elevation of the king, remained uncertain. Enough to know that it was planned; it now remained to learn the full extent of all the preparations. What more was to be ascertained could best be gleaned in Semya's own home city. This famous stronghold lay at a distance of some forty miles, or twice that far, reckoning in the turnings of the road.

The warriors soon departed to catch up with their train, swearing that no mammoth had passed them on the road. But where an hour since Kioga would have wished to turn about, it pleased him now to argue that they had been deceived. "He was suspicious of ambush, and so evaded you. Likewise he would have hidden as they passed and then gone on. If we would take him we must follow."

Meru, leader of the ambush which had thus far failed, sat deep in thought and finally voiced it, his eyes upon Kioga with an odd intentness. "I cannot think how he could have evaded us. He was described as tall, much like yourself, and wearing such a robe. His beast was to be patched with gray upon the neck, as is your own—no common mark. Indeed, save for our glimpse of your face, you must have fallen to our *kuris,* so like are you to him we waited for."

Kioga laughed to hide a faint uneasiness. "Death skimmed me close," he answered. "I vow it never has passed closer."

"I cannot understand," persisted the other stubbornly.

"Better to be off in search of him than sitting idle here," the Snow Hawk answered. "Time may resolve your doubts. Meanwhile, remember that Semya is a hard master, not easy with those servitors who fail him."

"That is the truth, at least," said Meru, still thoughtful. He rose; whereat all did likewise, mounted, and were on their way again. The route was now at greater altitude and climbing steadily. The road, from being broad, grew steep and ever narrower as they slowly neared their objective, Semya's stronghold city. Between the place of earlier pausing and their destination, a deep and seemingly bottomless gorge cut through the mountains. Across this narrow chasm hung a bridge of heavy planking laid on solid beams, which were anchored to the rock on either side with chain. Across this bridge the mammoths thundered, and on its other side came to a division in the road.

Meru, until this moment still wrapped in his thoughts, there checked his animal and called a parley. "We cannot know which road this Akra took," he said. "We must divide, going separate ways." He turned then to Kioga. "We two are equal to their several. Let us go on together to the left, while they search out the right-hand road."

Since this arrangement did not affect their ultimate arrival at Semya's stronghold city, Kioga found nothing objectionable in Meru's proposal, and suffered him to mount behind him. Meru's men on their two beasts took one trail; while Meru and Kioga took the other, more precipitous and perilous by far.

A while they rode without event, until they reached a turn, below which there stretched downward a sheer drop of several hundred feet, terminating in a chaotic heap of broken stone.

Suspecting nothing until this instant, Kioga heard the voice of Meru speak the word that checked the mount they rode together, and simultaneously felt the prick of metal near his spine.

Meru's voice was in his ear. "Get down! And do not turn or I will run my *kuri* through you."

Kioga obeyed, without a word.

"Your weapons. Throw them on the ground," the other ordered, and again Kioga acceded, avoiding the temptation to resist. "Now turn about," said Meru.

"Wherefore such great precaution, Meru?" Kioga asked, in hope of gaining a moment of time. " 'Tis clear that you intend to kill me, though why you should, I do not know."

"You know too much," answered Meru. "Think you that we should let you live to carry back to Semya the fact that we have lost our quarry? Life is too good. You die, that he may never learn of it."

"But he will learn that you have murdered me."

"When I have done, no one will ever know that you have gone. Look behind you, brother. Your bones will all be rent apart when your body strikes below. I shall not even hear it fall, so deep is that valley. But enough of talk. Prepare to die."

With the words Meru fixed his eye upon the point below which beat Kioga's heart. The Snow Hawk did not flinch, and Meru paid him one last compliment. "You are a bold one, brother. I must admire you. But life means much to me. And so, prepare. . . . *Now!*"

CHAPTER 15

In Mahri's splendid house, upon the main road in the City of the Kings, the handsome noble sat wrapped in bitterness; what had galled Mahri so deeply was a remark, purporting to have been made by Loalli herself, that if it came to choosing between the noble Mahri and the slave who had saved her from the maddened bull, her choice would fall upon the slave and not the noble.

Whether a true quotation or not, young Mahri well knew the candid high-born Loalli to be quite capable of saying it; and raging inwardly, he swore to find that long-sought slave of whom she spoke so highly. Loalli should have her wish, he promised himself grimly; but the slave, when she received him, would be less well-favored than on the first occasion!

Since his new servant Akra was not available, Mahri called into action several trusted employees of longer standing, and set for them the task of running down all clues concerning that elusive slave, promising a thousand *kuls* to whosoever found him. Had Mahri known that Akra and the slave were one and the same person, he would have trebled that reward. But he did not know; nor did Munro, Flashpan, Tokala or myself, who sat in on these conferences, all unconscious of Kioga's huge deception and completely convinced, by now, that he was dead.

We had the freedom of the city by this time, a freedom which each of us made use of in his own peculiar way. Tokala, when he went abroad, was ever accompanied by a heavy guard who bore him in a curtained palanquin, as was the custom of the high-born who desired to pass through streets too narrow to admit their mammoths. Along his route he daily received such cheers and adulation from the throngs as left no doubt about his popularity. He acted well his ordained part, emerging unspoiled through these demonstrations.

Flashpan, with a faultless nose for gold and kindred treasure, roamed here and there in search of the sources which supplied the royal goldsmiths with the metal which they worked. He took with admirable ease to this new life among a strange and half-barbaric people. His sole regrets were for his faithful dog Nugget, and that companion of his checkered past, the almost human little rhesus monkey Placer. Lacking his old pistols, with which he was a dead shot, Flashpan soon acquired no mean skill with the native *kuri,* causing some embarrassment to us by neatly skewering one of Mahri's own warriors who dared to tweak one of his long moustaches.

Munro, following his scientific bent, gave his attention to deciphering the ancient M'Anda records. Translating these, he gained knowledge of their staggering antiquity. For if the facts recorded thus were true, the T'emaho were proved the oldest race on earth, a human fragment of well-nigh incalculable age, survivals, like their mammoths, of the glorious Age of Mammals.

When early European man was rising from the twilight of the ages to defend himself against the beasts with his first clumsy hand-ax, men of M'Anda had already learned to work meteoric iron.

When Egypt's ingenuity, six thousand years ago, was still at work reducing pictographs into phonetic signs to form a written language, the simple and ingenious M'Anda form of writing had already been in use for centuries. Scribes of that far-distant day in Egypt had been compelled to cut their thoughts in stone. The old-time T'emaho had even then known the use of ink made from the soot upon his cooking pots, mixed with gum and water, and applied with a split and pointed reed upon the thin but lasting membrane of a mammoth's stomach.

Munro could not well connect the living men of M'Anda with the Incas or the Aztecs, since the latter had been of uniformly dark skin and eyes, whereas the T'emaho varied in complexion. And so he hazarded the guess, and wrote it in his notebooks, that they might be the root-stock of the famed Mound Builders, surviving where their continental cousins had vanished.

That penchant on the part of Flashpan for getting into trouble often took our thoughts from scientific subjects. It had become Flashpan's habit, in the endless round of seeking hidden treasure, to visit daily with the M'Anda barbers, smiths, hucksters, menders and men of trade—gossipers all —who might throw light upon his search.

In one deep drinking cellar he was already by way of

being one of its best customers, imbibing freely of the native mildly stimulating *lohe*. The drink had the effect upon Flashpan of but quickening his already active wit. And, for all his years, Flashpan had now acquired quite a reputation as a fighter and a comical eccentric on whose words men had but to hang if they desired to laugh. Not only men, indeed.

For in the land of M'Anda, as in other earthly realms, the drinking places have their share of loitering women; of these, one in particular returned a smile to Flashpan's shameless ogling. Having learned not much of value from the men with whom he spoke, Flashpan convinced himself, aided by a swift glance at the lady's pleasant person, that he might gain knowledge of the kind he sought from her.

But what he learned put from his mind all thought of gold and treasure. It left Flashpan, for once, without a word to say, albeit his head was full of leaping thoughts that tumbled on each other confusedly—for from the woman's lips, loosened by the *lohe* with which he plied her, Flashpan had a tale straight from the den of thieves over which one Ameeg presided.

One of Ameeg's own men, with whom she had been friendly, had blurted out the fact, in an unguarded moment, that Ameeg had abandoned his lucrative career of thieving and turned instead to politics—had joined forces with a former slave named Akra, and— But Flashpan interrupted there.

"His name was Akra, didst thou say?"

"Akra, indeed. But what of that? It is a common name."

"Mayhap, mayhap. What did he look like, this slave who could make a thief turn honest man?"

"Oh, tall," the woman answered vaguely, "and very handsome—until Ameeg painted on his other face."

"But why—his *other* face?"

"He had escaped the dungeons of the slaves."

The gulp of *lohe* Flashpan had taken all but choked him.

"The dungeons of the slaves," he echoed. "When? How did they paint him?"

"Upon the day the nobles came," she answered, adding a good description of the mask Kioga had worn since the hour he quit the den of Ameeg. Her facts but served to plunge Flashpan the deeper into speculation. Now that he had a grain of hope, he scrutinized it with suspicion, loath to reveal to Munro and the others what might later prove to be without foundation. Yet here was something not to be let go until investigated. Who better could inform him further than that sly cutpocket of whom the woman had spoken—Ameeg the thief?

Ascertaining where Ameeg might be sought, Flashpan thrust a handful of coins into her fingers and bustled out upon the street. His carry-chair, with which all higher members of Mahri's household were provided, was ready and waiting. Flashpan leaped spryly in, and snapped quick commands to his bearers, who conveyed him down into the close and foggy warrens in the lower city, haunted by such as old Ameeg.

He felt his chair set down, and raising the curtain poked forth his head turtle-wise, to look about him in that forbidding place and sniff the air distastefully.

"Highness has arrived," one of his bearers murmured deferentially.

" 'Highness,' bah!" growled Flashpan, and set foot gingerly upon the pavement. "Be off, the lot of you! I shall return on foot." His gesture sent them on their way, their copper ear-bells jingling.

Flashpan stood alone amid an utter silence, peering round about him in the shadowed doorways and hidden coverts. Then he took a metal coin and dropped it on the pavement, waiting. A head thrust from an upper window.

"What do you want, who come by night with such a clatter?"

"I seek Ameeg the thief."

There came a jeering laugh from up above. "Who seeks him not!" A metal grate slammed with a ringing crash. Flashpan, indignant, walked on a way. He tripped upon a foot thrust from a doorway. "Ho, there!" cried the little miner, dragging forth a man who lay within. "Get up. Direct me to the thief Ameeg."

"Would that I could! He has just picked my pocket," the other said.

"Your foolish fault, for letting him come near," said Flashpan.

"Be careful," warned the other. "He will hear your coins rattle."

" 'Tis what I wish, if only I may come upon him," said Flashpan, proceeding on his way and jingling his *kuls* at every step. For in the lower City of the Kings, there is a truthful saying that when money rings, it is like the smell of mammoth cheese to rats. But to Flashpan, it seemed that all the rats were keeping to their holes. He went unchallenged, and saw no one until at last, having put his money-bag away, he came upon a hunched-up figure weeping on a doorway. Touched, Flashpan drew near.

"Why do you cry, my little one?" he asked in the soft M'Anda tongue.

"I have been robbed," croaked the other, with a fresh outburst of sobs.

"Ameeg?" Flashpan demanded fiercely, and when the other's shoulders shook: "He is an ogre, this vile pocket-picker. But never mind. Here is to console you—" He reached in for his money-bag, to find it gone. *"He-ya!* I likewise have been robbed! Again this Ameeg!"

"Again Ameeg," agreed the other quietly, rising up to bow in mock deference, holding forth the while Flashpan's money-bag, and showing his seamed old face at last. "You search for me?"

"Wal, I'll be cussed!" exclaimed Flashpan. "That shore was slick."

"Your pardon?" queried Ameeg with a leering grin.

"I said," Flashpan replied, "that I had long desired to meet you."

" 'Tis done. What do you want of this poor thief?"

"There was a slave who recently escaped—"

"Ah!"

"His face was painted to resemble someone else."

"Ah?"

" 'Tis known that Ameeg harbored him; and for that act there is a penalty. A head stuck on a pole is not a pretty sight."

"Especially if it be one's own," said Ameeg.

"You catch my meaning admirably, thief," said Flashpan. "Speak straightly, and your secret shall be kept. Where is this man whom you call Akra?"

"I do not know," said Ameeg, turning up his palms expressively. "He is the only one who ever could elude me and my many eyes."

"Before you painted him—"

"He had a handsome face, a little mole below one ear, and on his back a long faint scar from hip to shoulder."

Flashpan arose, moustaches quivering with excitement. He tossed Ameeg the bag the thief had returned. "Your words are worth ten times this sum!" he said. And shaking little Ameeg by the hand. "We'll meet again."

"I hope so," said Ameeg in wonder, gazing at the money-bag. . . .

Wheezing after his hurried return to Mahri's house, Flashpan burst in upon Munro and me as if a war had been declared, and broke the news excitedly. "Kioga's Akra. Akra is Kioga. He's alive, s'help me! He works for Mahri. Oh, didn't I tell ye that cat had nine lives? That rumor of his death among the slaves was bunk!" And having dropped that shell among us, Flashpan sat down in near-exhaustion.

"It clicks," said Munro to me.

"What d'ye mean, clicks," said Flashpan.

"We had an inkling of it from another source," I answered, for Munro, and postponing explanations led Flashpan through the crowds which now camped perpetually on Mahri's doorstep. We paused some streets away, and entered a low doorway in a shadowed alley, Flashpan following me. Upon my knock, repeated in a way agreed upon, a door was opened. Within a dimly lighted room an old man stood, who greeted us in the M'Anda tongue, and told in substance before Flashpan what he had earlier told Munro and me.

"My name is Mingo. One of my guards helped me to flee the slave dungeons. While there I met and talked with Kioga. He was not slain, but escaped, my robe his only cover."

"How came you to be in the dungeons?" demanded Flashpan.

"I am a Shoni, part of the outer world, like you. My mother wandered here before my birth. When I was still a child, she told me by what route she came beneath the mountains. My memory is good. I wish to see my father's land before I die. If you will go with me, mayhap I can show the way of your escape."

Flashpan turned to me.

"If Kioga was alive, why didn't he give us some sign of it when he came to visit Mahri, lookin' like a soldier of the T'emaho?"

"He must have had a reason," I replied. "Perhaps he feared we might unwittingly betray him. We'll hear from him when he is ready. Meanwhile we'll act as if we didn't know he was still alive, and go with Mingo. If he can show us the path his mother used, we shall be ready, any time Kioga is."

CHAPTER 16

Upon a mammoth bearing the forehead shield of Mahri's stables, we entered the deep sub-mountain burrows of the T'emaho, free from interference, and with our path made smoother by that identifying sign. But unhappily, although he led us accurately for a way, old Mingo's memory finally proved at fault, so that the route his mother long ago had described to him must be located, if at all, by sheer deductive reasoning on our part.

We were compelled to think back to our first entrance into the hermit kingdoms of the T'emaho, seeking to choose from among the many abandoned borings that one which most nearly paralleled our route of entry. Logic said that since the mother of old Mingo had been one of the Shoni people, she must have made her way into this area north of her ordinary haunts by some route other than the tombs, which had presented to us such obstacles as no lone woman could have overcome.

Since Mingo's aid was exhausted, we chose at random one of the nearest tubes, closed off by rough-hewn barricades bearing a royal seal forbidding further labor here. By linking our great mount's chain to the lower logs, we thus could swing the barriers far enough aside to give us ingress.

The tunnel which we followed ended in a solid wall. Coming forth from it, we likewise tried out several others of varying length, eliminating one by one from consideration as that through which a stranger from the outer world might have passed.

We came at length upon a barrier so long untouched that its lower logs lay under several inches of rock dust. Entering here, we found a lane of many turns and branches. Following its main artery to the farthest end, we saw this time not solid stony wall, but a chaotic mass of tumbled rock, evidence of the greatest hazard which the excavators ever faced, a cave-in of many years ago.

Having actual knowledge of the several branches of the abandoned tubes, and recollection of the route which we had followed upward through the tombs, we surmised from our calculations that this old tunnel pierced the rock not far from where we and Kioga had passed. But though we suspected such proximity, lacking means of boring farther, we could conceive no way to bring it to a proof.

But suddenly our movements in and near the fallen rubble sent a darting shadow bounding almost from beneath our feet. One fleeting glimpse was all we had of that quick-moving form, but that sufficed. It told us that the Shoni forests could not be far away, not farther than that creature could have wandered searching for a place to den; for what we glimpsed had been a panther cub, half-grown, of a variety we had seen a dozen times while roaming in Kioga's native wilderness.

Along some such route, perhaps this very one, old Mingo's mother must have passed, seeking, perhaps, escape from some great hunting cat, only to fall captive to the race who had tunneled here before the cave-in had occurred to force a discontinuance of the work.

Following on the heels of the disappearing animal as far as crevices in the rock would permit, we brought up at last against a junction of the walls through which we could not squeeze.

Awhile we toiled, exerting all our strength upon the mammoth goad, seeking to pry the rocks apart, that we might follow through. Our labors were in vain.

We paused, returned to refresh ourselves with water from the leather bag hung at our mammoth's shoulder, then once more crouched before the crevice, to study out some means of enlarging it. That this gave exit to the forest beyond the kingdoms of the T'emaho, we had no doubt, since through the crevice faintly came the scent of pine and hemlock.

And suddenly, with straining ears and tilted head, Flashpan listened. He heard, as we did, from a distance yet with perfect clarity, the sound of singing. Our blood ran swifter in our veins. We knew that stirring chorus—the chant that fell from Shoni warriors' lips. Indeed, we even thought we recognized the leading voice for that of Kias, bound to the Snow Hawk by the closest ties of friendship. Flashpan let forth a yell.

"Kias! Can ye hear me? *Kias!*" Silence followed, and he called again, without result. Another pause ensued while we listened for the answer which would put us in contact with our friends beyond the hermit kingdoms of the T'emaho. But only the hollow echoes of his own voice returned to mimic him.

Some freak of the acoustics in these under-mountain caverns enabled us to hear them, but were our own voices being diverted elsewhere? Could they hear us? Again Flashpan signaled, but not now with his voice. Instead he whistled on a low peculiar note which echoed and reechoed in those tortured caverns. The sound of chanting ended.

Flashpan crouched before the crevice with a tense expectancy. And now a sound did come, a sound which I had heard somewhere before in my travels, without being able instantly to identify it. It was shrill and growing in intensity. The explanation darted into mind, but not before the reality was among us.

The shrill sound multiplied, and then became embodied in a leaping shadow which sprang through air, alighting on Flashpan's shoulder. Placer the monkey hugged Flashpan's skinny neck, screeching and chattering monkey confidences into Flashpan's hairy ear. Whereas a man might not pass through the narrow clefts between the solid rock, this little keen-sensed creature had heard his master's call and easily passed among the crevices. Our contact with the outer world had been established!

"Ye've got a lot to say," grinned Flashpan, stroking his active pet, "but it's all over my head. Now, if ye c'd tell us how all our friends be out in the forests of the Shoni—" Flashpan paused, his blue eyes calculatingly asquint. "Mebbe ye can't, but you *can* let 'em know we're still alive; and Miss La Salle at least'll be glad to know her man is still around."

I saw at once Flashpan's intent to make the agile little rhesus act as courier between ourselves and whoever was beyond the reach of our voices. Upon a strip of skin torn from his over-robe he scrawled a penciled message, to which I added my name. It read:

We ben tryin to git through the mountin an all air alive an kikin whats what out thair with you look in Placer's collar fer this note send us an answer same way.

Flashpan tied the note flag-like to Placer's collar and faced him in the direction whence he had come. The bright-eyed little animal well knew what was expected of him, but was loath to leave the side of his master, so lately met with after so long a separation. Several times he started off, glancing back to see if Flashpan followed. Each time he returned with deep perplexity written on his wrinkled simian face. But Flashpan had a way with animals. Presently the rhesus went back into the crevice and did not now return.

In silence, listening, we waited, all our hopes pinned on that agile flitting little form which bore our message to our friends outside. For though the kingdoms of the T'emaho were large enough for an entire race, to us they were a prison. As prisoners waiting for reprieve from their surrounding walls, so now we crouched expectantly. An hour passed, and two, before the long high call of Placer sounded once again; and like a ghost he swung into our presence.

Inside his collar was an answer, written on a strip of thin white bark in lieu of paper. Flashpan unrolled it, and by our smoking torches we read:

> *Your message received. Where are you? What can we do to help you? Now and then we hear a heavy thumping which seems to come from deep within the earth. Are these your efforts to escape, or what? Longer message being prepared. Good luck!*
>
> *Dan La Salle.*

"They hear a thumpin' in the ground," said Flashpan swiftly. "The T'emaho are gettin' nearer to the end of their tunnelin'. One of these fine days they'll break through. An' when they do, we'll make our get-away! We'll sure have news for Munro. But we can't linger here. Our place is in the tunnel of the T'emaho, if we're to leave the land of M'Anda."

We sent one last note to our friends, advising them of our intentions, dispatched the note by monkey-courier, and went as we had come. We thought to join with Munro and Tokala, to be on hand when the slaves holed through the tunnel, then to escape and meet our friends beyond the mountain wall which had until now held us incommunicado.

Well for our strength of heart and courage that we could not foresee events that yet remained between our hopes of liberty and their realization!

For what had occurred in the world outside during our adventure in the land of hermit people I am indebted to a record kept with utmost faithfulness by Beth La Salle. With her permission I am free to quote from it.

Placer, Flashpan's little simian pet, faithfully returned to them with our last message, telling of our safety and the nature of our strange captivity.

Dan, who received the message, at once relayed it by Shoni Indian runner to his sister Beth, and turned his full attention to the sounds of distant digging emanating from somewhere deep within the mountainside. It was an eerie sensation to listen to those muffled thuds and know them made by living men who knew of, but had never seen, the world beyond their peak-girt kingdom.

The sounds were intermittent, but increasing in volume, until one day they ceased entirely, as if all work had been abandoned; and this was true in fact, occasioned by the threat of cave-in which required full attention to the bracing of the tunnel ceiling.

Three days of silence passed, but Dan did not sit idly by. To dig through solid rock toward the sounds with the poor tools at his disposal was not practicable. Instead, he and his men attacked the stone at likely points of cleavage. These they enlarged, and deepened several fissures leading somewhere inward, until Dan could crawl in, and with sound from outside thus eliminated, listen to better purpose.

Upon the fourth day, thumping recommenced, continuing without a further interruption. Time and again Dan sought to gain attention from the unseen excavators, by blows struck with a heavy stone against the rock. He tapped in Morse, of which he had a working knowledge, in hopes that Munro, also familiar with that code, might hear and so communicate. But his efforts met with no success.

Undaunted by his failure, Dan made other preparations. Intending to blast a way toward his missing friends, he long ago had cached a good supply of powder, brought up from downriver. To this a stroke of luck had added several sticks of dynamite, stolen by one of his Indians from the mining-camp headquarters of the *Pirate's* gold-seeking company.

Of powder Dan packed a quantity into the inmost crevice of the rock, nesting in the blackish grains the sticks of high explosive. Ingenuity provided Dan with fuses made of twisted cedar bark, which he had moistened, dipped in powder, then set out to dry. Into the explosive core he introduced the ends of two fuses, then with a buckskin blanket covered it and weighted all with dried-out sand and stones brought from the river, achieving thus a tolerable mine, which could be detonated from a distance by setting fire to the fuses.

Such preparations made, Dan kept his vigil. The rumblings

beyond grew hourly louder. Now and again it seemed to him that other sounds came through the rock; sounds as of great horns hard blown—no doubt the trumpetings of laboring mammoths; and finally—this time beyond all doubt—the sound of human voices raised in mighty unison, followed instantly by hours of silence.

While Dan kept watch, one of his red-skinned runners, who made liaison between the divided parties in the Shoni forests, brought news: Down at the miners' camp all was bedlam and excitement. Gold had been struck in quantity that men had never dreamed about before. Three full canoe-loads had been taken down the river, sack by sack, to their waiting ship the *Pirate,* and there been melted into rough ingots and stored aboard.

This preoccupation of the hostile miners with the hunt for mineral treasure worked to the advantage of Captain Scott and his men, who thereby went unmolested during the building of their craft, now well advanced. The framework of a little ship already stood erected, like a skeleton, on which the men were now at toil attaching rough-hewn planks and reinforcing stringers. For sails they intended using the deerskins brought in by the red-skinned friendlies, and cut and sewn together at the blockhouse by Beth La Salle, her father and the men there stationed.

So much and little more did Dan know of events out near the coast; for since Kioga, Flashpan and Munro, with Tokala and me, had vanished in the mountain caverns, Dan had not once relaxed the search for us.

One fact gave him cause for constant apprehension: Internal strife had long existed in the savage Shoni nations. The flash of scalping knives was reported with a growing frequency. His runners told of war bands moving on the rivers, freed of ice by an early spring thaw. And the blockhouse down the river lay directly in the path of such scalp-hunting parties.

Worst of all news came from the mining camp. There had been firewater, killings and retaliations. Several cruel atrocities had been perpetrated by the miners on red-skinned visitors to their camp. A number had been shackled and forced to labor in the miners' frenzied search for quantities of gold. And the Shoni, now thoroughly aroused against the whites, would not discriminate between their persecutors and others with pale skins.

All the more cause, reflected Dan, to stand by to aid the Snow Hawk and his friends, if aid were needed in the final piercing of the rock. For with Kioga's knowledge of the Indian mind, chances of safety were vastly multiplied.

And with Dan waited Kias, lifelong friend of Kioga, who had persuaded near a score of Shoni braves to join him in his vigil. They speculated on what manner of men would presently come forth, and what was happening to us.

CHAPTER 17

Kioga was not the man to let himself be slain without a struggle; yet on the narrow ledge he had but little room in which to make a stand.

As Meru's blade licked forward, Kioga dodged, evading it by very little margin, and with the movement slipping abruptly until he had but hand-grip on his ledge. Now he was utterly at Meru's mercy, had not a kindly fate intervened. For drawing back to thrust a second time, a whiplike blow across one cheek distracted Meru, accidentally flicked by his mammoth's swishing tail. It was a sharp and painful cut, and angrily he kicked the beast behind him, full against one of its ankles, which was red and sore from scuffing on the long up-trail.

Then Meru returned to his job of murder—and an instant later yelled in terror. For a hairy trunk had curled around his waist. Then with a mighty swing the mammoth catapulted Meru screaming into space. His yells grew fainter as he plummeted.

Kioga hauled himself upon the ledge, one eye upon the mammoth for fear of being dealt with likewise by the pain-crazed brute. Instead he heard it sobbing wheezily, infallible indication that its rage was past, and glanced into the void below. Far down, he saw a dark misshapen lump bound from a jutting ledge—the last that any man would ever see of Meru.

Kioga's eyes came up, attracted by a moving train along a mountain trail far in the distance and coming toward him. They were as ants so far away; yet his keen eye made out a mighty host of men and brutes, undoubtedly the minions of Semya's city bound for the City of the Kings to put him on the throne by force.

Kioga mounted on the beast which had been Meru's and retraced his earlier steps to the bridge across the gorge. Its chains defied his strength. He hitched the ponderous mammoth to their rings and urged it forward.

Up on the winding trail above, the vanguard of the mounted warriors appeared, and glimpsing what he did, rushed down with threatening yells.

The second staple broke away. Kioga drove his beast across the bridge, now resting only by its weight upon the side he quitted. Chained to a timber of the bridge, Kioga's bull strained mightily, hauling it within the fraction of an inch of slipping off the other ledge. But there it somehow jammed.

The oncoming foreguard thundered out upon the bridge, two abreast, until the weight of four great mammoths tramped on the quivering structure. Turning to unhitch his beast before escaping, Kioga saw the bridge sag with the weight it bore, and shortened thus, slip from its distant seat.

Men's yells, and shrill wild trumpetings of mammoths mingled. The bridge sagged farther; unable to advance along its steep incline, the brutes slid backward until their combined weight was all at that weakened far end. One of the warriors sprang from mammoth-back to safety on the road above his head, before the bridge gave way completely, precipitating beasts and men to eternity.

Stunned by this severance of their artery of war, Semya's soldiery gathered opposite Kioga, the gorge and dangling bridge between. The Snow Hawk wheeled his brute and sent it on. From the other side a heavy war spear hurtled, shod with meteoric iron. It struck Kioga's brute a glancing blow and clung, but did not pierce the mat of hair.

Kioga snatched it up and hurled it back, with better aim, to strike its owner squarely in the breast. Then, urging on his mount, he started down the trail, part of the enemy still remaining to be passed. There was not time to replace his earlier disguise which Ameeg the thief had contrived, and by which they would recognize and give him way. Yet he must attain the City of the Kings, to inform Mahri of the danger threatening in the mountains. He must also contrive that those ahead of him did not attain the city.

Encountering that earlir war train, he joined them, offering their leader a fabricated message from the forces in their rear. "You are to wait for them upon the river bank. All will approach the City of the Kings at once, with show of mighty force. A messenger will greet you at the gates, and give you further orders."

Adding thus to uncertainty, Kioga hastened on. Arriving

at the river, he beheld, amid its murky fogs, six of the broad flat riverboats with Semya's shields nailed at their peaks, waiting to bear the noble's men-at-arms.

Avoiding these, Kioga turned upriver, swam his mount across and paused before the city gates.

"I am from Semya's city," he announced. "I bring news of disaster to his army. Delay me at your peril, gatemen!"

This threatening response was well conceived; for cunning Semya could be counted on to post men friendly to his cause at such a strategic point. The gates swung in. Kioga passed through swiftly. He had not gone a hundred paces when his name was called. He glimpsed a crooked form—the thief.

"Ameeg! Your face is pale! You tremble!"

"Not for myself—for you, my friend. Ten of Semya's men are seeking you, the pick of his best fighters. 'Tis well you have returned without your old disguise. They know you only as Akra the warrior, or you would have been slain before the gates. Dismount! Be not conspicuous."

It was good counsel. Kioga obeyed, abandoning his mammoth and mingling with the crowds. "Wherefore such multitudes?" he inquired.

"It is the coronation day," Ameeg replied. "Tokala is to be crowned within an hour, if the spies of Semya do not kill him first."

"Your men?" the Snow Hawk questioned hastily.

"I have but twenty faithful left. Of one of them I am not sure. Semya's wealth has bought the rest, and more than half the nobles too. All is lost—we'll be dead men, my friend!" wailed Ameeg dismally.

"Not yet! Bear up, good thief! Do not forget that Mahri is our strong ally, commanding many men." The Snow Hawk thought swiftly. "Come with your men into the hall of state, well armed."

"Beware of Semya," muttered Ameeg swiftly. "One of Loalli's chamber-slaves told him that you were the slave who saved her from the mammoth and later marked his face forever with its scar. He will remember you. Beware!"

"This for black-hearted Semya," Kioga answered, slapping Ameeg's knife-blade sharply. The thief grinned fiercely.

" 'Twill be a pleasure. Tell me when."

"Place yourself near him. At the first sign of treachery, strike hard and true! I go to Mahri. Luck to you, friend!"

"And to you also," murmured Ameeg as Kioga quit his side.

The coronation march had begun; hastily Kioga neared the hall of state. Its doors had all been taken down to open the great hall for these historic ceremonies. Crowds milled before the portals and densely lined the street down which the royal procession presently would come.

Within, the foremost nobles, attended by their slaves and glittering in rich white robes of royalty, sat on the ornate chairs which flanked the central golden throne.

Semya was there. He gnawed his lips. His face was pale, with pearls of sweat upon the brow. Well Kioga knew the turmoil that was in him. With all plans made to foil the nomination of Tokala, the force which he had counted on was not available, since the soldiery from his home city had not yet arrived. Another hour or two would see Tokala king, with power to destroy him at a whim. The other conspiring nobles shared in his frustration.

Mahri's seat was vacant, as was Loalli's. Kioga met Mahri entering the hall of state to take his seat, and stepped before the noble to tell him of events upon the highroads out beyond the city. As if he saw a ghost, Mahri checked. Kioga noted it, but spoke out quickly, that no time might be lost.

"Semya's warriors will soon be at the gates. He knows that I am in your service and faithful to the king-to-be, Tokala. Be warned and ready for whatever comes. See that the boy is guarded watchfully. I shall be near if worst should come to worst."

Mahri's lips were white. "So thou art Akra, slave at first and false warrior in the second place! Now I remember thee, who stepped between Loalli and her bull, and later bore my gifts to her, to bring no answer back. I did not know thee in that other ugly mask."

"This is no time to talk of gifts and maidens," said Kioga sharply, without the deference which Mahri would demand. "Semya's men, I tell you, will undo your making of a king if it is possible. I have delayed their army on the road, eluding the assassins Semya put upon my trail. But the army may find another route and so undo my work."

"Thy tone is sharp—nay, insolent," complained Mahri through lips that trembled strangely. "I like it not. I say, I like it not!" His voice rose to a note almost hysterical. Kioga, startled by the change in him cast quickly through his mind for some good reason for it. He had not far to search.

He knew that Mahri loved the noble Loalli. If it had come to his ears that she had scorned his gifts and spoken of love and power to one who seemed to be a slave in Mahri's own employ, the deep affront of such a thing would rankle like a mortal wound. That only could account for Mahri's sudden change of face.

Kioga was aware of deadly danger in this circumstance. But Mahri, outwardly controlling his emotions, swept on to occupy his place among the seated nobles. As he sat down, a slave from Semya's retinue bowed in obedience to an order and left the hall in seeming haste.

All eyes now turned upon the entry of Loalli. Never more strikingly beautiful, she slowly strode toward her seat, aware of Mahri's eager eyes devouring her, yet utterly indifferent.

Attempting to depart unseen by her, Kioga saw her stop and stand at sight of him, a glad expression on her face. He moved away again. She checked him. "Wait! They said you were in danger, wounded, killed—that Semya sought to murder you. . . . Why did you not come back to me?"

He cautioned her. "Do not delay. There is no time for explanations now. The horns blow for the entry of the little Ru. He is in peril, as are all of us. Do not dismiss your guards."

"I am a noble. You order me. Yet I obey, because—because I am a woman," said Loalli, with her eyes upon him softly. "Do you need warriors? My men would follow you—"

A sound of chanting drowned her words. Kioga waved her on. She went, head proudly high again, to her chair.

The roll of rhythmic chanting rose to shake the ground. Kioga stood aside, to watch the slow unfolding of scenes as from the old Arabian Nights: Three score of finely muscled slaves strode into view, bound wrist to wrist and limb to limb in chains of clinking gold. They were the symbol of the nation's servitude to its new king.

Behind them came as many golden-bodied girls, free maidens of the upper class, each likewise chosen for her beauty and magnificence of form and bearing. These symbolized the choice which any M'Anda king may have among the marriageable maidens of his realm. Each bore a snow-white pigeon in her hands, which, as she passed between the double rank of slaves, she cast aloft to circle in the great rotunda dome above.

Now came men of the upper class and lower nobility, in mammoth-leather suits of scarlet and bright orange. Upon each wrist a sable hawk was perched, blindfolded and bound by a leash of silver chain, and wearing silver bells about its ankles. These passed between the rows of slaves and maidens, standing then to either side, in token of submission by the rich to their new ruler.

Came next the royal soldiery, with *kuris* bared and flashing, marching to the alternating roll of drums, with bucklers and helmets agleam by torchlight. These paused before the open doors of the great hall, to act as protectors of the peace during the coming ceremonies, and hold the throngs in bounds.

Watchfully Kioga eyed these dispositions, taking note of everything transpiring. The face of Semya was now calm but pale. Mahri's was a study in conflicting passions, his eyes ever and again upon Loalli, who sat unperturbed and cool between the other nobles, gently wielding a hawk's-wing fan.

The *rat-a-tat* of drums, and sound of chanting slaves increased, and mingled with them was the trumpet of approaching mammoths. Now splendor reached its brightest height. A train of beasts hove into view, albino mammoths of the royal stables. Their ears were hung with sparkling jewelry. Their thick white outer hair was twisted into looping scalloped braids, under which the inner wool lay curled and curried till it glistened. Their curving tusks were carved, blue ivory inlaid with threads of silver and of copper. Torchlit, they glowed as beasts of living gold, requiring no other ornament. Each with its trunk swung up and down a smoking ivory censer, whose heavy perfume hung along the streaked air. Their bare-skinned mahouts checked them just outside the portals, and ranged them in an open row.

Between them now came one afoot whom Kioga knew, in stunning vestments of the royal house. Flashpan bore himself with comic majesty, though tripping now and then upon his over-robe of saffron-colored mammoth wool. He carried a shield of yellow metal, inscribed with the heraldic coat-of-arms of the M'Anda ruling house. This would be handed to the king on his accession, in lieu of head-crown, according to an ancient M'Anda usage.

In his other hand Flashpan held a chain which led back to a pink-eyed mammoth calf, also albino, its silk-like hair dressed and decorated with all the artistry of the royal M'Anda grooms. Cross-legged on this lesser mammoth sat the king-to-be, Tokala, his message hawk before him on the richly polished leather saddle. The beast he rode would be his own for life, to grow with him and bear him through his realms. His robe was made of iridescent overlying feathers, open at the breast to show the flashing golden plaque of office.

Behind him, one to either side, strode Munro and I, who had been with Tokala on his entry to the kingdom, and so were rated worthy of the honor of escorting him.

At glimpse of him, the multitude sent up the roar of their approval, breaking through the restraining cordon of warriors, to surge about Tokala, eager to behold the person of their young ruler.

Foremost among the crowd, and blanking out the others from our notice, stood one the rumors of whose fate were settled now forever: Kioga stood there, by his living presence raising from our minds all fear that he was dead!

Tokala, with a yell of gladness, would have leaped down from his perch, but for the Snow Hawk's voice close by. "Remember, you are a king," Kioga said in English, comprehensible to ourselves alone. "Act like a king." Tokala heard, and obeyed—composed again, although joy and excitement surged in him.

Kioga turned to us who rushed to greet him, lost for words to show our joy that he was still alive. I cannot express what fresh and reassuring confidence surged up in me to know that he was still with us, working for a reunion with our friends which we all craved, despite the pagan mummery we acted out to save our skins. He did not leave us time to talk.

"Go through with this," he told us, shouting to be heard above the roaring press on every side. "Watch out for Semya. Keep Tokala closely covered. Once he is actually king, it will be too late for them to harm him. Loalli is on our side. But all the rest are hostile. I shall be near, in case—" He sought to tell us more, but now the soldiery had controlled the mob again. With it, he was hurled back. The march moved on. Tokala, with ourselves as escort, neared the empty throne, dismounting just before it. The nobles rose to honor him.

A warrior clove the slender chain in half with one blow of his *kuri.* Tokala mounted and sat in the empty place. Flashpan stood waiting, with the shield of kingship.

His action was the signal for a sudden silence. A heavy gong rang deeply with a brassy tone. The men of wealth and low nobility unbound their hawks, drew back their leathern hoods. Then at a signal all the hawks were freed, to rise with beating pinions high above the swarm of milk-white pigeons.

Swift then were the vicious blows with which the killer-birds struck and struck again. All the silent court was filled with sound of jingling bells, as the sharp-beaked hawks struck down the fluttering pigeons.

When every hawk had borne its victim down and covered it upon the stones, the owners came to gather in their taloned hunters, retiring to their several places.

A cry went up:

"Thus may the little Ru strike down his enemies!"

This ceremony ended, Loalli rose, received the royal shield from Flashpan's hands and presented it to Tokala with the ritual words: "O Ru, long absent, now returned, the ninety-seventh of thy line, long may this shield defend thee whom we shall acknowledge by our hails as king. May thy rule endure for many decades! May the maidens of thy choice one day give thee many sons to carry on thy line. May thy mammoth herds be multiplied. I give thee homage. Hail!"

Her voice rang clearly in the silent hall of state, and that of Mahri and of several others followed promptly, until only Semya was unheard from. His voice alone was now required to make Tokala king, unanimously.

Tall Semya's glance leaped through the crowded hall, as if in search of someone. His brow dripped sweat. There came a rumble of condemnation at his delay; for Mahri had well established his puppet's popularity, and the people hungered for a ruler of the old king line.

Uninformed of their delay, and hourly expectant of the arrival of his warrior force from the mountains by which to execute a *coup,* Semya did not dare delay his answer longer. The word came out of him reluctantly. Yet it was clearly heard, the one word *"Hail"* which made Tokala king.

A moment's deep hush ensued, before the storm of accolade which would follow. Then suddenly a cry rose somewhere amid the throng: *"Slaves of M'Anda, rise and strike! The outer world is reached! We shall be free, to spread our tribes upon the outer earth!"*

In the ears of all who heard, the news seared like a white-hot flame. Here for the hermit race of M'Anda were the tidings for which they and countless generations of their ancestors had been laboring down the centuries.

For slaves, here was new freedom. For royalty, new fields for power and conquest.

And for ourselves, the prisoners within a captive kingdom, here was escape back to the world and friends we knew, release from this strange mummery to which we lent ourselves perforce.

Kioga, his eyes not upon the ceremonies but on that slave of Semya whose shouted rumor had been intended to disrupt the ceremonies, lashed swiftly out to fell the shouter in his tracks. But now the winds were loosed. The nobles, ever fearful of just such consequences of their cruel misrule, were frozen momentarily. All save tall Semya and Loalli.

The wolf-faced noble leaped with *kuri* drawn, to skewer Mahri's new-made king, probably intending later to justify his act by proving that Tokala was not of the royal blood, of which his spies had only recently informed him.

Tokala raised his shield to fend the blow. But Loalli was yet quicker. Her slim hand moved as the lightning strikes. There was the flash of metal as she drove her dagger home, and Semya wheeled, with blood afroth upon his twisting lips, to cut her down.

Hardly had Loalli endangered herself by striking to save her youthful king, when from behind there sprang the figure of Ameeg the thief, supported by his score of nimble-fingered and well-armed rascals. Ameeg swung swiftly upward with a long and heavy blade he carried. The noble's *kuri* shivered on the stouter weapon, and then Ameeg sprang wolflike at his throat, snatched out the metal Loalli had planted in the noble's breast and plunged it back repeatedly till Semya stirred no longer.

And now suddenly, out of the milling press, Kioga appeared, to join Ameeg and throw a ring of armament about Tokala, the boy-king. Things moved with speed when guided by his judgment. Kioga's voice rose up above the din. "The king! Protect your king!"

Among the throng were some not yet insensible to loyalty. Of these a number rallied to us, making a clear way out of the desecrated hall of state. We caught a glimpse of Loalli, separated from us by a milling mob, moving rearward to another exit, well guarded by her warriors and slaves, most of whom were loyal to her kindness.

Of Mahri I saw nothing. I never dreamed—but of Mahri more in its place.

Kioga had thrown his robe about Tokala, to hide the royal vestments from too-covetous eyes. Now, on account of violence and rioting, we were the safer for being afoot and inconspicuous. Several of the lesser nobles favorable to Semya had taken to their mammoths, seeking to ride through the press of humanity in the streets, careless of whom they trampled in their rush for sanctuary. A roar of fury followed them, and some were dragged down from their mounts and killed by infuriated relatives of those they had trampled.

The royal soldiery, disorganized by rumors of a contact with an outer world, were derelict in duty, as mercenaries anywhere are wont to be in times of crisis. They had disbanded, scattering to rejoin each other when chanced to meet, but offering no serious threat to the menace of the mob.

Led by Ameeg, to whom the byways of the city were familiar as its runways to a fox, we found a safe retreat at last in an old abandoned subterranean slave-keep near the great outdoor arena. And it was here, by special courier—a thief in Ameeg's service—that we learned the irony of these events, and the depths to which the treacherous Semya had sunk: Reports of contact with the outside world were false and baseless. Semya had created them out of whole cloth in order to prevent another from becoming king; but his slave had bungled matters, delaying his outcry until too late.

"You speak with certain knowledge?" demanded Kioga of the messenger.

"I have just spoken to Tali, the overseer, fresh from the workings in the tunnel to see a new king made. He left his slaves laboring to brace the ceiling of the tunnel, which threatens to collapse near its far end."

Here was information which we must believe, since Tali of all men was best qualified to speak on tunneling. It was a moment dark with disappointment for each one of us.

And still from afar the roaring of the tempest which the rumor had unloosed mounted steadily in volume.

To take stock of the altered situation, Kioga left us, going out into the City of the Kings.

With *kuri* loosened in its scabbard, the Snow Hawk strode the troubled streets, and turned toward the wall, where by this time, there should be some sign of the warrior forces approaching from the hills. He felt that since the mass of them did not know what end they were to serve, he might divert them to join with Mahri and Loalli in a strong alliance to support the new boy-king, and subdue the growing uproar.

He neared the city gates, one point still held by the old authorities, and suddenly glimpsed Mahri being admitted to the challenge platform, from which palaver may be held with friends or foes beyond.

Kioga thought to hail the prince, but had one fair look at the noble's face. Mahri's features were lined and pallid, the eyes deep-sunken, feverishly ablaze as if an inner fire were consuming him.

Warned in time, Kioga let him pass unspoken, and mounted atop the wall to where he could command view of the challenge platform on which the other was emerging. Below, Kioga also glimpsed the warriors and beasts arriving after long delay before the city gates. He heard them call identities, demand admission. Mahri answered in a deep yet penetrating voice:

"He whom you came to serve is dead. A new king has been made, who has no drop of royal blood in his veins. I am not rich, as was Semya; but if you help me overthrow this false impostor, each man shall be a leader in my realm, and there shall be no kings hereafter. Refuse, and it is death to all of us!"

All that Mahri had wrought, he now sought to destroy; the young boy-king, the ruling class, and all established government must fall if he succeeded. Here was a rouser of rabble incarnated, faithful to no friend or party, the archetype of nihilist, who would throw down all things to serve his private ends—of jealousy and love of power.

Near to the Snow Hawk's hand, arranged one on another in wooden racks, were numbers of the sickle-bladed *molas* he had seen upon the forges of the arm-smiths, razor-sharp except at one short gripping place. Kioga took one up and poised it, eyes upon Mahri's shoulders just behind the neck. From up above, at such close range, a well-directed throw might easily behead the faithless noble in his tracks; and the realm would be well rid of such a traitor. Back went Kioga's hand, the *mola* glittering brightly. The muscle on his shoulder twitched. But suddenly he paused, assailed by doubts about his right to kill.

After all, he had dined at this noble's board, and served him well while they were friends. Kioga put the *mola* back, unable to bring himself to strike thus, thug-like, from behind. . . . He would regret his failure to destroy this Mahri before the day was old!

Kioga heard the leader of the forces shout back his acceptance of Mahri's terms, and heard the noble call: "Throw wide the gates!" Came then the rumble of a lifting bar, as a warrior inside leaped to obey. There was a louder clang as the long broad bar dropped back. The warrior fell, speared from behind. The slaves, in roving through the city, had reached the gates at last.

Mahri, aware of something going wrong, vanished from the outside platform, reappearing yelling frantically for the soldiery to put their beasts against the gates and force them in. But already the slaves, as if led by one versed in the arts of war, had braced the gates with timbers to withstand assault of any kind.

Balked in attempts to rush, the soldiery outside ranged their tall beasts up close to the wall, then from their large equipment broke out crude flexible ladders, made of mammoth leather, and wooden scaling devices. Swift though they worked, they were outwitted by an active figure on the wall above, who when the hooks upon their ropes took hold, immediately cut the strands; and when their ladders were upraised, pushed one after another backward, laden with climbers who sprawled in howling confusion on the slope before the city wall.

Kioga could not long hold the top against the multitude beyond. But aid came swiftly in the form of one he knew and well remembered—one who had first befriended him and taught him how to drive a mammoth.

"Tahro!" cried the Snow Hawk, and the other met him with a hard quick grip of friendship. As he came, a stream of slaves appeared to man the wall.

"My men," said Tahro swiftly in explanation.

"You lead the rising slaves to liberty?"

"Or death, I know not which," Tahro replied. "But we shall at least die fighting to become free men. Ah, see them go to battle!"

It was a scene Kioga found worth watching. The attacking soldiery, now better organized, had planted broader ladders at the walls securely and stormed with valor suited to a better cause. They came up two by two in twenty places, presenting helmets and breast-of-metal to blows the slaves rained on them with the arms kept on the parapets for such emergencies. The wall was as a ship between two waves—the one of naked slaves arriving from within, the other of the storming soldiery—which met and crested in a whirl of fiercely fighting men.

The soldiers were outnumbered, but more suitably equipped. Their heavy swords sheared naked slaves almost in twain. Their armor turned the hardest blows; but its weight encumbered them, whereas the slaves, light on their feet as cats, could leap and circle nimbly, waiting for the chance to run their *kuris* deep into any vital unprotected spot.

Now back, now forward surged the battle on the wall. Swift as the flight of hawks, glittering *molas* whirled through air; and where they struck, no helmet or armor could withstand their force and deadly keenness. Fast as the soldiers mounted, even faster came fresh levies of slaves to take the places of their fallen comrades and force the fighting until the last attacker fell.

Kioga struck no blow save occasionally in his own defense. His life was necessary to another cause than this contention of the slaves and former masters. When he departed from the scene the slaves had dominated, throwing wide the gates at last to admit the weakened enemy, laying hold of them as they came in, diminished by the number of fallen stormers, and slaughtering them without compunction.

The whirlwind now was in its fullest power. Turmoil, pandemonium, reigned within the city walls. The city was like some giant anthill overturned, as from every dungeon, liberated slaves poured forth, a wild and pitiless horde unleashed upon the ruling classes. It now was generally known that rumors of a contact with the outside world were nothing more than rumors. Yet though the slaves had struck prematurely, their gains were great; already they held half the city. Many of the nobles had retreated to their cliff-side houses, easily convertible to fortresses, and here were in a state of siege, surrounded by their faithful.

Near the open theater arena, where the carnivals were to have been held, the former rulers still held out and partly dominated; for it was near here that Mahri's fighters had assembled and rallied, joining with the men-at-arms of other nobles.

Much of this Kioga saw or learned when presently he rejoined Ameeg and the rest of us who anxiously waited his safe return. We learned of Mahri's treachery with sheer dismay, for on his forces we had counted to the last. Now he too was an enemy, the bitterer for the personal motives that drove him.

Yells from without foretold fresh misfortune. One of Ameeg's thieves burst in to give us warning. "Mahri and his warriors seek the new boy-king! Hide him away before they come!"

Kioga bounded to his feet at that and turned to Ameeg.

"You, Ameeg," he said, "know some distant exit from the dungeons underground. Lead on. You—Munro, Flashpan, Kirk, Tokala—follow Ameeg. Quick, now!"

Five of Ameeg's men accompanied us as their leader picked a way through these tortuous mazes which rival the famed Parisian sewers in complexity. Men have been lost for weeks in these blind passages, and we saw skeletons to prove that others had been lost forever there. Undoubtedly these died from lack of water. But Ameeg knew the passages as the old Romans knew their own deep catacombs, and led the way toward safety without a slip or one false turn.

With the remainder of Ameeg's men, Kioga waited to defend our rear, or to throw Mahri off the scent, as necessity dictated. How readily and confidently men did his bidding, I thought as we left him; they were caught up and drawn to him as by some strong magnetic power.

Mahri himself was one of those who came in search of us. He found his entry disputed by Kioga and a dozen resolute thieves, each one of them skilled in the art of thrust and parry. It was with some astonishment that they beheld Mahri accompanied only by a small military bodyguard.

"We wait to serve you," said Kioga coldly, as they neared.

"With *kuris* or in friendship?" observed the noble softly, as with hurt feelings.

"Whichever you prefer," Kioga answered. "Your friendship, like your dagger, has two edges."

"Your men outnumber mine," said Mahri, speaking swiftly. "I come to seek your aid, not to do injury."

"Out with it, then! What aid is it you want of us?"

Mahri made great show of frankness. "Things go not well with us. The slaves are almost in control; the noble class is doomed, its warriors scattered. Out of the strife will come another government. Join with us to support the new boy-king."

"That from you—who not two hours since called on Semya's minions to enter and destroy him as an impostor!" Kioga answered with ironic reproach.

Mahri bore his thrust with equanimity. "You overheard me speak? 'Tis true. I frankly do admit it. But I was overwrought by the uprising. My words were not my own, and I repent. Call on me for the proof of this repentance."

"It rings deceitfully," Kioga answered. "But put down all

your arms in proof," he added, distrustful more than ever, but well aware that Mahri's strength of warriors might still be advantageous to us all.

The noble and his men obeyed unhesitatingly, whereupon Kioga and his men came forth for parley. The noble's gaze passed over them. He talked at length of plans and purposes —at too great length, Kioga thought. "Art vague," he answered brusquely, at last. "Get to the point, and quickly."

"The point is reached," said Mahri with an undertone of triumph which Kioga caught at once. "You are all my prisoners."

"Prisoners!" one of the thieves replied, with derisive laughter on his lips. But suddenly his laughter died, stopped by a flying *mola* that struck him from behind. Two others of Kioga's men dropped where they stood. The Snow Hawk took one glance behind and knew the worst.

One of Ameeg's own men must have betrayed this hiding place to Mahri, for from behind, out of the very exit Kioga and his men had used, a file of Mahri's warriors came, armed to the teeth.

Mahri smiled sinisterly. His voice was soft with purring triumph as he gave orders to his men. "Seize that one," pointing at Kioga. "Kill the rest."

The grim work done before his eyes cold-bloodedly, Mahri's laughter bubbled in his throat. "For you"—to the Snow Hawk—"I have a better entertainment waiting. I would Loalli could be here to see thee dance." He made a sign.

All entered where so recently the new boy-king had hidden, and by dark passages came toward the open-air arena, catching as they did the reek of wild beasts from the forests of the realm, whose snarls and growls reechoed in the lantern-lit darkness. "They bid thee welcome," said Mahri to Kioga, meaningfully.

A patch of light appeared beyond. A full moon lit the great arena brightly, showing its oval enclosure, high polished walls surrounding it on every side and rising twenty feet. Beyond were tiers of empty seats.

"Shalt run before a silent gallery," muttered Mahri, and to his men, "Throw him in!"

"A moment," said the Snow Hawk. "Give me some arm to make a fight of it. 'Twill make it better worth your watching."

"I came to see thee flee and scream for mercy, not to see thee fight," was Mahri's contemptuous answer, and to his warriors. "Down with him! Why do you wait?"

The warriors obeyed, but before he fell Kioga seized a lance and *kuri* from the nearest, hurling it below. A moment later he found himself upon the earth within the wall, with Mahri and his men looking down on him. Worked by a chain manipulated from the wall, one of twenty traps was slowly rising. Behind, gaunt with starvation and long confinement, a shadow rose upon hind legs. Kioga knew it for a pit bear from the hills, chosen for its savage disposition and formidable armory of claws and curving teeth, more deadly than a tiger.

The pit bear dropped down to all fours and came out with a raging impetus, straight at the crouched and muscular figure waiting to defend himself.

Ameeg had taken leave of us to search for food in places known to him. Munro and I sought rest and sleep, weary from this day's activities. One of the thieves among our company stood guard, though we were in little danger of discovery.

Tokala, not yet king for a day, alone was wakeful. It had been through these very mazes that Jemmu the city urchin had lately led him, to view the penned-up beasts and slaves. Kioga was somewhere behind, perhaps in danger. Round about him were the snores of weary men. The single sentry nodded, taking frequent swigs of *lohe* from his ivory flask.

Tokala turned, sat up. The sentry took no notice. Tokala gained his feet. The man was breathing heavily, thanks to the mildly potent drink. Tokala passed behind, paused to pick up a lantern, then quietly slipped away as he had come, skirting the skeletons with averted eyes.

He heard a sudden multiplying uproar of the beasts, followed by mocking laughter and a voice which sounded much like that of Mahri, whom he had always known as a friend, which cried, "Well dodged! Now, at him, beast!"

Tokala bounded forward, glimpsing through a barred opening the sight of man and animal contending in the arena, with Mahri and his warriors applauding from the wall. The bear made short and vicious rushes, finding at each charge the keen blade of a lance which pricked him on the head and shoulders. Then suddenly Tokala's blood ran cold, for he who faced the animal was Kioga.

Again the pit bear charged, and Tokala turned in frantic haste—not to desert his friend, but to summon help.

Within the dungeon chambers Tokala ran on flying feet.

Somewhere near were allies, could he but find them and enlist their aid. He cried out loudly: "Slaves! Slaves whom I fed when you were starving! Reply to me!"

"This way! This way!" a deep voice answered.

Stumbling, Tokala found a door, on which someone was pounding. He raised its outside bar. The door swung in. The faces of the slaves, no longer emaciated from starvation, were unfamiliar. But he was known to every man of them—the little Ru, who had not been too proud to visit them and now had come to keep his second promise, that of freedom.

A roar of acclamation rose. The slaves, destined to be nobles' sport, saluted him. In leaping words he told of what transpired in the near arena.

A burly hearty ruffian tossed Tokala on one shoulder and led the rush up toward the wall which skirted the arena.

Other ears had heard Tokala's cry. Flashpan, Munro and myself, alarmed by his discovered absence, had traced him, and encountered those whom he had summoned to his aid. We joined them, bursting out upon the wall a little distance from where Mahri and his companions were engrossed in baiting another living human being.

The slaves just liberated by Tokala crept stealthily upon the other party under cover of the wall. I know not what Munro or Flashpan did. But speaking for myself, I was transfixed. I never shall forget the dreadful terror which I felt, beholding our stanch friend in his extremity. The bear indeed he had killed; but Mahri had ordered loosed against him four of the great dire wolves. His back against the wall, Kioga was fending them off, but even the tireless Snow Hawk was gasping in exhaustion; and the four fearsome beasts pressed ever closer.

And then I saw that even in this extremity he had kept his wits about him, for he was edging along the wall toward the door of the wolves' own den. And now he made a furious berserk sally before which the wolves gave ground. Then whirling like a flash, Kioga leaped into their den. The trap fell heavily behind him. Like hammer blows against the wood he heard the hard impacts of the baffled beasts as they were stopped short by the heavy bars.

Again, from up above, the cry of Mahri rose imperiously. Then terror, fury and surprise were in it also. Kioga caught the sound of shouts, the impact as of bodies falling in the arena, and cruel laughter from the wall.

He looked out through a ventilating hole, to witness Mahri

rising to his feet, his face a waxen mask of horror. A cry of dread was in his throat, yet passed his clenching teeth in but a whisper. His own fierce harriers, baffled by the sudden disappearance of the other prey, knew nothing of discrimination—and shrieking Mahri was their victim. He went down threshing like a stricken animal. His heels beat a hard tattoo against the trap which hid Kioga.

A fellow man was being rent and torn beyond Kioga's sanctuary, one who had sought his life with an unparalleled ferocity. By every tenet of right or justified revenge, Kioga should have stayed his hand. Instead, assailed by pity, he raised the trap a foot and seized the stricken Mahri by the ankle, intending to haul him from the jaws of the wolves.

But suddenly the Snow Hawk's grasp was broken by a fierce tug from beyond. The snore of snarling tight-locked jaws told him that he was too late.

We who beheld the grim finale from above turned sick from the spectacle. Not so the slaves, who loosed the other captive beasts to join the dire wolves.

But though we turned away, sounds followed us—men's voices being choked off, the crunch of cracking bones.

The Snow Hawk emerged from the dens to join us on the wall that overlooked the arena. Hardly had he greeted us when yet another company of slaves, leading nobles in their clutches, arrived upon the opposite edge of the arena and threw their victims to the beasts.

Such was the indication of the general temper. Tokala, representing nobility at its highest, was now endangered too. The time had come to make our bid for liberty. The route toward it led through the City of the Kings toward the tunnel in the mountain.

Upon the tide of slaves ebbing and flowing in the streets, we could contrive best by seeming also to be slaves; to achieve that end, we put off outer apparel obtained from Mahri's wardrobe, and wrapped ourselves in ragged cloaks.

With Ameeg and his men for company, we set forth through the troubled city, riding on three mammoth laboring-bulls which were provided by Tahro. Thus, masquerading as toilers bound for labor in the tunnel, we slowly neared the opening. Scenes on the route informed us what we might expect were we recognized as attendants of Tokala, who still was king, though fleeing his domains.

With the scaling ladders originally used by the soldiery in attempting to force the wall, and others improvised upon the spot, the slaves were now engaged in bitter warfare against their former masters, who had taken refuge in their sumptuous cliff mansions, defending them with desperation from the former slaves who, climbing by ladder and agility, sought to oust them to the clutches of the mob.

Some of these lesser strongholds already had fallen. Slaves paraded from them in the finery seized at the time of victory, or fought about division of the spoils. Others looted in the households of freemen. Smoke and fire told of uncontrolled incendiaries at work.

A wild shout rose upon one side of us. A band of scaling slaves had just gained ingress to a noble's dwelling from a neighboring house. The defenders made their stand upon the topmost balcony. In full view of the cheering throngs upon the streets, the naked ravagers attacked, hurling their unlucky victims to the stones a hundred feet below. There was the crash and roar of destruction within the cliff-side mansion. Then someone hurled a torch, and smoke began to curl from every orifice.

Pillage, terror and destruction, held the beautiful City of the Kings in thrall.

I could but wonder: Where was the lovely noble Loalli now? How many of the other nobles would survive this holocaust? I did not realize as yet, the deep astuteness of that high-born princess.

CHAPTER 18

As we approached the inner entrance to the tunnel, we had become part of a flowing river of humanity, still acting upon the false rumor that the tunnel had been holed through. Slaves of less angry temperament strode side by side with poorer freemen, laden with their few possessions, and heading toward that hoped-for exit to a newer and better existence in a larger outside world. The endless tramp of multitudes was that of men migrating—toward a tragic disappointment. For at the entry to the tunnel they found the human tide dammed back, confronted by the information that the tunnel still was uncompleted.

Here Tali, overseer of operations in the tunnel, met and joined us. As they had done for countless generations, the mammoth labor-beasts made their exit, dragging forth the rumbling sledges, laden heavily with rock. Their toil was interfered with by the presence of those hopefuls crowding near the entrance. As yet no one, save those entitled to pass in and out, had been admitted by the strong guard at the entrance.

But with Tali in our company, we had no difficulty gaining access to the borings and passing through to the far end, where slaves still toiled, bracing up the cracking ceiling with timbers which to my unpracticed eye seemed hopelessly inadequate.

Because of the danger from falling fragments and the risks attendant upon the movement of slaves and mammoths in such close quarters, Tokala had been left in the company of Ameeg the thief and those loyal slaves whom he had released from confinement under the arena. These faithful guarded him some distance in our rear.

And now we set to work, like common slaves, to compass what we knew was nearer realization than the M'Anda toilers thought. If what Dan's message from beyond had said was true, now more than ever sounds of our toil must be audible to them in the world beyond, since many tons of rock had been excavated since that time.

On our arrival the wall ahead was honeycombed with borings about the diameter of barrels and ranging eight or ten feet into the solid stone. It was Munro's idea to enter one of these, head first, and seek to make a contact with Dan La Salle beyond. Dan, he knew, was skilled in radio and knew the Morse code well. Munro's own knowledge of Morse, acquired of necessity in order to talk back and forth while Dan was learning it, might now prove useful.

Armed with a chipping rammer from the heaps of digging tools nearby, he tapped out sharply in Morse the triple letter S.O.S., listening then for some reply. Faint and seeming far away there came a dim response—his S.O.S. repeated and the words: *"I hear you. What can we do to help? Dan."* The answer came with practiced speed. *"Stand by,"* returned Munro, not so quickly, since his skill in code did not equal Dan's. *"Will advise."*

Munro emerged then to consult with us.

"Find out how many men Dan has available, and what arms they carry," said Kioga, already thinking of our final exit from the M'Anda realm. Munro crawled back and made inquiry in code.

"Twenty Shoni braves," was Dan's tapped-out reply. *"Armed with smooth-bores, ball and powder from the store at Fort Talking Raven."*

"What is the state of things among the Shoni?"

"They're on the warpath now. No telling what may happen, or when. Can't you hurry?"

"Doing all we can," replied Munro. *"Can you help?"*

"Have planted mine of powder. Say when!"

"Not yet. Rock still too thick. Wait further word. Stand by!"

Munro came from the boring just as Tali and his laborers drew near, again to attack the rock with all their force, though little realizing how near success was in their grasp. Nor did we enlighten them, lest intimation might reach that dammed-back mob beyond the entrance and cause a concerted rush and consequent interruption of the labor.

But interruption came in other guise, and danger, which we thought had been left behind, appeared with stunning suddenness. The laborers had worked a second day and night, hewing yet another layer from the rock which separated us from freedom. The time had almost come when

Munro would signal Dan to detonate his charge of explosives, in the hope of doing in one blow what might yet require many days if left to slave labor on our own side.

The tunnel now was filled with sounds of mammoths, trumpeting as they toiled, the clinking fall of hammers on the solid rock, the shouts and cries of slaves, the crack of whips on leathery rumps, when out of turmoil leaped a cry of warning, followed by the piercing whistle of the overseer.

The slaves, well-trained to the instant obedience on which their lives might depend, stopped work at once, alert to the supposed danger of a cave-in. But the threat proved not from nature, but from man. Advancing came a troop of soldiery, led by two of the nobles who had sat within the hall of state and somehow evaded the fate which befell so many of their peers.

With dagger blades drawn and *kuris* bare, there could be little doubt of their hostility. Arrayed against them were ourselves and the laborers in the tunnel, armed only with the tools with which we toiled. Faced thus with show of force, the leading noble advanced alone, his eyes upon Kioga with instant recognition. He spoke.

"Well met, O maker of spurious kings! What have you now to say before we put an end to you and this impostor whom you call the little Ru?"

"No more than this, High-born," answered Kioga coolly, though we knew he sparred for time. "To put an end to him, you first must put an end to us, then find him. If you do that, who then will hole your tunnel through? Will your proud soldiers stoop to do the task of slaves?"

"Not so," the other sneered contemptuously. "The slaves will do the bidding of my soldiers. Is this not so, O tattered rabble? Dare you defy the orders of your masters? Turn and destroy these interlopers! Disobey, and you shall be entombed and left to die!"

The noble's words came forth whiplike to lash these laborers who all their lives had done the bidding of a higher caste. Knowing only by hearsay of events transpiring in the City of Kings, they cringed before this wrathful harangue. Eyes slid from the noble to Kioga, then to us. Toil-calloused hands fingered heavy tools nervously. Kioga signaled to Munro, Flashpan and me to group ourselves together, ready for the worst.

Swift to seize upon the indecision of the slaves, the noble cracked the whip of his voice again. "Put down your tools and file between us, and no harm shall come to you. Obey! A noble speaks!"

The slaves were vassals still—eager to defy, but too long trained in the habit of unquestioning obedience. A moment later we stood alone, four men against four hundred or four thousand, we knew not which. All that had been gained was lost. And what would become of Tokala?

But we had left one person out of consideration. Her intervention came like light in darkness, preceded by a crash as if a mammoth had been put against a creaking gate. Part of the wall burst outward like a shell, revealing the offshoot of some old abandoned work. Our present tunnel had apparently crossed just before the point at which another boring had been discontinued. Begrimed with marks of travel underground, but nonetheless superb and beautiful, Loalli came in view upon a giant bull. Beside her, to our surprise, sat Tokala, the royal plaque exposed. Behind Loalli came her faithful retinue, both soldiery and slaves, among them Ameeg and his men, met with in their explorations for a hiding place in which to secrete Tokala their king.

Loalli's voice was keen with scorn. "O men of mighty voices and little courage, who would destroy the little Ru—first you must destroy Loalli and her following!"

"Hast ordered, High-born. It shall be done!" cried one of the nobles in a tone that dripped with venom. He raised a *mola* from his belt and swung it for a throw designed to catch her in the breast.

But Kioga was before him by the fraction of a second. A pointed bar used in prying stones apart, hurled with mighty force, impaled the noble where he stood. The *mola* spun through air and missed Loalli by no more than a hand's-breadth, lodging with a thud in a timber upright just beside her.

A moment later her supporters and the other soldiery were at grips. The slaves, released from the fears which earlier had weakened them in favor of our enemies, gained courage and supported Loalli against the other nobles. Between the two, they routed and drove them several hundred yards before them, leaving only our small group to give thanks for this timely interruption.

The sounds of combat now abating in the distance, we heard the insistent tapping on the wall, frantically calling on us for an explanation of our silence. The tapping now was clear. Munro stepped to the wall and sent his message out.

"Explode your mine."

The answer came back quick and clear. *"O. K. Stand back!"*

A minute passed, then two. I glanced back into the tunnel, to see Loalli, swept back before her men on the crest of the fighting wave, now returning toward us on her stately bull. She was perhaps three hundred yards away, and clearly visible in the tunnel, Tokala waving to us from beside her on the stately mount, while Ameeg and his men swung lanterns at their side triumphantly.

Then from behind me came a terrific concussion. Rock dust filled our nostrils as Dan's mine exploded. Behind I saw a ragged hole appear—which led out to the world we knew. I turned back toward Loalli, who suddenly had checked her mount and wheeled the bull in the opposite direction. A moment later I saw why she had turned.

An upright timber, loosened by the impact of a passing mammoth, and, shaken by the blast we felt, had fallen. The shoring of the tunnel roof was now collapsing at that point. I saw the next supports give way and buckle. The falling debris shut out the sight of Loalli for a moment before we had a glimpse of her again, well on her way in swift retreat.

Then with the deep and booming roll of thunder, complete catastrophe and chaos ensued.

"God help us! The tunnel's cavin' in!" cried Flashpan.

A blast of air thick-laden with rockdust hurled all of us back. The rock above where we had stood fell rumbling. The tunnel through which we had come was sealed, beyond all possibility of unsealing it, deep within the mountain.

This much I realized, before my head struck hard against the ground; whereafter, all was throbbing blackness.

CHAPTER 19

I came back to the world of consciousness to hear the excited gutturals of the Shoni warriors who bent above me, dashing icy water on my face and neck. The first face I saw was Kioga's, cut and bruised. Dan stood beside him. I heard his voice:

"Feel all right, Kirk?"

"Not too bad," I managed. "How about Munro and Flashpan?"

"Bruised like yourself."

"Tokala?" I could not quite remember what had happened.

"That's something we may never know," Kioga answered thoughtfully, in a tone which told how deeply he was moved. "We saw him with Loalli last. Whether they got back successfully to a safe place inside the tunnel, we can't surmise. We can only hope."

"And the hermit people of M'Anda?" I rose to shake myself into some kind of self-control. Flashpan sat nearby with Munro, resting. Kioga pointed at the chaotic mass of splintered rock and rubble which filled the hole Dan's powder mine had blasted.

I saw a hand thrust from the dusty heap—a human hand clenched tight in death. Upon its back was burned the brownish brand-mark of a slave. But in the rigid clutch there was a jeweled dagger, the emblem of a man who at the last had fought for liberty. About the wrist there was a shackle, clinging only because the hand rested within it on the ground. The shackle itself was broken.

"He was the only one to see the light of outer freedom?"

"The only one," Kioga answered me.

Munro spoke: "I hope the broken shackle is an augury of liberty amid their old surroundings for those we left behind; for they are destined to remain a hermit race, perhaps forever."

We four stood thoughtful, while Dan threw earth upon the hand and its broken shackle. The hard-gripped dagger Munro pried loose. "The only memento, except the rags we wear, of the adventure among the T'emaho. He'll never need it now."

"And Tokala?" reiterated Dan. "Must we go without him?"

"We must," Kioga answered. "Don't forget that Loalli is the king's ally. If he survived the tunnel, she will find a way to protect him."

Whatever Tokala's fate might be, we had not time to linger over it. From the forest, to our meeting place here at the mountain's base, there came a runner, spent and gasping, with news which told Kioga there was to be no rest. The Indian jerked the words out in the Shoni tongue:

"Shoni braves on—warpath—passing down the river to burn the white men's lodges." This meant the miners' cabins, as well as the blockhouse wherein Beth waited, Kioga realized.

Pausing only long enough to take the exhausted Indian's weapons, and inform the rest of us of his intentions, Kioga set forth downriver, relieved to tread once more the forest trails which he had known since boyhood.

The ground was soft and Kioga did not wish to leave a trail; he therefore chose to travel by the strength of wrist and arm, swinging thus below the overhanging thickets which brushed the river. He chose his hand-grips with unerring instinct, and passed through semi-darkness with the facility of a nocturnal cat. Though there were breaks in his highway here and there, necessitating foot travel on and near the river bank, his pace was nonetheless as swift or swifter than a speeding longboat on the river.

Ultimately it was he who overtook a Shoni war canoe, laden deep with braves, all painted as for combat. The messenger had been correct. The war canoe joined others in a cove not far from where the riverboat *Amazon* had destroyed a dozen of the finest Shoni craft with that one shot from her forward gun.

Kioga knew palaver would precede action, and a bravery dance would give him extra time now the while it spurred them on to more cruel outrages later. He had at most a few hours in which to work. It took him one of those to reach the blockhouse. To avoid being mistaken for a hostile, he called Beth's name as he approached.

The girl, until this moment all but certain he was dead,

sprang up as if electrified. She met him at the swinging rough-hewn door. He stood a moment, hardly recognizing her, what with the stains of tragedy beneath her eyes, unprecedented hollows in her cheeks, and the fragile slimness to which his long absence and the uncertainty of his fate had reduced her.

Until this moment of reunion Beth had not once let down. But now she saw him nearing her as through a mist, and felt a helpless welling of the tears from between her lids. Despite the thousand things that clamored to be uttered, she could not speak, nor act more than to wait for him with open arms.

For once Kioga's perception slumbered. He did not note the stealthy swinging of the rough-hewn door behind him, nor glimpse the two shadows, one well behind the other, stealing up along the trail which he had left from riverbank to blockhouse entrance. He did not hear the silent footfalls on the threshold, nor the faint metallic *click* of rifle-hammer being thumbed. No inkling of his peril came to warn the Snow Hawk until—two shots rang deafeningly out.

For sheer capacity and industry under most extraordinary circumstances, the palm is due to Captain Phineas Scott; for the bones of his ship the *Bearcat* had hardly been battered out of sight by the waves which combed the reefs, when he, abetted by his men, set out to build another vessel to replace her. Now, with the work all but completed, Scott stood almost knee-deep in chips and shavings, beholding with fair pride the handiwork of himself and his men.

" 'Tis all of a miracle, lads," he told them. "She's built! She's caulked and made to battle ice. We've but to knock the blocks away come next high tide, butter the skids a bit, and down she'll slide, down to the briny, a proper ship, though I warrant she's no Eel de France." The doughty Captain rubbed his horny hands. "Sven Svenson, you were born and raised a whaler's gunner. There'll be a chance for you to shoot again. We salvaged the *Bearcat's* harpoon gun, and above a hundred of her bombs and good black powder, for which we may have use. MacGregor, here, will help ye bolt it on the foredeck. Lose no time."

Scott turned then to Tom Codd. "What news from Kias, whom we set the task of freightin' down the cannon from Fort Talking Raven?"

The words had hardly left his lips when someone called that Kias was approaching. Scott glanced and swore with hearty gusto. The Indian, flanked by a score of red allies, bore in the Captain's answer—four of the fort's crudely mounted, hand-cast cannon, small but serviceable, together with a supply of rusty iron scrap and ball. There was another gun of smaller bore hidden in the rocks above their heads, as a defense should enemies approach down either rocky beach. This, with its ball and powder, was now brought down.

The Indians also carried in the fort's full supply of smaller arms, the greater part of which had been hand-fashioned within the walls. These several arms, together with supplies of bows and arrows, should need for them arise, were stored between the decks.

All such precautions were taken against no foe of Scott's imagination. The ship must be launched and floated at high tide, then immediately worked several miles along the coast to gain the sheltering bay in which the *Pirate* lay. Only from that point could we attain the channel leading out to sea. And, for a day or possibly for several days, we should be in view of the raiding miners ashore or on their hostile ship, and vulnerable to some extent to possible attack.

Scott's Indian friendlies hunted in the neighboring forest for elk and moose, whose meat was smoked and stored within the hull as reserve victuals for the final voyage from Nato'wa. Water, too, was taken on, but not in great quantity; for Scott well knew that once at sea, fresh water could be found almost at will atop the floes. A monster bear was killed, and its fat was used to grease thickly the skids down which the ship would slide when all was ready.

Scott had also kept a weather eye upon the *Pirate's* crew, by means of one of Kias' roving scouts; and learned that since they had already found great quantities of gold, they might at any moment put to sea, to take advantage of the seasonal break-up of the ice floes.

From Dan he had no other word, though young La Salle, accompanied by ourselves and his own warriors, was heading swiftly down the turbulent Hiwasi, tossed in their creaking bark canoes. In these we rode no longer than was necessary to reach the river boat the *Amazon,* moored up a little creek under cover of the overcurling thicket growth. At once the *Amazon* was got out on the river, her skin sail raised to take a following wind; at fair speed we descended toward the blockhouse, where, long before we came, Kioga had preceded us.

Nearly deafened by the explosion of two firearms at such close range, the Snow Hawk wheeled, thrust Beth behind him, and saw a warrior sprawled face down across the threshold of the blockhouse. Behind, with gun now clubbed and held in readiness, John La Salle stood crouched, waiting for the hostile brave to move.

"He's dead," Kioga told him, stepping forward to seize the hand Beth's father had extended in a cordial welcome, and with the grasp to drag La Salle in to safety.

And only just in time. For as Kioga swung the great door to, the twang of bow cords came from beyond, and two arrows from the forest chugged into the panels venomously. Dan's information had been well-founded. The Shoni braves were hostile to all whites. A scouting party, of which the dead warrior was undoubtedly one, waited now for one false move, to take the scalps of those within the blockhouse.

They would not attack in open front, Kioga knew well. Nor was he deceived by hours of uninterrupted silence which ensued; the Shoni braves, true Indians, could wait with panther patience until the prey, lulled to a false sense of security, did one wrong thing.

Within the blockhouse Beth, Kioga and the elder La Salle laid their loaded guns beside them and kept their eyes glued to the firing-slits in the walls. The short hours of faint light which was Nato'wan day at this time of the year gloomed into night, and still they heard no sound. At intervals Kioga related to them all of our strange adventures in the realm of M'Anda, to occupy their minds with other things besides the danger which hourly multiplied.

For if the Shoni force was great, Dan and the others, returning down-river in the *Amazon,* might walk into an ambush unawares. He must devise the means of precipitating action before that could occur. Pondering it, Kioga saw a point of light flame up and spring through space like a meteor. There was a thud upon the roof, the smell of burning resin, followed by the crackling sound of fired wood. Thus had the Shoni chosen to strike.

As the flames took hold upon the blockhouse roof, the shadow of the *Amazon* appeared upriver, and we aboard her beheld the blazing blockhouse with horror. The wind still favored us, but it seemed hours until we neared the bank on which the small log stronghold stood.

We heard a shot ring crisply out, followed by a shriek of pain and fury from the woods. Dan grabbed his gun and sought to spring out into the water, but Flashpan checked him with a yell of warning. A naked shadow with straining bow stood on the bank. The miner brought the threatening savage down with one clean shot, then hurled our anchors over, fore and aft, within good rifle range of the blockhouse.

A shout apprised us that Kioga heard our shot.

"Come out!" cried Flashpan. "We'll cover yore retreat." Without an instant's hesitation John La Salle, Beth and Kioga bounded forth. Simultaneously we on board the *Amazon* sent our bullets crashing through the brush on either side of them, so that they reached the bank through a veritable lane of flying lead. The savages, bewildered by the sudden break for safety, were late in sending forth their shafts, the more astonished by having three swiftly moving targets at which to shoot.

The three were at the bank, then knee-deep in the river, before the first reeds whistled through the air to cut them down.

But now the Snow Hawk employed an old device, and threw his two companions headlong on their faces in the water, with the quick words "Dive and swim!" Arrows skittered close about, but a moment later eager hands were hauling them aboard, unhit.

Although we had expended ammunition, we had had no targets at which to aim and did the hostiles no hurt; and so, perceiving us up our anchors and slowly gather headway, they bounded from concealment, drew forth their long canoes from somewhere and set out in pursuit.

"They must be from the far interior," La Salle declared, "or they'd know better than to attack us in the open."

"They'll l'arn!" said Flashpan, pouring powder down his pistols' mouths.

"Wait!" said Kioga sharply. "I'm all against unnecessary shooting. We'll have better use for our powder later. Hold off, and don't fire unless they try to board."

I could not blame Flashpan for his enthusiasm to protect his friends, but I liked the Snow Hawk even better for that humaneness in the face of deadly danger.

The *Amazon* forged along. On either side and well within our range had we been disposed to shoot, two longboats came in hot pursuit, the muscles of their paddlers rolling in their efforts to pass ahead and cut us off. And they presently succeeded.

We others kept low, to avoid the occasional arrow that

whipped across our deck. Dan, at the tiller, looked for his orders from Kioga as the nearest longboat set a course that would bring her up against our bow. The danger of hand-to-hand fighting could not be risked now. Kioga gave a sign, which Dan interpreted to mean, "Do what you must."

He put the tiller over hard. The *Amazon* went on another tack. The longboat, misjudging by a matter of inches, shot squarely across her bow; and the larger craft ran the longboat under like a log, hurling men and weapons overboard, and passing on to leave them bobbing, yelling, to the surface, in her bubbling wake.

Another longboat darted forward from the other direction. Again Dan moved his helm; but in maneuvering, the *Amazon* had lost some way, and responded now less quickly. We did not this time cleave the longboat, but passed instead before it.

Close overside a dozen eager painted Shoni braves rose up to spring upon us, brandishing their knives and tomahawks. But simultaneous rising of every other man was their undoing. For as our craft came slowly round, her swinging boom struck like a flail against the risen savages, and beat them pell-mell before it, like dominoes set in a line. Pandemonium broke out behind us as we passed, leaving them almost swamped and entirely helpless.

At the junction of several rivers leading into the fardeep-forested interior, Kioga ordered the *Amazon* checked. To one with knowledge of the savage Shoni ways, this was a point where information might be had, as fast as it was signaled forth between the tribes.

No African drum signal system can compare in its intricacy with that in vogue among the red-skinned tribesmen of Nato'wa. In equatorial jungles the messages are sent forth through air for all to hear. But the Shoni drummers send their warnings and tidings through the water of their river highways.

Their talking drums are cask-like in shape, with ordinary drum-head tops, but having open bottoms. Five drums of varying size joined together comprise a signaling unit. These units are placed so that their even bottoms are several inches deep in water on creek, stream or river, and the message is beaten out with heavy skin-wrapped sticks, and thus transmitted directly through the water, of itself a splendid conductor.

Within close range, a skillful listener may feel the vibrations with his dipped-in hand or foot. Farther off, the listener must immerse one ear, or preferably both, to take the message—a trick involving some gymnastics, if he would breathe while listening; and it is no uncommon sight, at river camps, to see one brave alternating with another, lying on his back in shallow water with ears awash, taking in the signals and translating them into speech for the benefit of his feasting fellows—ofttimes a cold but always an informative task, for Shoni gossip-drums are never still.

But at more startling distances at which the distinctive drumming sounds continue audible, some amplifying device must be employed to pick them up. Kioga sought and found what was required for this purpose, a wide strip of thin hard bark, which he rolled into a curving cone, the large end of which he put below the water, the small end into one ear like a hearing trumpet.

Crouching thus, the while we lingered close in perfect silence, the Snow Hawk listened, indicating with a nod that he could hear the signaling. And strange it seemed to all of us that for Kioga the rivers actually spoke. He listened thoughtfully for half an hour, now and then advising us of what he heard.

"The drums speak of white men who dig the earth." That means the miners from the schooner *Pirate*. "They say a hundred Shoni braves have been enslaved to do their digging for them." This squared with rumors Dan had heard before. "Hostile bands from all the villages have put aside their differences to make war upon the whites." Of such, no doubt, were those who had attacked and burned the blockhouse. "Four hundred warriors are heading for a rendezvous on the coast, to lift the scalps of all white men they find."

"They be no fools, those bloody murderers," muttered Flashpan below his breath, the while he hitched his smoothbore nearer.

Kioga tossed his hearing cone aside, and swiftly rose. "No time to lose. Come on!"

We followed him, on through the forest and toward the coast, regretfully abandoning the river boat which had served us so well.

We achieved the overland march without noteworthy incident. Scott's men cheered our arrival. Once again we were a single party, joined in a strong alliance of hearts and hands. Save by Tokala—whose fate lay with Loalli in the hermit land of M'Anda—our numbers were undiminished since our first landing, and I recall with what a surge of confidence we beheld the new spring sun, now rising on the south horizon, as if to beam a benison upon our fortunes. Alas for all the hopes of such as I!

With nothing to hold us back, and the tide almost at the full, Scott gave the order to knock the blocks from under his new-built ship. Down the slight incline she slowly slid, checked by the ropes on which we pulled, to ease her in. One by one we went aboard from her small-boat to make ourselves familiar with her rude but adequate 'tween-deck appointments.

But not one of our Indians would accompany us. No persuasion could induce a single one to set foot on this craft. Even Kias, whose bravery and courage were far above all criticism, stood on the land, with both Kioga's hands in his, begging his former chief not to embark upon the vessel. Kias, of course, reflected Kioga, must be torn between two loyalties; for he'd heard gossip of an attachment between Kias and the Wacipi maiden Heladi. And so with a word of hope for Kias' future happiness, he bade his old friend farewell.

If sailormen may be believed, every ship possesses a soul. And *Bearcat II* proved no exception. She handled well beneath a rag, but proved a trifle cranky when her full suit of heavy skin was unfurled to the wind; perhaps she was a trifle oversparred. But she would serve; and serve with honor, those who put their faith in her. Scott worked her wheel. MacGregor cast a stone up forward as we sounded south and westward for the sheltered harbor which held the *Pirate*.

Against the danger which we hoped would not materialize, our cannon all were packed with powder, wads rammed in, rusty round shot rolled into the muzzles. Below, men fell naturally back into shipboard habits. Beth and her father were quartered aft, the crew amidships, with all the armament stowed forward and provisions centrally located.

Compared with the greater *Pirate*, plank for plank, *Bearcat II* must have appeared a puny war vessel, save for her really formidable armament—five smaller mobile cannon, two to a side and one to serve as stern chaser, and a fixed whaling gun up forward, capable of swiveling—to make no mention of our small- and hand-arms, with which each man was well equipped.

We rounded the rocky promontory which hid the *Pirate* from our view. Scott put the spokes hard over and brought her in right handily; and we saw the shadow of our enemy looming dark against the cliffs. She showed no running lights, nor did *Bearcat II*, moving slowly in.

We had not come too soon. The sudden ebb, peculiar to the tides about Nato'wa, set quickly in. The waters drew away, save from that great natural basin in which the two vessels now rested safely, landlocked until the sea came in again.

" 'Twill be a fair surprise to the *Pirate* when she wakes up in the mornin' to find a fighting ship abeam," said Scott, and ordered all guns rolled to port and laid to bear upon the other ship. "Just to remind 'em we can sting if they attempt to touch us."

Kioga's eyes and listening ears were toward the shore; and in his head were mental images of what must happen when the Shoni warriors descended on the unsuspecting mining camp. In fancy he already heard the screams of the attacking savages, foreseeing all the hideous aftermath of torture and bloodshed that would follow. He knew what fate was in store for the several pale-skinned women in the camp. Knowing that, although he felt but little sympathy for men who would enslave other men, pity for their women rose in him.

He turned to Captain Scott. "They must be warned."

"They'd shoot you down at sight, man!" Scott exploded. "Ye must be daft to even think of it!"

"They must be warned," Kioga repeated quietly. "I'll take the risk."

"Then you will not go alone," Scott answered loyally. "Some of my men will go along to cover ye. Here, Svenson, Stumpf—"

But there his words were interrupted. A scream, almost too inhuman to have issued from the throat of man, apprised us that it was too late already to do anything to aid those ashore. Warning and massacre had come on them at once. Now we heard the rising shouts and yells of men hard-pressed, the crack of rifles and the lesser sounds of smaller firearms. It was a running battle, judging by the nearing, multiplying volume of those sounds.

Suddenly men burst into view atop the cliffs, now partially illumined by the dawn glow in the south.

It was a rout, undoubtedly. The whites, known by their garments, showed but one single thought—to scale the cliffs and gain their ship. The greater number won the lower rocky beach; but laggards, four of them, were captured by the savages, knifed and scalped at the brink, and hurled down among the others who preceded them.

A few men from the *Pirate* who had been camped in the rock shelter on the shore rushed forth. Perceiving the danger, they ran at once to the *Pirate's* boat, and without waiting for any of their companions, pushed off, intent only upon their own salvation. But before they could pull away, a dozen miners swarmed upon the craft, and in the savage scramble for possession, several were felled before it drew toward the mother ship.

Those who were left behind plunged in and swam—or drowned before they reached their vessel. More would have died had the tide been at the full and sharks on their dread visit to the land. As it was, their loss was great enough, for on the shore the Shoni war bands swarmed; and in their clutches, too shocked to scream, and apathetic with their terror, three white women faced a fearful destiny.

Upon the *Pirate* all was wild confusion in the rush to reach that forward gun and put a shot into the assembled body of the savage warriors.

We on *Bearcat II* saw with horror what impended, and cried protest and warning, which went unheard amid the bedlam on the other ship. In the act of putting down a boat, at all hazards to attempt the rescue of those white-skinned women, Kioga was checked by the jarring boom of the *Pirate's* gun.

The shell screamed toward the shore, plumped on the rocky beach and burst. And when the smoke had cleared, Kioga saw that he could do no more to aid the three white women.

The savages, astounded by the shattering destructive shell, retreated from the heap of intermingled dead it left, scattering among the rocks. Our eyes went back once more to the *Pirate,* to witness the final cold-blooded acts of which her company were capable.

Perhaps a dozen of her men still struggled in the water, as they neared the sanctuary of their ship. Some who sought to haul themselves aboard were beaten off. Others near enough to have been saved, were let sink down, no hand raised to give them aid. Such was the example set by white men for those watching savages ashore.

But we alone could comprehend the despicable motive at the heart of it. A snarling voice from off the *Pirate,* distinctly heard across the water, put it into words: "Don't let 'em board. That many less to share with!"

Uncertain what the Indians could achieve in the way of attack by water, the *Pirate's* men raised her bower and swung their ship a length farther from the shore. Then for the first time those aboard her had a view of *Bearcat II,* whose berth was inconspicuously to one side, within the hook formed by the promontory we had rounded. Men rushed to the *Pirate's* rail.

"What ship is that?" a voice hailed over, sharply.

"*Bearcat II,* Captain Phineas Scott," was Scott's answer.

"Where are you bound?"

"Back to America, come next high tide."

"In that hogshead?" came the derisive question.

"She'll sail—an' that's more'n that mud-burnin' scow of yours'll do," Scott answered furiously.

"Have you provisions, or do you think to eat the sail?"

"We've stocked with food to last two years with no one going hungry," was our Captain's answer—to which he added almost instantly to us: "I've said too much. They can't go back on land; and they spent all their time in huntin' gold, not deer meat. They've nothing in their commissary, and they can't put to sea without it."

"Then let 'em rot here in Nato'wa!" Dan cut in angrily.

"Aye, but they'll not be content to rot—not when we boast how rich we are in what they lack. Aye, I've said too much."

A voice was hailing from across the water. "We've got a bit of gold below. We might pay well for half of them provisions."

"I knew it!" muttered Scott, below his breath, and then in answer bellowing: "Aye, that ye might, if we would sell."

"And you won't sell, will you?" The question came heavy with sarcasm.

"Nary a poond to the likes o' you!" cried back MacGregor, Scott's associate, unable longer to contain himself.

"You'll wish you had before we're through!"

"Quick, Mac," Scott interrupted in a quiet voice. "See the decks are cleared. Brace them iron plates we salvaged from the *Bearcat* up against the bulwarks."

"Aye, sir," MacGregor answered quickly, sobered by the tone.

"Svenson! Stand by your whale gun!"

"Codd! Stand by with Flashpan at the portside cannon.

"You, Kirk, Dan, John La Salle, hark now!" We stood silent waiting on his words. "Take orders from Kioga, who will direct matters on the deck. I'll work the ship as need be." He paused in these swift instructions to send a word of warning toward the *Pirate*.

"Don't bark at me, ye friend-killing swine! We'll give back more than we receive."

Derisive laughter from the *Pirate*. "A good bluff, skipper, we'll call it." There was the flash of binoculars on the other craft, and then came the voice again: "Who is the handsome wench beside ye, Captain?"

I saw Kioga's eyes flash with the glint of cold gray steel.

Scott turned to see Beth standing near. "Below, Miss Beth," he told her. "Remain there. Your service may be needed, if it comes to fightin'."

And then commands broke swiftly from Scott.

"They're coming round to hold their bow gun on us. You are to fire when you like, Flashpan. Bring down her foremast if you can. You, Svenson, let them have it when she comes to lie bow on; and if you put their gun out of action, so much the better. I do not know what other arms she carries. Try to cripple her, but not to sink her unless you must." A ship was something living to Captain Scott, not to be destroyed except in last emergency. "Above all else, oppose their boarding. That's all from me. Kioga is in charge from this time on. There's a fairish breeze which ought to freshen. I'll work the ship."

The *Pirate* was slowly swinging. Flashpan crouched by his gun, carefully laid and elevated, awaiting the instant when the *Pirate's* foremast should almost cross the gun's line of trajectory. That instant came. Flashpan worked the flinten lock, which showered sparks into a little pan before the touch-hole. The gun roared with a belch of smoke and flame, and a recoil that shook our timbers.

From where I stood, I clearly saw the dark sphere hurtling. The little miner's aim was good, all crudities of his weapon considered. The ball actually did strike the foremast, too much to the side to bring it down, though damaging it severely, and hurling deadly splinters like shrapnel in all directions.

Three men went down as if machine-gunned, and dragged themselves to shelter. The others on the *Pirate,* all unprepared for such a greeting, scurried suddenly for cover.

Came then the crisper answer of the *Pirate's* forward gun. A shell screamed through our crude hide sail and burst beyond, fragments scattering like a fiery hail upon our decks.

On land, enthralled by sight of this, to them, astonishing engagement, the native Shoni redmen beheld with wonder this first combat of white men's ships about Nato'wan waters.

From the *Pirate* came the voice of command. We heard the rattle of chains as she took up her claws. We had our own hooks already in, in order to be ready for her when she came. Until her auxiliary motor started, we held a slight advantage in being on the move, with all sail up. But what would happen when her screw began to turn?

Some such thought was also in the minds of Flashpan and the rest, who waited for the moment when we should pass the *Pirate* to let her have our second gun. We passed to starboard as she faced us, and Flashpan fixed his eye and sights upon her hull, aft near the waterline. I heard him muttering to himself repeatedly. "Hit 'er in the engynes, or miss and blast the bloomin' rudder off!"

He pulled the trigger actuating his flint. Sparks flew, but no explosion followed. Flashpan worked the flintrock madly, while from the *Pirate,* slowly passing, hidden riflemen sniped at him, their bullets *ping*-ing fiercely from the iron shield that sheltered him. The gun went off at last, but unexpectedly. The shot hurled up a spout behind the enemy which doused her cursing helmsman but did no other damage.

Both of our port guns were now discharged, and it takes time to charge, load and prime an old-type cannon such as we must use, while under fire. Scott saw this state of things at once and helmed to come about, so that we might discharge our starboard guns into the *Pirate's* sides, if possible before her auxiliary went to work.

But halfway through the maneuver, he heard the motor cough and stutter, then settle down into a steady drone of power. We noted with a grim satisfaction that there was no further derision from the *Pirate.* She and her men all knew that they were in a fight, dependent on their utmost efforts to avert disaster, and already wounded in their foremast, which several men were now repairing hastily.

Nonetheless the motor gave her great advantage over us, who were dependent on what wind there was in order to maneuver, and praying more would blow into our sails. Responding to her helm, the *Pirate* slowly turned and brought her gun again to bear.

Scott brought our stern around, so that we faced her bows-on, presenting thus the narrowest possible target.

Now the *Pirate* fired again, and on the echo our craft shivered like an arrowed deer. The shell had burst two feet before our cutwater. The enemy gunner was reloading.

The *Pirate* now appeared to have her motor in reverse, to hold her stance so that another shot might find us in a relatively unchanged position for a truer shot. But Scott was equal to the situation, and came up strongly with the wind, so that the *Pirate's* third shot sang above our heads as had the first, and burst behind us.

Now Svenson had a good bead on the other ship and fired one of the whaling bombs, which caught the *Pirate* just below her sprit and severed the anchor from the chain, to drop into the depths. *Bearcat II* ranged up close now, and our two port cannon, reloaded in the meantime, roared loudly.

Close and distinct there was the crash and rend of smashing timbers. This time the *Pirate* had sustained two heavy blows, unluckily above the waterline.

But now *Bearcat II* lurched to the crash of an exploding shell. Gazing aft, I saw a suck of water entering us, and called the fact to Scott, who put the spokes over swiftly, threw her on the other tack, thus elevating her dangerous open wound sufficiently to be up out of water.

Three of our men swung swiftly out on ropes, to nail spare planks across the opening. This operation necessitated that *Bearcat II* be held upon her course. And since the bay was not a quarter of a mile in width at any point, her way must be reduced by taking in some sail, else she would bring up on the rocks before repairs were made.

In this unpleasant case the *Pirate* gave us chase and swiftly overtook us, roving up along our lower bulwark, secure from momentary danger, since our cannon could not now be elevated high enough to hurl their balls into her. And the *Pirate* swiftly took advantage, to put a shell square amidships, the first direct hit made upon the deck of either craft. I saw a stain of red appear on John La Salle's sleeve; and Flashpan's jaw bled from a wound dealt by a flying splinter. The *Pirate*, by virtue of her extra power, seemed in a fair way of settling us.

But luck held, for the time. Repairs effected, Scott swung her full around, had all sail hauled up again, and while she hesitated just before her skins filled up, our starboard guns bore full upon the *Pirate's* quarter. Like thunder they discharged, the double echo rolling from the cliffs and back among the forested hills.

This time we had dealt a telling blow, betrayed by the crash of steel and the sudden silence of the *Pirate's* muttering machinery. Her power plant was killed. Now we held the advantage, since, counting on her engine for all power, the *Pirate* had not a rag of canvas out to catch the wind. Still moving forward, she answered but slowly to her rudder, and being dangerously near the rocks to start with, was on them in a moment, gently but firmly.

Now had we been bent on vengeance, we might have come alongside and given her our broadsides at pleasure. But seeing her stopped by the situation, Scott crowded sail and headed for the open sea, now accessible through the channel in the reefs, thanks to the rising tide and freshening offshore wind.

The *Pirate* and the mainland of Nato'wa fell astern. At long last we were on our way out to the open sea, the other ship a threat no longer, so we hoped.

But Scott in glancing back for one last sight of her, was moved to swear. "By God, she's off the rocks again! The tide did that. They've got sail upon her, and she's comin' like Halley's comet. Now, lads, it is a race. Trim ship and shift them iron plates a bit aft, and two guns with them. She acts a little cranky with the weight as is. . . . Aye, now that's better; feel her surge! Now they'll see how a hogshead can run when rightly handled!"

It was a satisfying leap the vessel gave, urged by increasing winds. Yellow foam made song below her counter. With all strings pulling she was no lazy sailer. It was her rugged lines and curving swell, designed to cope with ice conditions we would have to meet, which gave advantage to our black pursuer, more than the almost double area of canvas which the *Pirate* carried. And slowly she closed up the gap between us.

A puff of smoke came from her gun. What with the flap of sail and song of wind in rigging, we hardly heard it speak. But in our wake, three hundred yards behind, the shell threw foam aloft. At intervals the *Pirate* sought our range, which each time was little shorter, until a sixth shell struck only a hundred feet away on a line with the wheel to which Scott clung.

From that time on the firing ceased.

Scott explained simply: "Without our knowledge of the

channel we could not have come this far. Since we know the way, they're followin', hoping to take us when we make the open water. If they sink us, they'll starve to death. If they turn back, as they dare not, the Shoni, will slit their throats." Scott laughed aloud. "We are at liberty to fire. They are not, for reasons stated. We have five guns and they have one that's equal to all of ours. She's creepin' up. Hi, Flashpan, let me see your marksmanship. Put me a ball upon the *Pirate*."

"Exac'ly whar upon her?" demanded Flashpan.

"Amidships," answered Scott, "where that rascal stands with glasses, watchin' us."

"And shall I hit or graze him?"

Laughter came in Scott's voice again. "Just knock the glasses from his hands."

Flashpan chuckled in his throat and took a long sight, elevating, depressing, elevating yet again. He fired finally and through a wreath of smoke observed the other ship. He saw men on her stare, then run to cover, all save him who stood with glasses trained. Bolder than the others, the man leaped suddenly aside. Where he had stood a great hole suddenly appeared.

No one was more astounded at the lucky shot than Flashpan himself, who saw the hit with falling jaw. But he was quickly nonchalant again, and feigned disgust. "Ah, bah! Another miss—he's still got the glasses in his hand. Me eyes ain't whut they used to be!"

Scott roared in high good humor, which changed to consternation as he saw our sail slashed twenty feet by a shell that cracked beyond the bow. The *Pirate* doubtless fearful of the worst from such uncanny gunnery, was crowding sail, intent on silencing us before we put her under water. The enemy meant to close, and drew up quickly, sending shells as fast as they could load and fire.

"All cannon to the starboard!" Kioga ordered crisply, and suiting action to the words, rolled one by main strength to the bulwark. "Aim low and fire at the waterline!" Almost as one the guns exploded and smoke enveloped us. We heard loud yells across the brine, yells of fury and of consternation. But on our own deck there was silence, filled with horror.

Death stalked among us. One of our guns had burst. MacGregor lay outstretched and still. Tom Codd hung limply on the wrecked barrel. Kioga's face was almost black with powder smoke. One of Flashpan's long moustaches had burned completely off, and the other was singed to half its former length. Dan La Salle had neither brows nor lashes left.

But evidently the *Pirate* was now taking water. Her speed had carried her ahead of us so that her gun was out of action, though rifle fire rattled against our makeshift battle plates.

One by one our guns went off. The range was close. The *Pirate's* wheel was shot away whole, spinning high in air, her rudder wild. Her fractured foremast toppled, fouling all her forward gear, her gun included. Her crew had only one alternative. They quickly glimpsed it, as did we, who made our preparations to receive them when they sought to board.

Theirs would be the wild assault of desperation, for the *Pirate* gave all indications of having taken a mortal wound. The duel of the gunners had resolved into the certainty of closer combat. To check them if we could, we hurled by hand the time bombs originally intended to kill whales.

Svenson threw up his hands and fell, a bullet through his forehead. Close-quarter fighting would destroy all that superior gunnery had achieved. But we could not avoid it now. The *Pirate's* standing sails were set to throw her hard against us, and on her rail swarmed those who had survived our fire.

One more broadside, our last for lack of powder, hulled the *Pirate* as she ground against *Bearcat II*. Her crew came over, rifles swinging. Kioga and his deck gang met them with keen lances, sharp flensing knives and deadly cutting spades, all whaling implements salvaged from the first *Bearcat*.

I saw the black boy Grant die like a hero, having done for three men with as many thrusts. I saw poor Flashpan hurled like a pitiable scarecrow against the mast, round which he curled inertly. Side by side with Dan and Kioga, La Salle the elder was valiantly fighting with a shining courage until a gun butt crushed him down in defense of his own. All this I saw, as through a reddish mist, and with the fascination of the terrible, from which I could scarce take my eyes to lay about me with my own smoothbore.

The ships were linked together bow to bow, like two fighting craft of old, and members of the *Pirate's* crew were fouling up the ropes to keep them so, until by force of numbers they should overwhelm and take us. But since they had elected a prow-to-prow connection, their men could come aboard us only at that single point, because the sterns and 'midships of the craft were thereby forced apart. Upon those interlocking bows would be decided our fate, and that of Beth La Salle.

I glimpsed the girl emerging from below. She paused above John Ford La Salle, and with a little moan sank to her knees beside her father. But courage blazed in her. The dead could not be aided. The living needed her. She rose and came to Flashpan, and with a strength born of the moment's need, picked his slight form up and carried him aft near the gun.

Beth reappeared, and this time came to me when I lay helpless from the blow of a gun butt. A dash of water from a bucket which she bore helped to revive me. I caught a hard and painful breath, and struggled to my knees.

Beth pressed a knife into my hands. Her voice was quiet, but vibrating with deep urgency. "Go forward. Try to cut the ropes that hold the ships together. I'll turn the stern gun round. Flashpan says there is a charge still in it. Be ready. When I give the signal, tell our men to drop down flat behind the cover of the deck house!"

I reached the forward cabin house; and there again became assailed with weakness and went to my knees, my muscles caving under me. Forward at the prow Kioga, Dan and Scott still held their own by virtue of the fact that only one or two could come against them at a time. But Stumpf was missing.

From the shrouds, high in the broken rigging of the *Pirate,* came the intermittent fire of a rifleman. And presently Dan, struck in one arm, must wield his clubbed gun with the other. Again the sniper aimed and fired.

Suddenly, from aft on *Bearcat II* came a simultaneous fire.

The sniper's head snapped back, slewed round grotesquely on his neck. His cap fell to the *Pirate's* deck, and presently the owner toppled almost full upon it.

I threw a glance behind. Flashpan had risen to his elbows to shoot, and now, hurt by the hard recoil of his gun, slumped back again.

Scott fell, his heart still willing, but his aging body failing him. Kioga stood alone, the shirt ripped from his back, his cable muscles rolling with his movements. Skulking in the background, Ifuago the little rat-eyed Asiatic, waited for the Snow Hawk's fall to leap and slip a knife in him. His thin blade glittered, ready to do murder.

Now, however, I was almost myself again, and had seized the lance which Dan had dropped.

Sneaking round to take Kioga from behind, Ifuago leaped with weasel quickness. It was my chance. I raised the lance, took aim and let Ifuago have it.

Straight through his back it would have plunged, had not *Bearcat II* lurched suddenly under us. Ifuago had escaped the lance to meet another end, more fitted to his deserts. The jar dislodged him down between the vessels, grinding together at the bows. Ifuago screamed. The sound of grating paused a moment, as if a mat had come between the ships, and then began again. Released, the body of Ifuago struck the water, sinking instantly.

That sudden lurch and fall of the *Bearcat's* bow disconcerted the enemy, giving momentary advantage to Kioga. He threw them off, glimpsed me, and dimly saw Flashpan, waving and yelling from astern. I shouted what I knew Flashpan would be trying to make heard:

"Drop down! Drop down—behind the deck house!"

Kioga understood at once and dived for cover, I beside him. The *Pirate*'s crew cheered with the hope of final victory and flocked aboard us in full force. The echo of their triumph had not died when Flashpan let his last shot go. Annihilation went before that blast.

Small bits of chain and scrap, a veritable hail of our crude shrapnel passed above our heads. The men from on the *Pirate* melted like lead soldiers. Not one survived that final fire. The battle ended on our own decks.

All suddenly became funereally still. We were victorious —but at what price!

Aboard the *Bearcat* five good men and good friends had died, and one was missing. All the rest bore wounds. Svenson, whaler's gunner; Washington Madison Grant, the valiant black boy; MacGregor, our lovable Scottish smith. Tom Codd still hung across the burst gun; all lay still just where death had come to greet them. Now, with the crisis past, Beth La Salle knelt and mourned silently beside her fallen father, with Dan himself, sore wounded, attempting to assuage her grief.

Kioga, who had borne the brunt of that last fighting forward, miraculously had taken but slight wounds—a tribute to his amazing quickness and agility. Scott, beneath the

Snow Hawk's ministrations, was coming round. Otto Stumpf, that lion-hearted German, was nowhere to be seen.

I still could get around, and moved to Flashpan's side, to find him semi-conscious, grimed with powder smoke. His dog had found a way up from below, to rest his muzzle on the master's breast and softly whine. Flashpan was speaking weakly. "Placer—whar be ye, monk?"

From far aloft there came a chattering cry. Down through the ropes and shrouds a spidery figure plunged. Placer, too, had a minor battle wound in one black little hand.

There was small time to patch him up. Victorious against the *Pirate* and her crew, *Bearcat II* now capitulated to the sea. That crash of ships together at the bow had damaged her severely. I ran below to find five feet of water in her hold, the level rising rapidly.

I called this news to Kioga, who, with Scott, now able to stand on his feet, surveyed the situation. "She'll founder, sure," Scott said. "She's fillin' fast. On deck, my lads! Take to the *Pirate*. At least she's got a boat that isn't kindling like our own."

In haste we worked to bear our wounded forward where the ships were still entangled bow to bow. Well for us now that I had not succeeded in their separation. It was a feat to get those still alive from one ship to the other, for now our vessel's stern rail was awash and visibly submerging. What with an added list to port, the deck was at an ever-steepening slant.

Air blew from the hawse hole with a hoarse and bubbling sound. It was *Bearcat II* sounding her death rattle. One of her guns escaped, to roll and crash in wild career into the sea, carrying away part of her rail. Tom Codd was draped across that gun and went down with it. As if endowed with sentient fury, the other cannon followed, almost as one, running down the dead.

Kioga leaped upon the doomed craft's deck, intent on saving La Salle's body from sinking with her. Then all at once the snarl of cordage parted. *Bearcat II* sank beneath her weight of gravel ballast. With her went her dead. And Beth cried out, for in the whirlpool on that swirling surface, the Snow Hawk spun a moment and was sucked under too.

Frozen by the suddenness of this chain of disasters, capped with Kioga's disappearance, we stared down almost in paralysis; then suddenly his head appeared, tossing the heavy wet thatch back from his eyes. We threw a rope. He gripped it and was hauled aboard. But of La Salle the elder and those others who had gone down with *Bearcat II*, we saw no more.

Why the *Pirate* had not sunk already was a mystery. We did not wait to clear her littered decks, but went immediately aft to where we had inflicted greatest damage on the *Pirate's* hull. Advancing armed, we heard the sound of stertorous grunting and the rasping of a saw—and by lantern light we glimpsed the sweating form of Otto Stumpf.

With planks and canvas, he had stopped the shot holes below the water-line, working while the *Pirate* had been dragged down at the bow—and consequently raised astern—by the sinking *Bearcat II*.

Thanks solely to Stumpf's foresight, we still had a floating ship beneath us. Presently below, we got her pumps in action, made fair repairs, and ascertained that none of the crew remained to threaten us. Then we went aloft to clear the littered decks and give the dead all decent burial overside.

At dawn the *Pirate* sailed from Nato'wa, leaving the last rock reef tower astern in four hours. Three days passed before we first encountered solid ice fields; but from then on, each day brought crises which we met and overcame, more by the grace of God than our own strength.

But the *Pirate* was not destined for destruction by the ice. She limped out of the pack weeks later, scarred and wounded by the floes, but still intact. Of water we had plenty. But her small store of provisions, doled out in daily smaller rations, had barely sustained our lives. Our strength grew less and less. When no food remained, one seal, killed by Kioga from the *Pirate's* boat, was all we shared to eat.

Land was sighted in the south by men so far gone in hunger that they dared not trust their senses. Scott calculated that it was the north coast of Siberia, and steered the *Pirate* east and south on that assumption. According to the final entry in my journal before I lost my senses, we passed between the Diomedes near Bering Strait in mid-July. We were walking skeletons, all but dead of hunger, drifting aboard a leaking ship that soon would founder for lack of hands to man the pumps.

CHAPTER 20

Forward on the *Pirate,* Captain Scott stood next to Kioga, staring out across the water with eyes that played strange tricks upon them. Through the mists Scott had thought he saw the outlines of another ship, and asked Kioga to confirm his vision.

"She looked to be right dead ahead," he whispered huskily. "I could have sworn. Aye! There she is again!" His hand shook, pointing. Kioga followed it, and in the mists he too made out the vague dim outlines of a vessel far ahead. Before he could affirm his agreement, she had vanished and the mists were thicker.

The *Pirate* held her course, her wheel lashed in position. An hour passed. The vessel long since must have cut across the other's course, if she had truly been a ship and not the figment of their own imagination. They watched on either side and suddenly, abeam, Kioga saw a distant gleaming broadside through the fog, and called for Scott to verify him. But Scott could not sustain him nor deny. "The mist is like a curtain," the Captain murmured. The minutes passed.

"Now! There!" cried Kioga suddenly, pointing toward the north, astern, whence they were sailing.

"Aye, thanks to God; I see her clearly cutting through our wake! But now she's gone again." A little later Scott began to chuckle in his beard.

Kioga eyed him sharply. "Why are you laughing, man?"

"Because she is abeam, now, to the west of us!" Scott answered in a voice that had begun to rise a little. Kioga wheeled to peer out through the fog. "My eyes are sharp, but I don't sight her," he said.

Scott nodded heavily, but he had controlled himself again. "Nor do I, friend. It is the hunger working at our wits. There was no ship out there at all."

With only Kioga now able to get around at all, there was no possibility of working the ship. Nor did Kioga wish to leave a group, any one of whom might lose his mind and perpetrate some dreaded act. As for myself, I had short rational flashes, but for the rest I must have been a trial to the others, babbling and raving other times. . . . In a moment of clearness I saw Kioga moving toward the port bow, to strain his gaze out through the fog. I could not see above the bulwark. But in my delirium I seemed to hear a distant hail.

"Ahoy, on board that schooner! Who are you?"

Kioga answered, but even I could not hear, much less that ghost voice from the distance. Another distant hail.

"Aho-oy, aboard the *Pirate!* Come about, or I'll put a shot into you!"

What mockery that was—come about, with not a man aboard who could handle rope or wheel! Again Kioga's shout was but a whisper.

I seemed to hear a gun explode, and thought it was the one near which Kioga crouched. A shell wailed over and struck the sea beyond us. The hailing voice again. "We've warned you. *Will you come about?*"

I seemed to hear the sound of bells. Came another boom. I struggled to my feet to see what was happening—only to collapse again, unconscious.

So this still silent dark was the Beyond. . . . In our crossing from the world of life, we must have come together in a company, bound for a common destination; for I could now hear Flashpan's voice, raised up in a cracked but happy song—a very earthly song, it seemed to me, sung to the tunes of a banjo whose sour notes would never pass in any proper heaven.

I caught still other sounds, the *jong-a-ling* of bells, the thrum of powerful machinery as in response. Then suddenly, assailing me with wondrous effect, the rich aroma of coffee and the scent of ham and eggs awoke me from that heaven of my own imagination to the world of living men—a very interesting world.

I awoke to hear the story of our rescue out of Flashpan's mouth: "The *Pirate* was goin' down, d'ye see, when what shoots into sight but a fine white lifeboat, six men at th' oars. The boat gits to us jest in time, like in the story-books, b'gosh! The mate says, kinda low: 'Migod, migod! These ain't the folk who stole this ship. They're starvin'! Look at 'em!'

"They picked us up, even to my monk and hound, and tuk us on their ship."

"What ship?" I interrupted.

"One o' th' Coast Guard boats. She—"

A voice interrupted from the doorway. I saw Beth standing there, a steaming tray in hand. Behind her in the passage loomed the mighty shoulders of the Snow Hawk. Scott was there, all smiles and ruddiness again; so was Stumpf, his moon-like face aglow; Dan grinned at me and all came in until the little room was crowded with friends and good will.

While I ate, they told me news of what had transpired in the world we came from.

And as the news was told, Kioga looked out through a porthole toward the north, Beth standing at his side.

The hour when the crew had taken us aboard had added *finis* to the great adventure of Nato'wa. They faced a different kind of personal adventure, but their happiness, like my own, was of the quiet kind, tinged by the memory of tragedy, of friends and loved ones never to be seen again. And as they gazed in silence northward, I did not need a crystal gazing ball to divine their thoughts.

Up there, on that last continent of vast adventure, another king was only taking up his duties. They wondered what was the destiny of Tokala—boy-ruler of the T'emaho, and master of all M'Anda.

After some further talk in the secure and comfortable cabin, they all departed, Beth and Kioga arm in arm. Beside me Flashpan picked up the banjo belonging to one of the crew and stroked out chords from the Lohengrin Wedding March. I turned to him in some surprise. "A little premature for that, isn't it?"

"Pshaw!" said Flashpan laconically, stroking the head of his dog. "Not premature. Late. I forgot to tell ye, the Captain married them this mornin'. Dan was best man; but out of deference to me bravery and service to the bride and groom" —here Flashpan struck an attitude of pride—"I held the ring."

Suddenly, through the porthole, I saw a little face peer in. Placer, Flashpan's pet rhesus, had just had floury adventure in the ship's pantry forward. Except for that, I could have sworn the human little rascal winked.